JUN 02 2015

450L

WELCOME TO
PASSPORT TO READING
A beginning reader's ticket to a brand-new world!

Every book in this program is designed to build read-along and read-alone skills, level by level, through engaging and enriching stories. As the reader turns each page, he or she will become more confident with new vocabulary, sight words, and comprehension.

These PASSPORT TO READING levels will help you choose the perfect book for every reader.

READING TOGETHER
Read short words in simple sentence structures together to begin a reader's journey.

READING OUT LOUD
Encourage developing readers to sound out words in more complex stories with simple vocabulary.

READING INDEPENDENTLY
Newly independent readers gain confidence reading more complex sentences with higher word counts.

READY TO READ MORE
Readers prepare for chapter books with fewer illustrations and longer paragraphs.

This book features sight words from the educator-supported Dolch Sight Words List. This encourages the reader to recognize commonly used vocabulary words, increasing reading speed and fluency.

For more information, please visit passporttoreadingbooks.com.

Enjoy the journey!

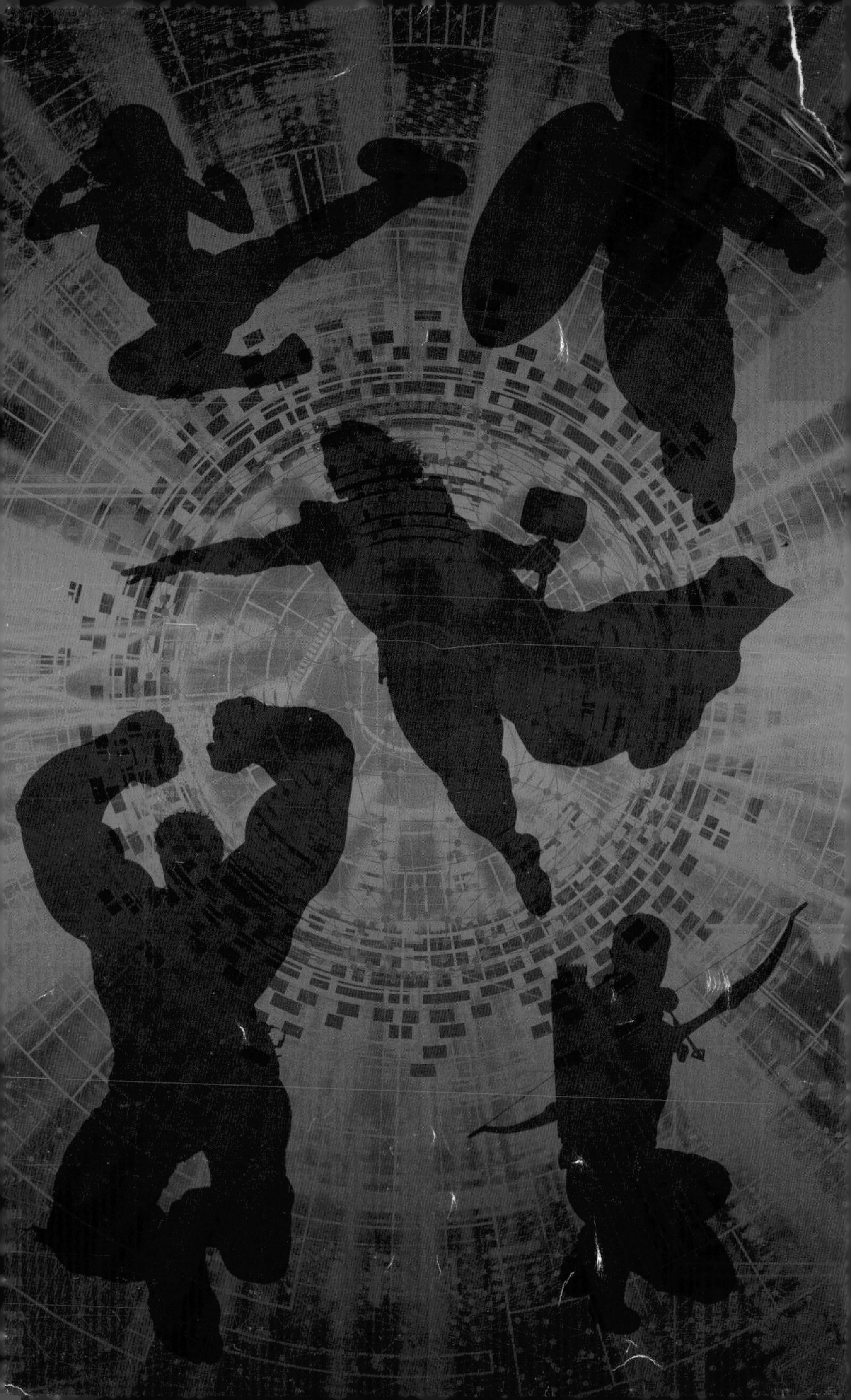

MARVEL

THE AVENGERS

READING ADVENTURES

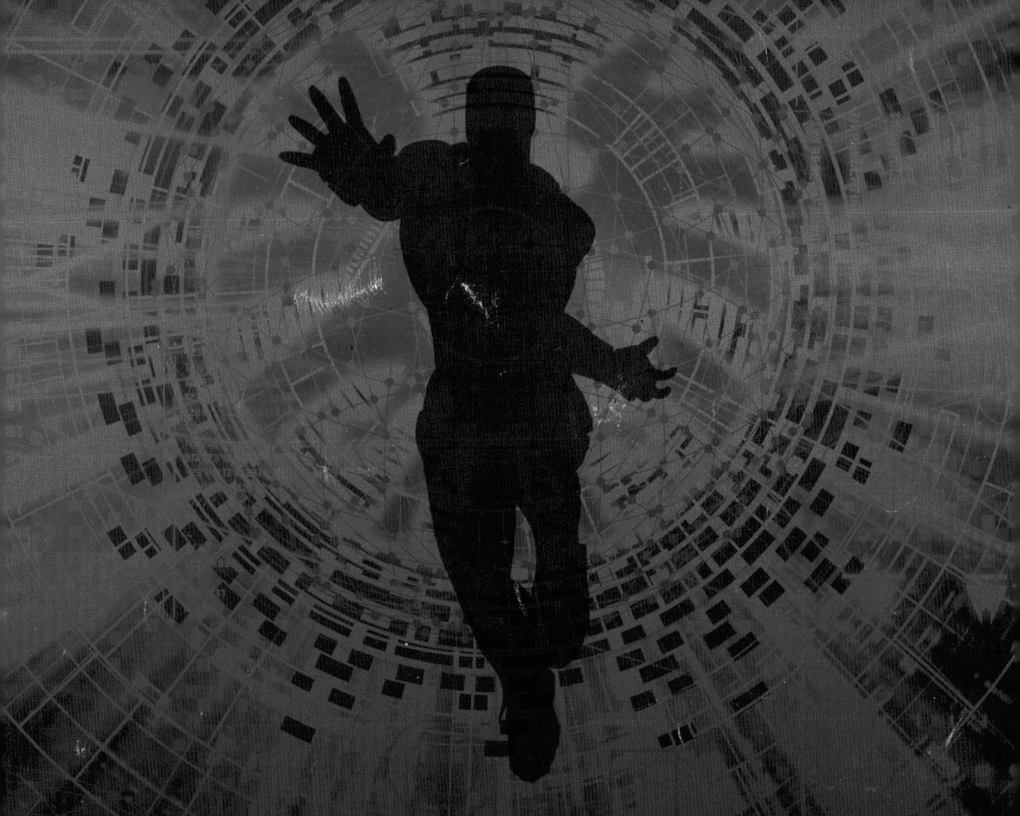

LB

LITTLE, BROWN AND COMPANY

New York Boston

marvelkids.com

© 2015 MARVEL

In accordance with the U.S. Copyright Act of 1976, the scanning, uploading, and electronic sharing of any part of this book without the permission of the publisher is unlawful piracy and theft of the author's intellectual property. If you would like to use material from the book (other than for review purposes), prior written permission must be obtained by contacting the publisher at permissions@hbgusa.com. Thank you for your support of the author's rights.

Little, Brown and Company

Hachette Book Group
1290 Avenue of the Americas, New York, NY 10104
Visit us at lb-kids.com

Little, Brown and Company is a division of Hachette Book Group, Inc.
The Little, Brown name and logo are trademarks of Hachette Book Group, Inc.

The publisher is not responsible for websites (or their content) that are not owned by the publisher.

First Edition: March 2015
Avengers: Assemble! originally published in
July 2013 by Disney Publishing Worldwide
Iron Man 2: Iron Man's Friends and Foes originally published in
April 2010 by LB kids, an imprint of Little, Brown and Company
Iron Man 2: Meet Black Widow originally published in
April 2010 by LB kids, an imprint of Little, Brown and Company
Iron Man 3: Iron Man Fights Back originally published in
April 2013 by Disney Publishing Worldwide
Thor: The Dark World: Heroes of Asgard originally published in
October 2013 by Disney Publishing Worldwide
Captain America: The Winter Soldier: Falcon Takes Flight originally published in
March 2014 by Disney Publishing Worldwide

Library of Congress Control Number: 2014949964

ISBN 978-0-316-25749-7 (pb) — ISBN 978-0-316-33839-4 (paper over board)

10 9 8 7 6 5 4 3 2 1

SC
Printed in China

Passport to Reading titles are leveled by independent reviewers applying the standards developed by Irene Fountas and Gay Su Pinnell in *Matching Books to Readers: Using Leveled Books in Guided Reading*, Heinemann, 1999.

Starring in

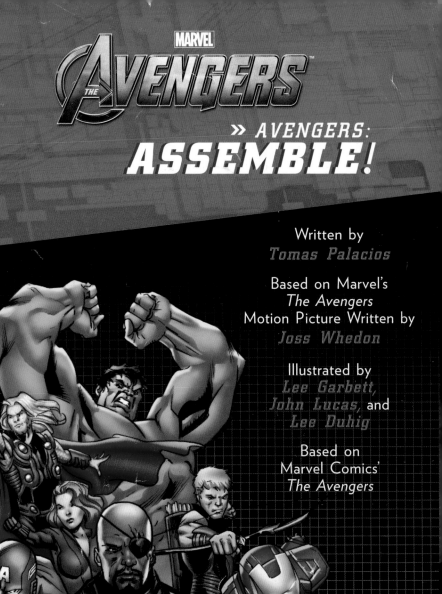

MARVEL

AVENGERS™

» AVENGERS:
ASSEMBLE!

Written by
Tomas Palacios

Based on Marvel's
The Avengers
Motion Picture Written by
Joss Whedon

Illustrated by
Lee Garbett,
John Lucas, and
Lee Duhig

Based on
Marvel Comics'
The Avengers

This is the story of the Avengers!

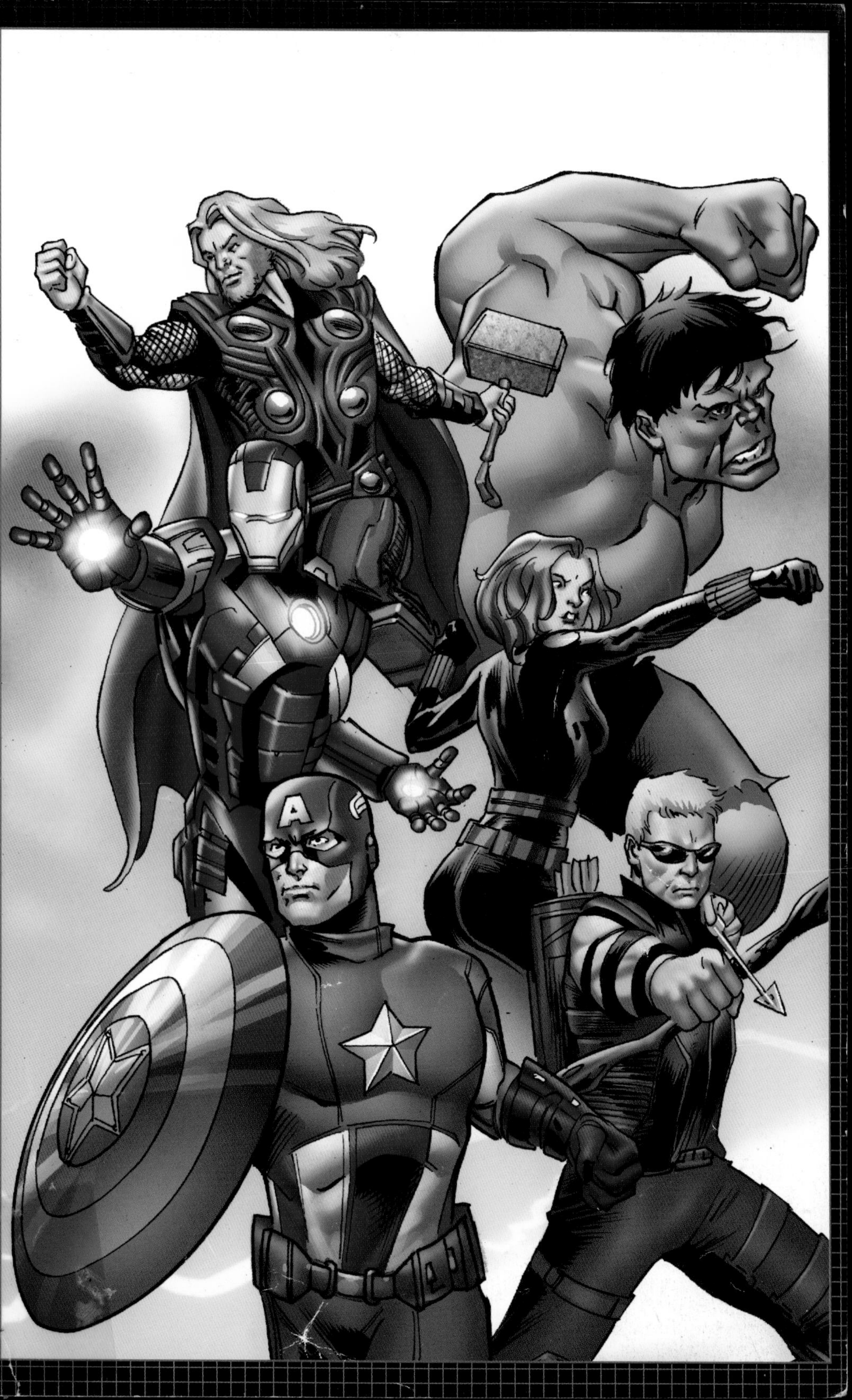

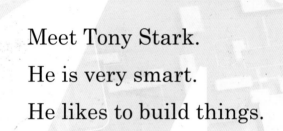

Meet Tony Stark.

He is very smart.

He likes to build things.

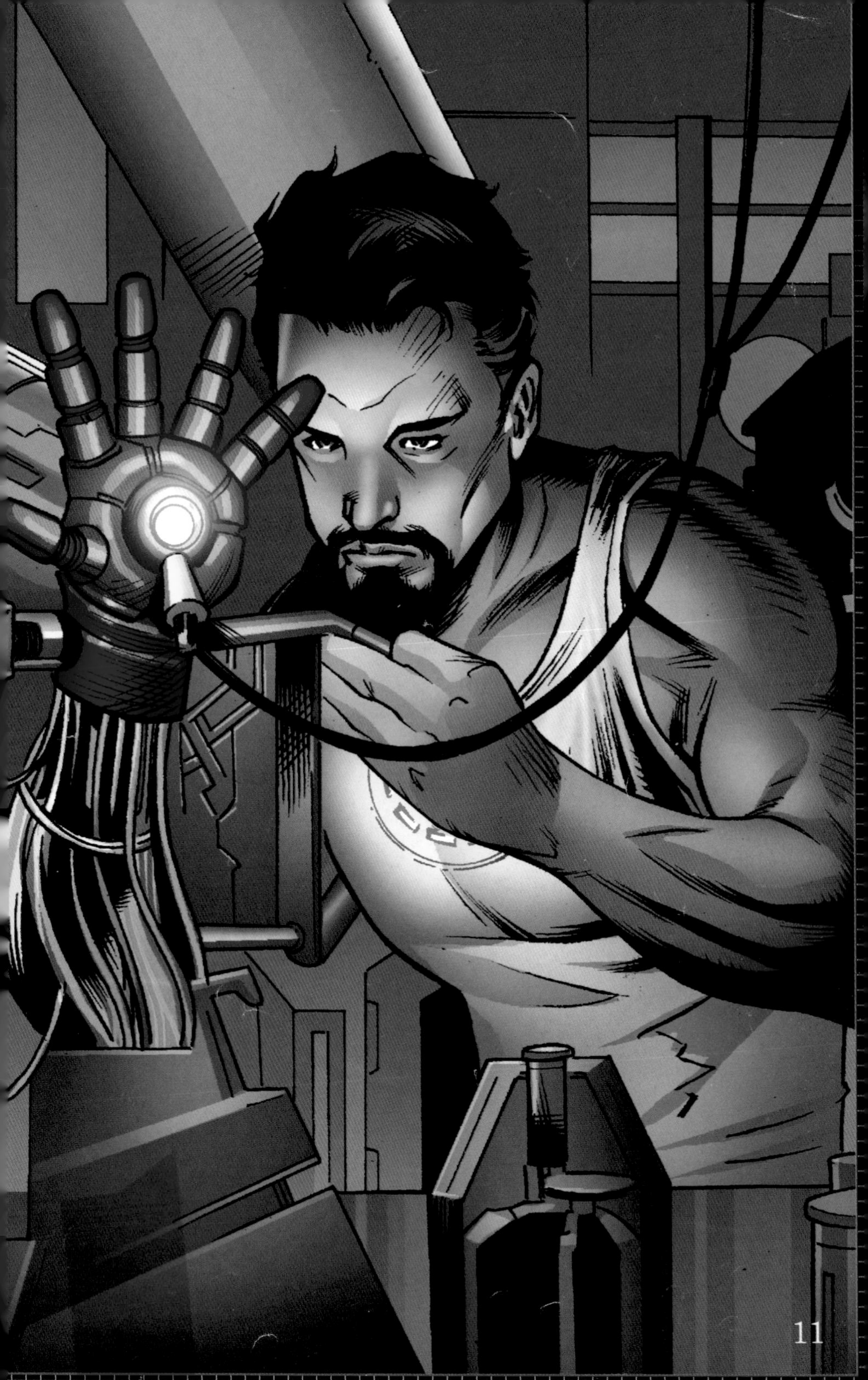

Tony built a suit of armor.

He is now called Iron Man!

Iron Man can fly!

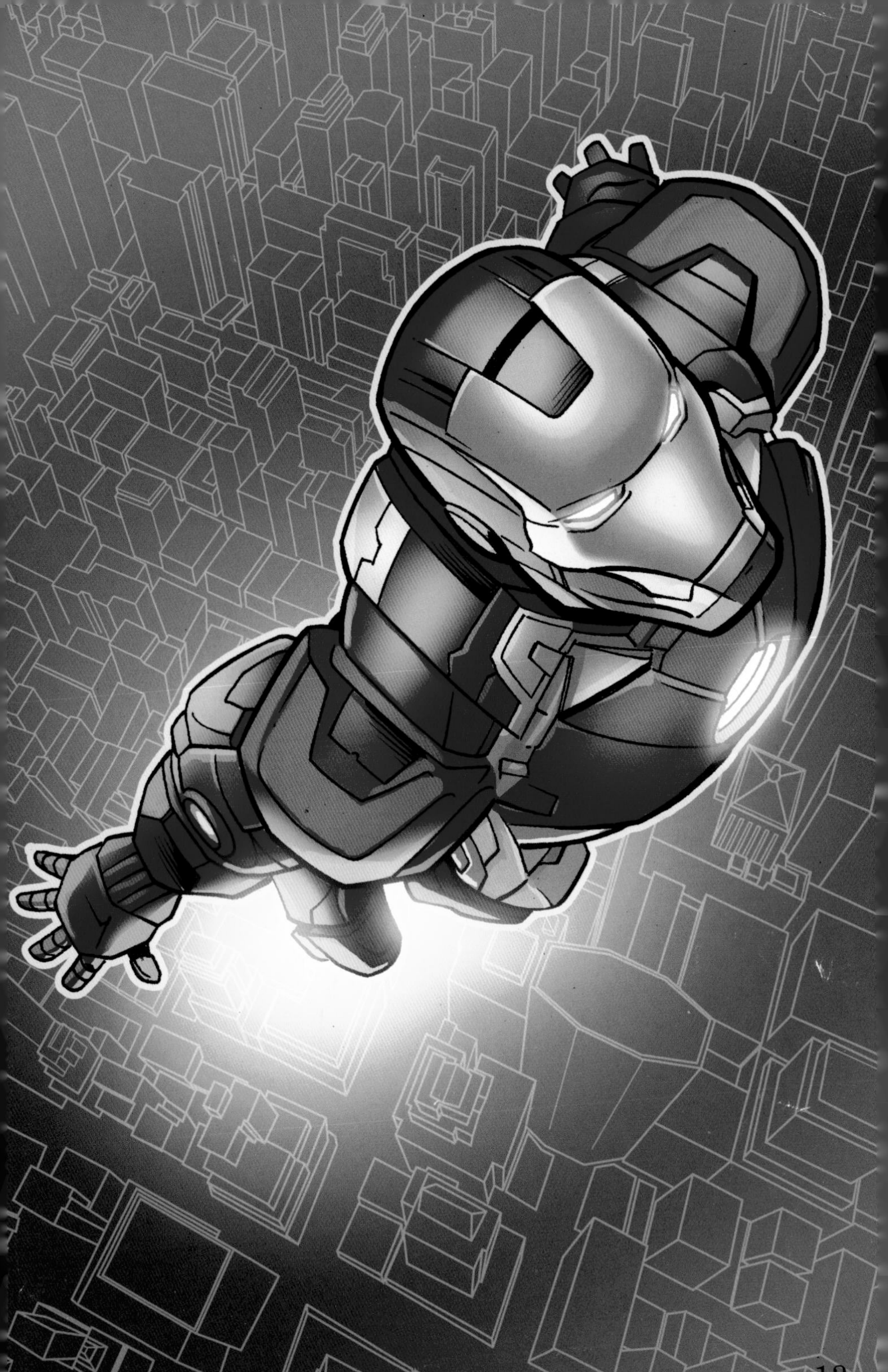

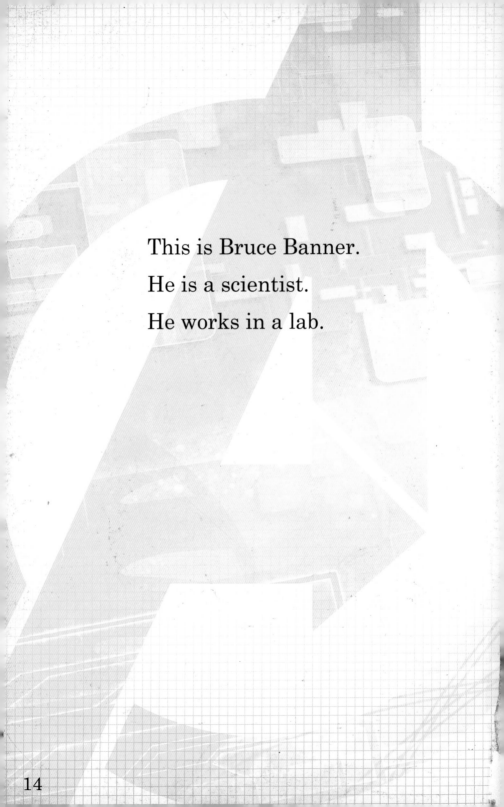

This is Bruce Banner.

He is a scientist.

He works in a lab.

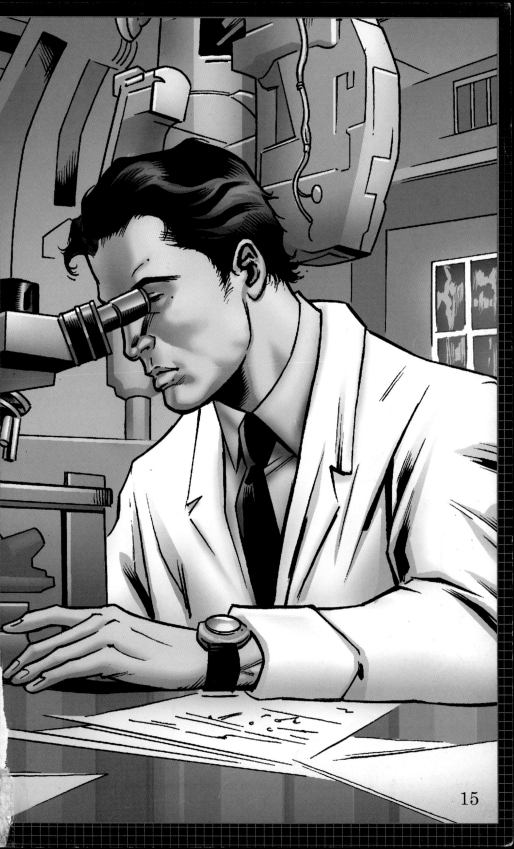

15

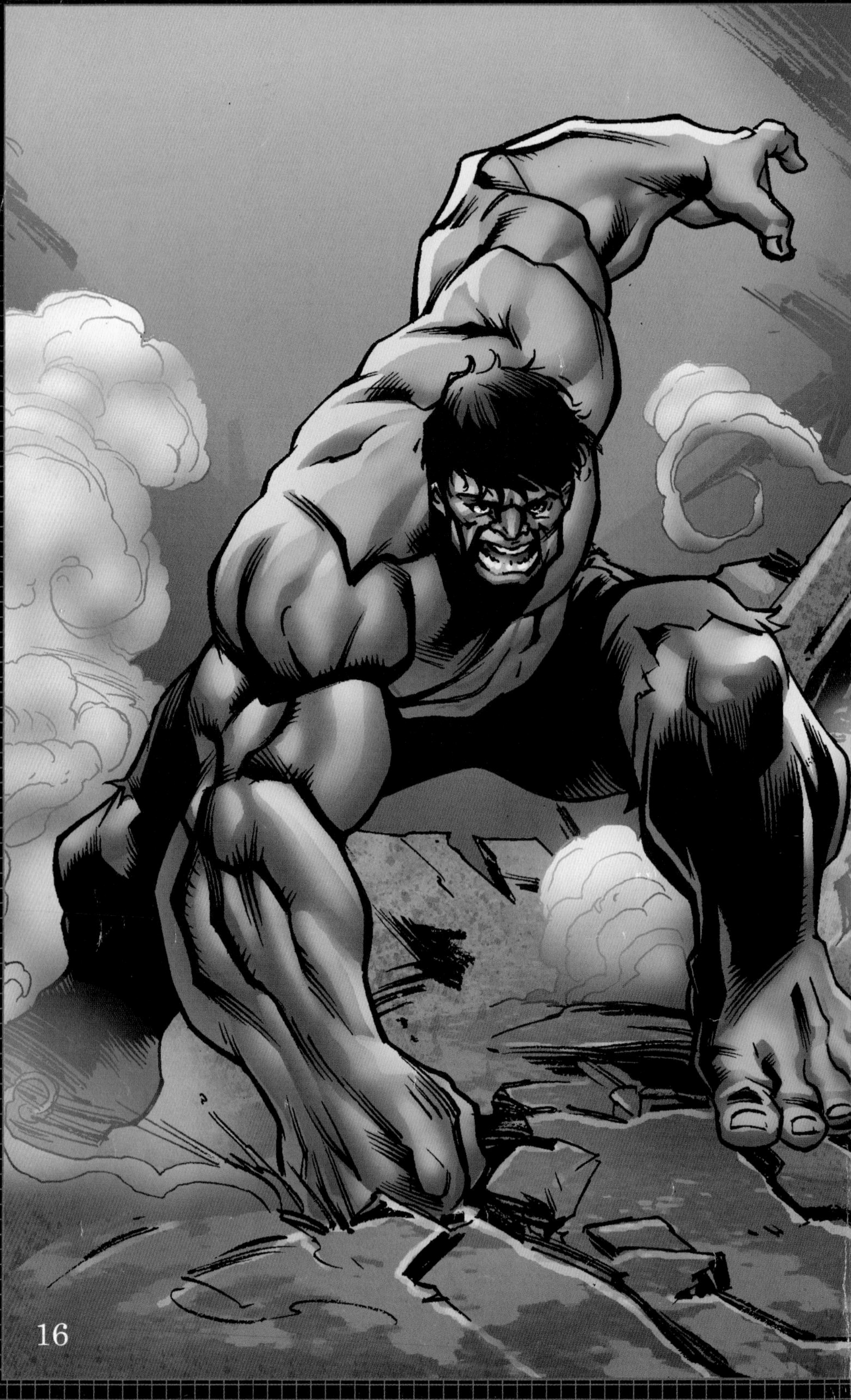

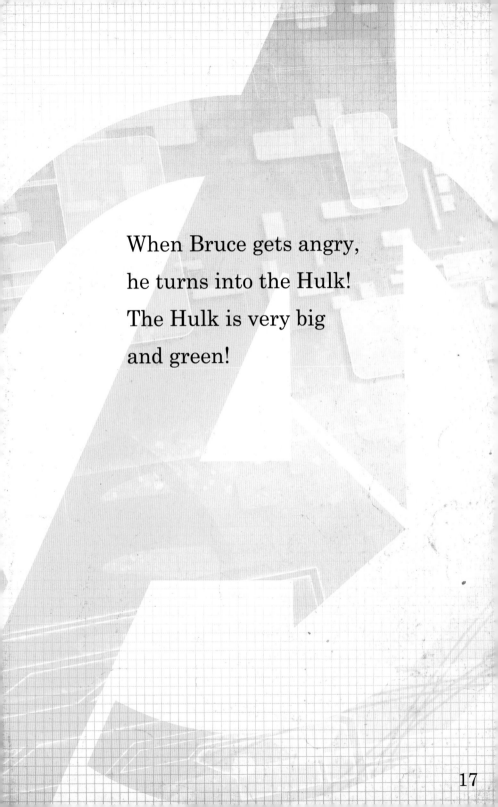

When Bruce gets angry,
he turns into the Hulk!
The Hulk is very big
and green!

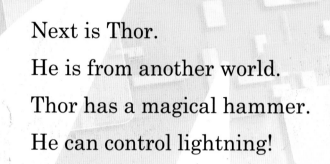

Next is Thor.

He is from another world.

Thor has a magical hammer.

He can control lightning!

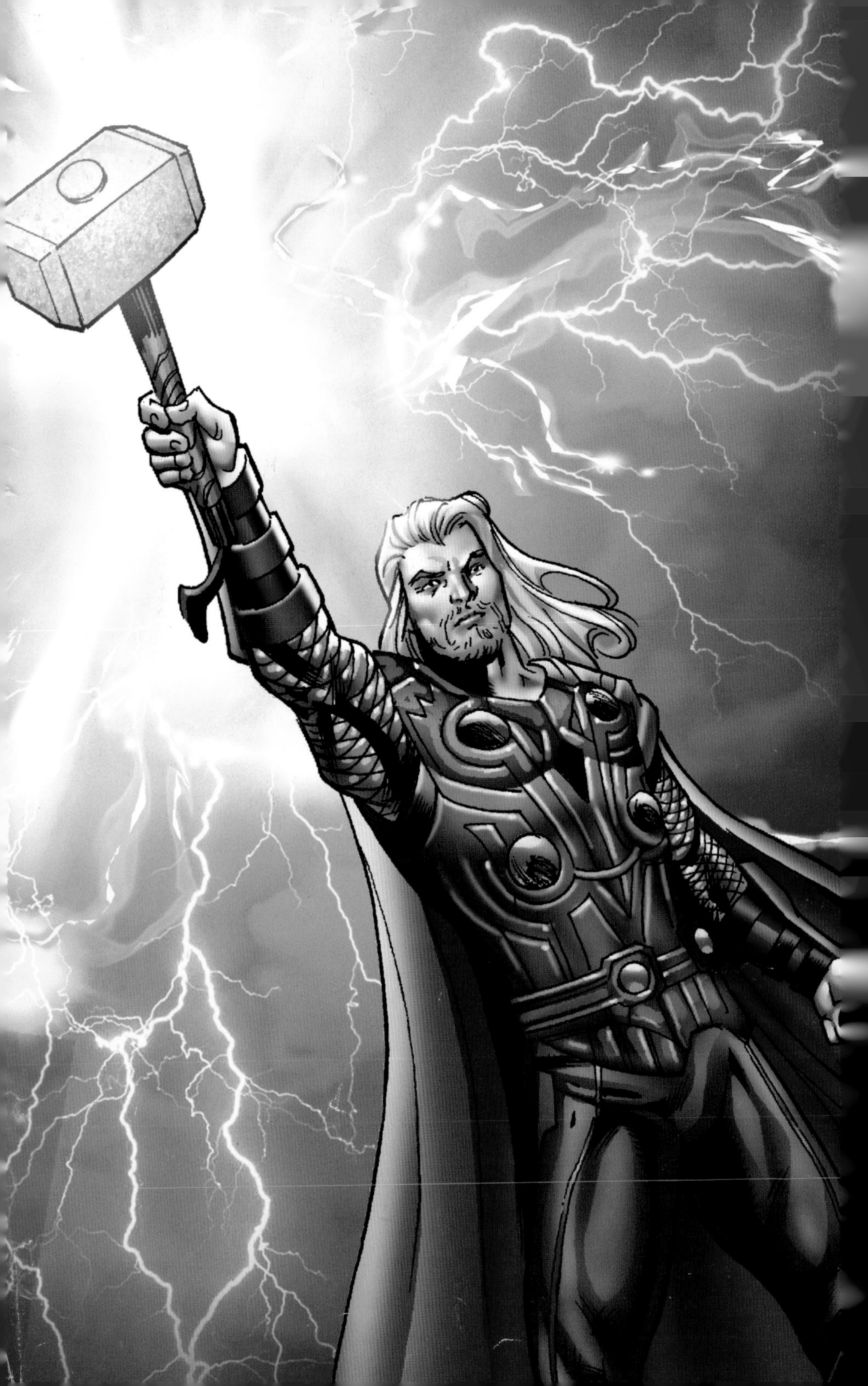

Thor has a brother.

His name is Loki.

Loki is a very sneaky villain.

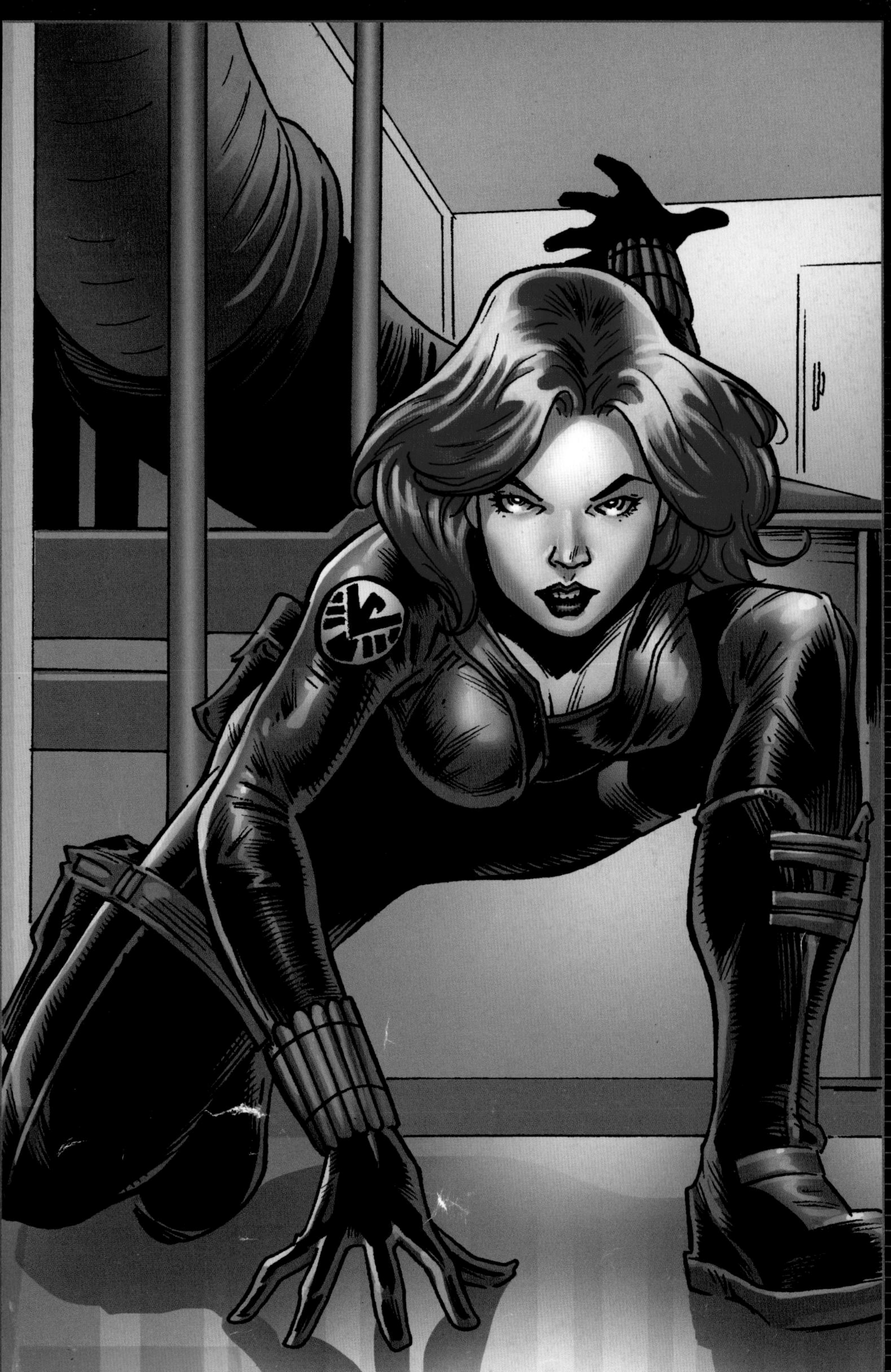

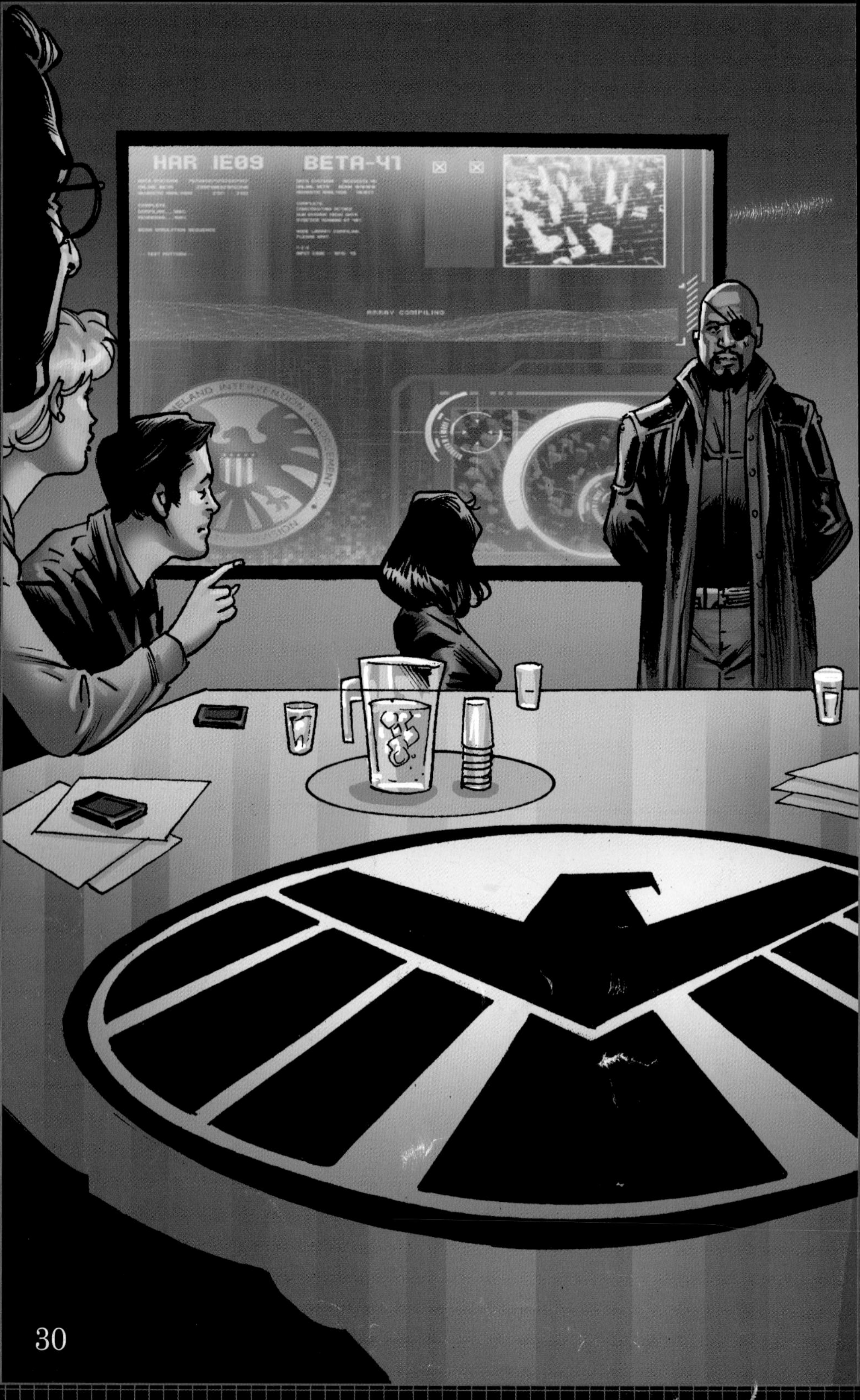
HAR IE09
BETA-47
ARRAY COMPILING

Finally, there is Nick Fury.

He is the leader of S.H.I.E.L.D.

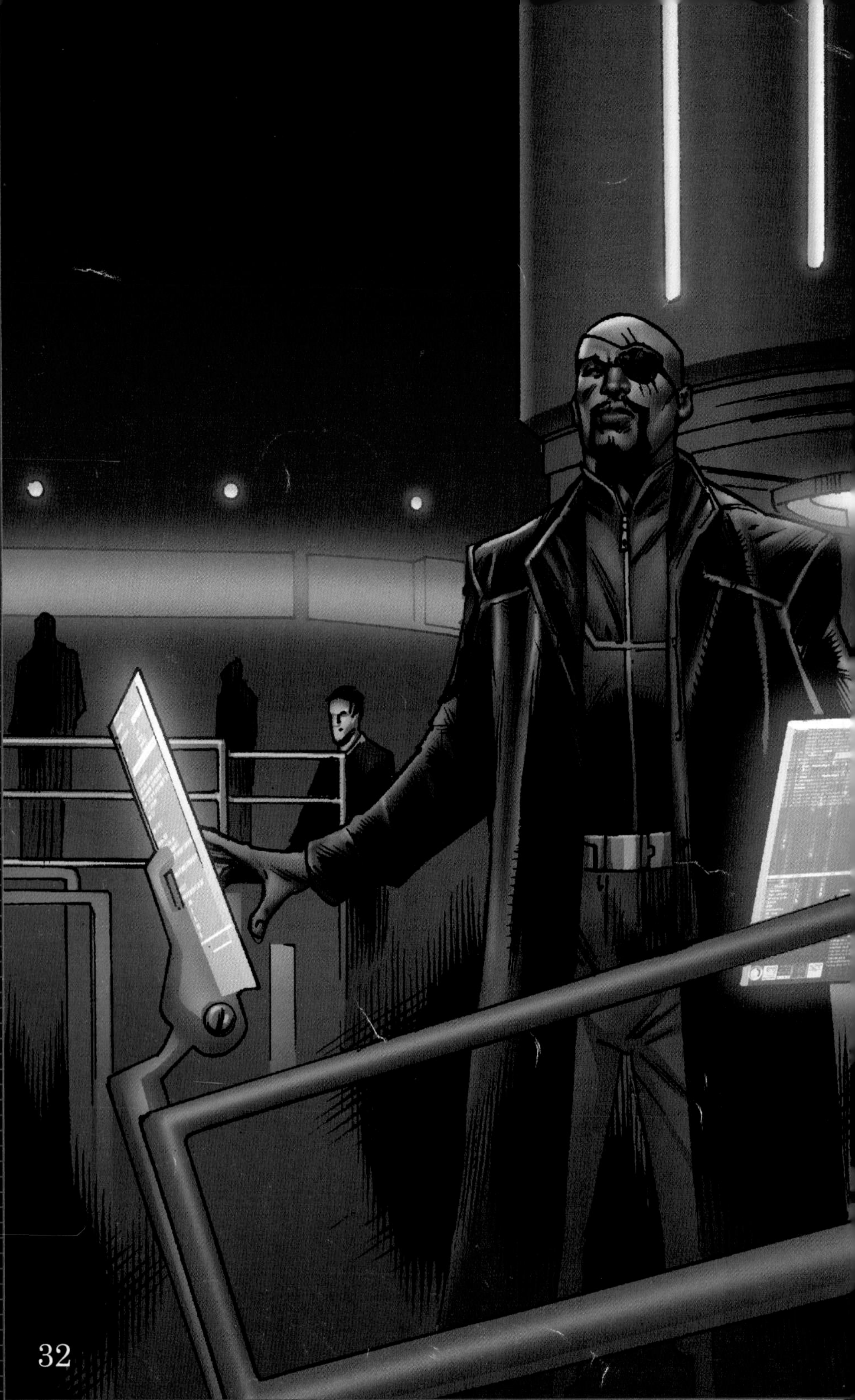

S.H.I.E.L.D. is a special
group that helps people.
Nick Fury wants to make
a new group to work with
S.H.I.E.L.D.

Nick Fury creates
a team of Super Heroes.
He calls them the Avengers!

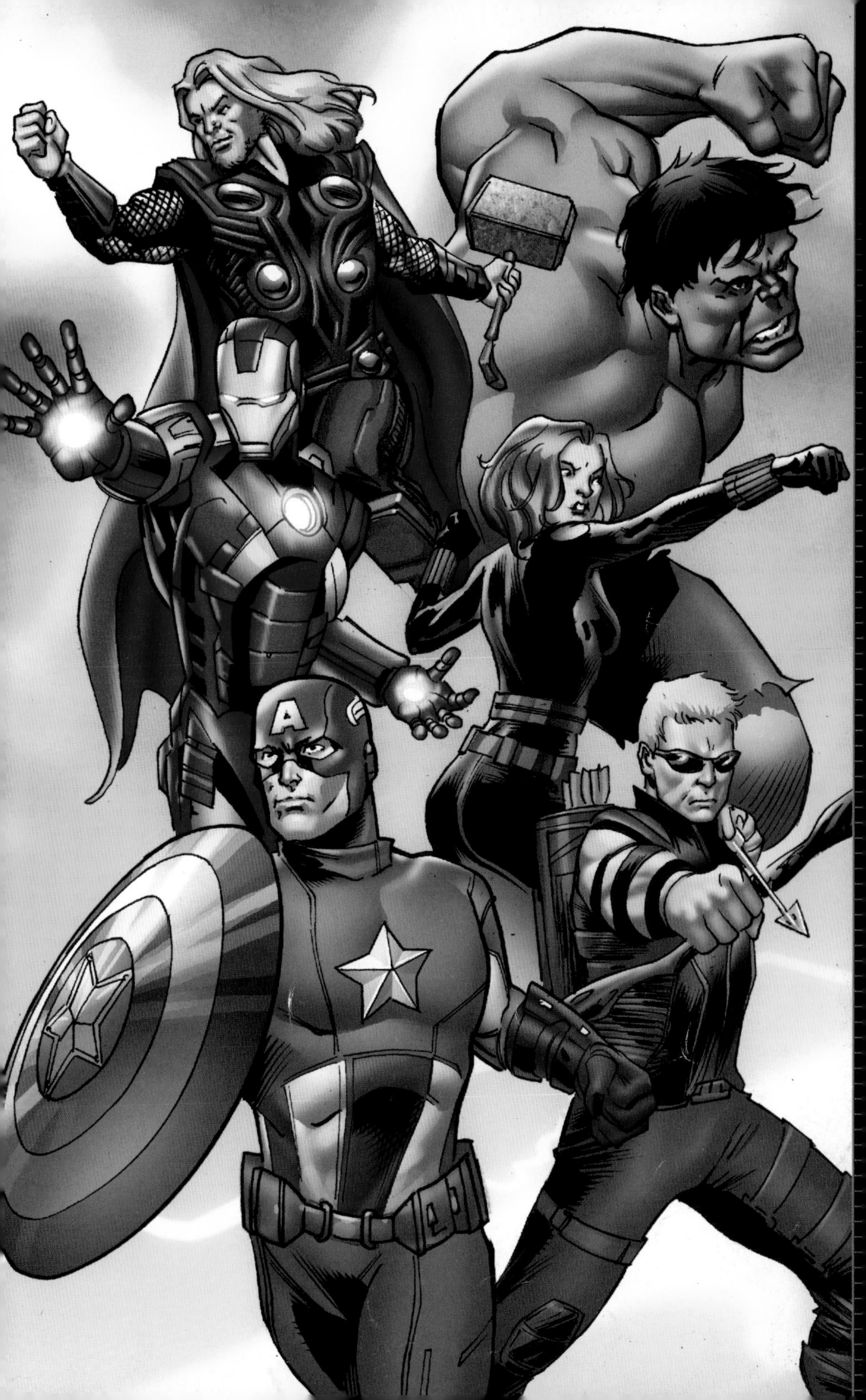

When there is trouble,
the Avengers assemble!

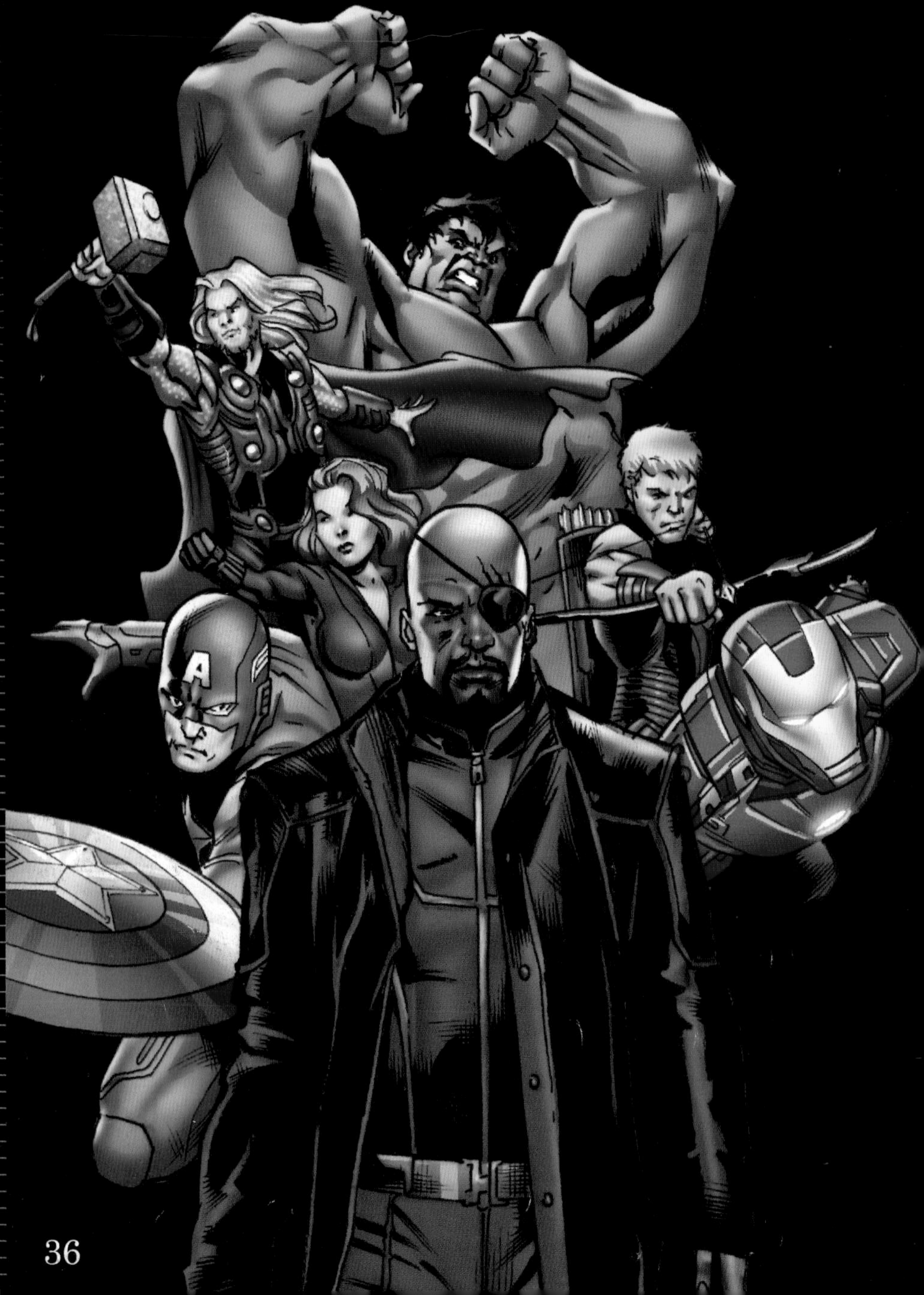

MARVEL

IRON MAN 2

IRON MAN'S FRIENDS AND FOES

100% POWER

Adapted by LISA SHEA

Screenplay by JUSTIN THEROUX

Produced by KEVIN FEIGE

Directed by JON FAVREAU

Pictures by DARIO BRIZUELA

Inked by MIGUEL SPADAFINO and LEANDRO CORRAL

When you are rich and famous,
you make lots of friends.
But you make lots of enemies, too.
The trick is to know the difference!

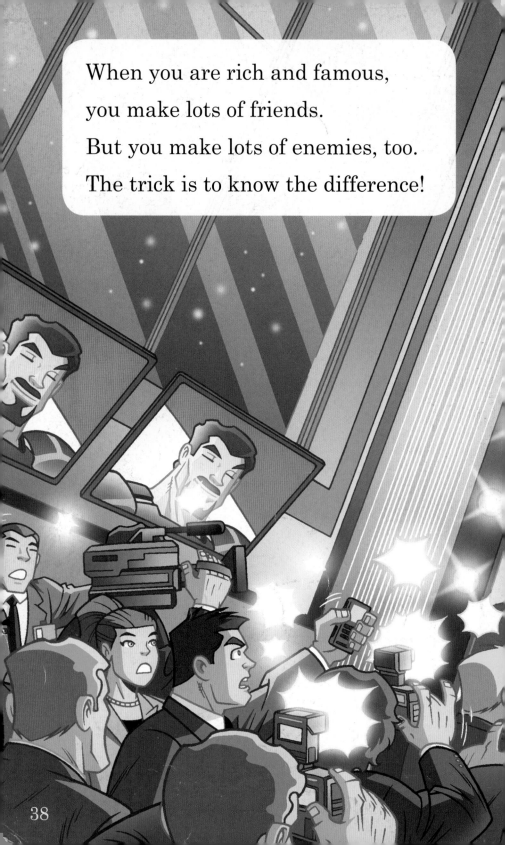

Rhodey works for the government.
When Tony stopped making weapons,
Rhodey started working with Hammer.
Tony does not like that.

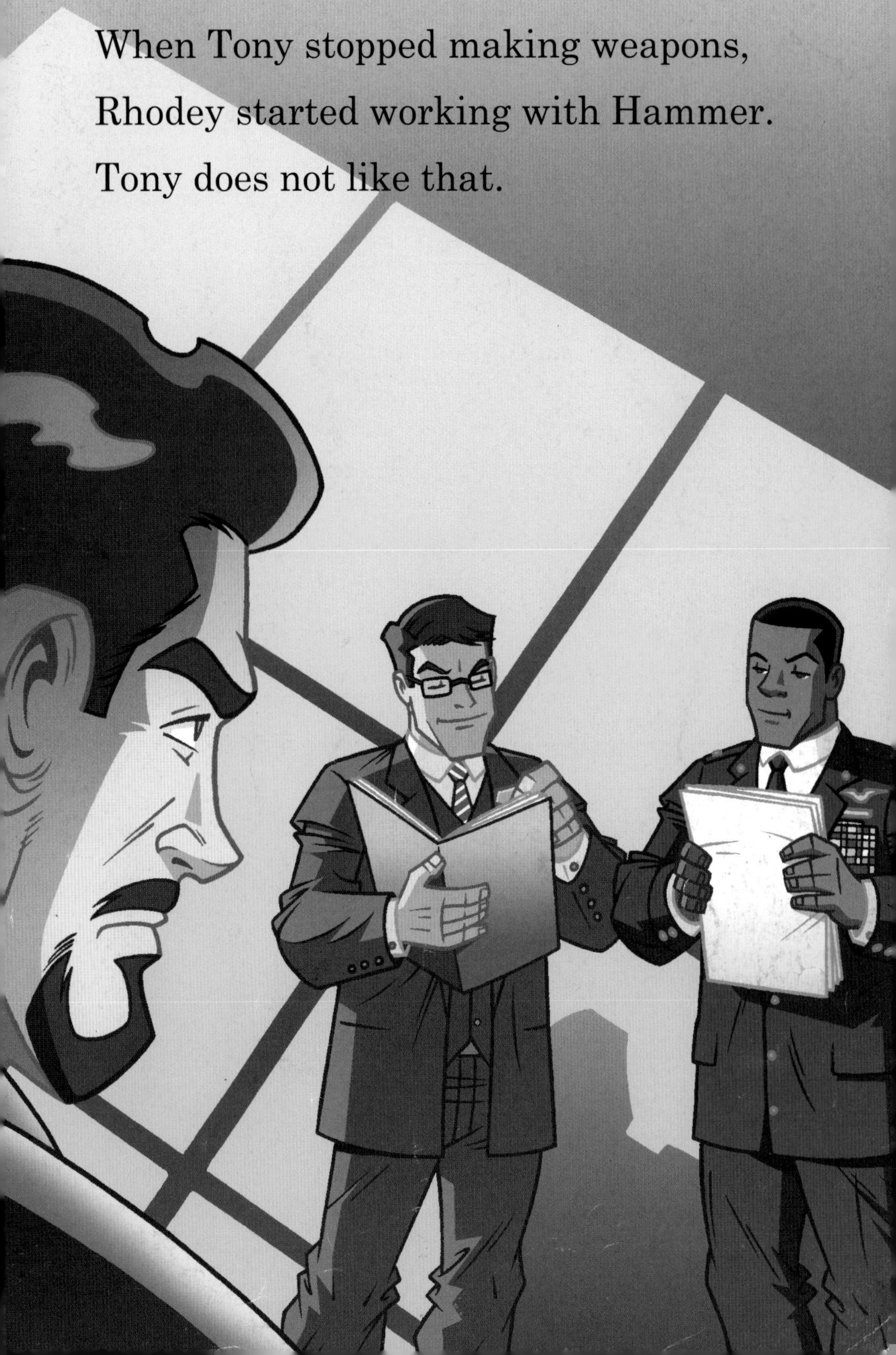

Pepper Potts is Tony's assistant.
She helps him with everything,
even when he is Iron Man.
She is always there when he needs her.

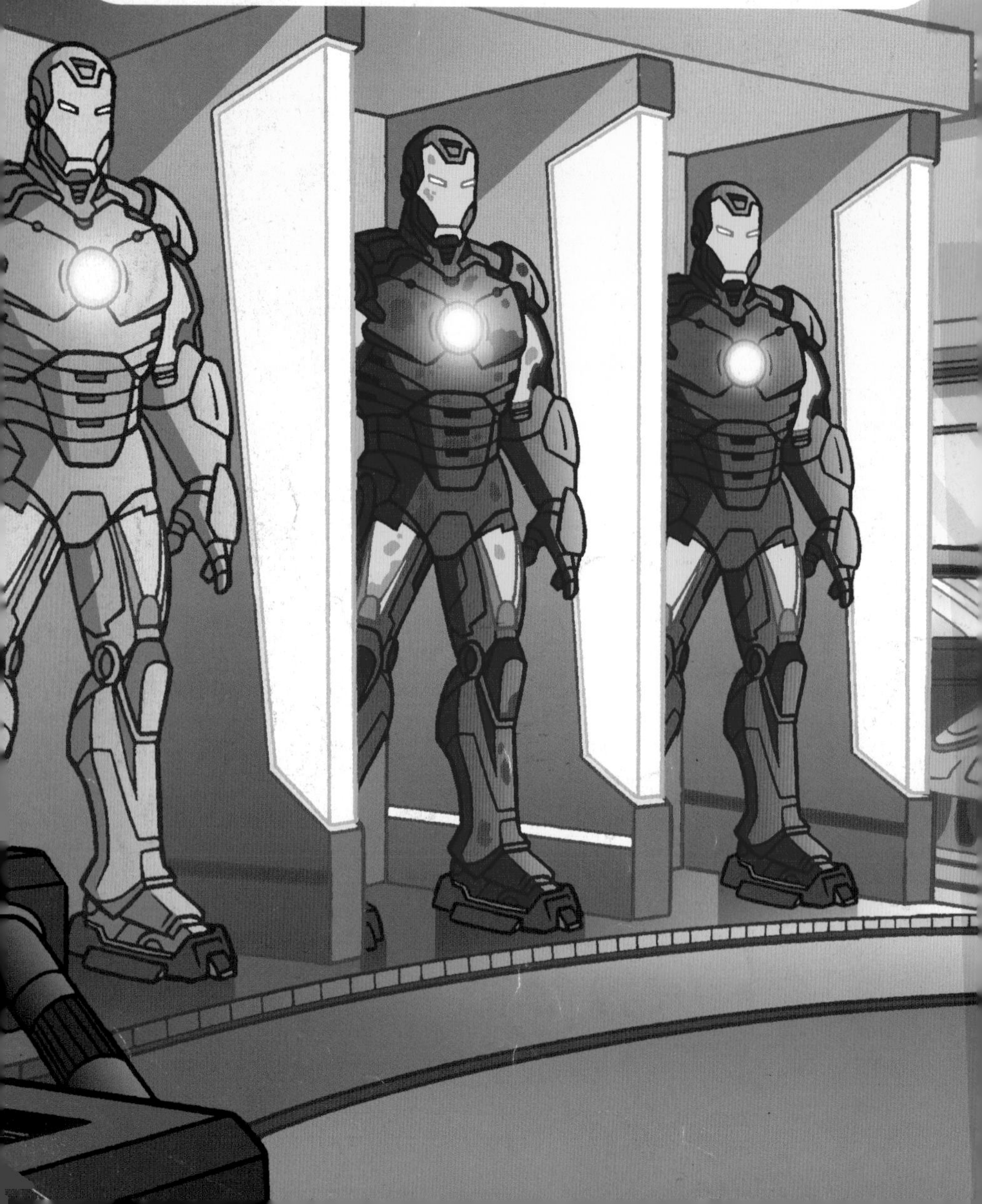

Pepper is so good at her job
that Tony gives her a promotion.
Pepper is thrilled!

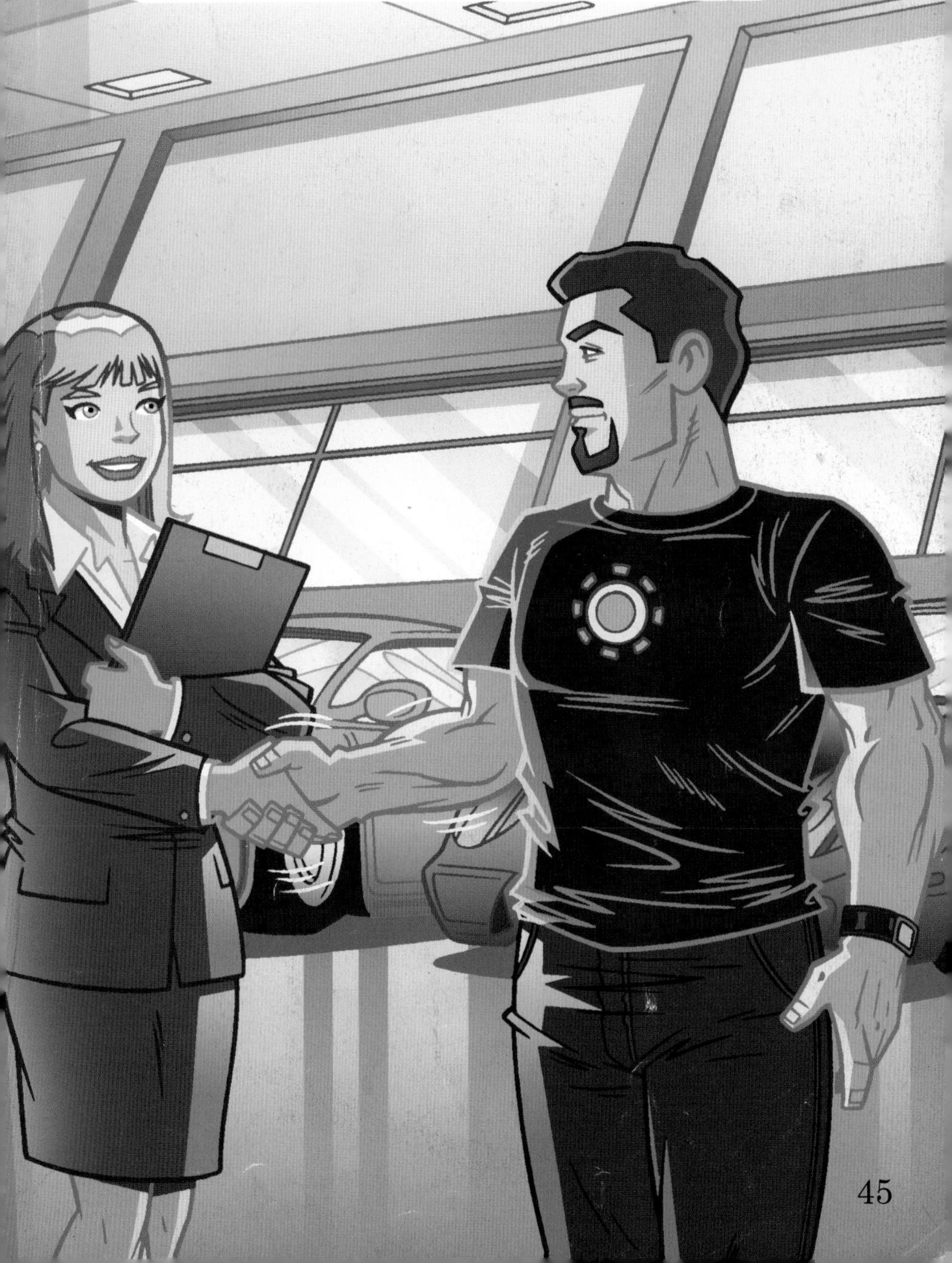

Pepper is not the only friend
who is always there for her boss.
Happy works for Tony, too.

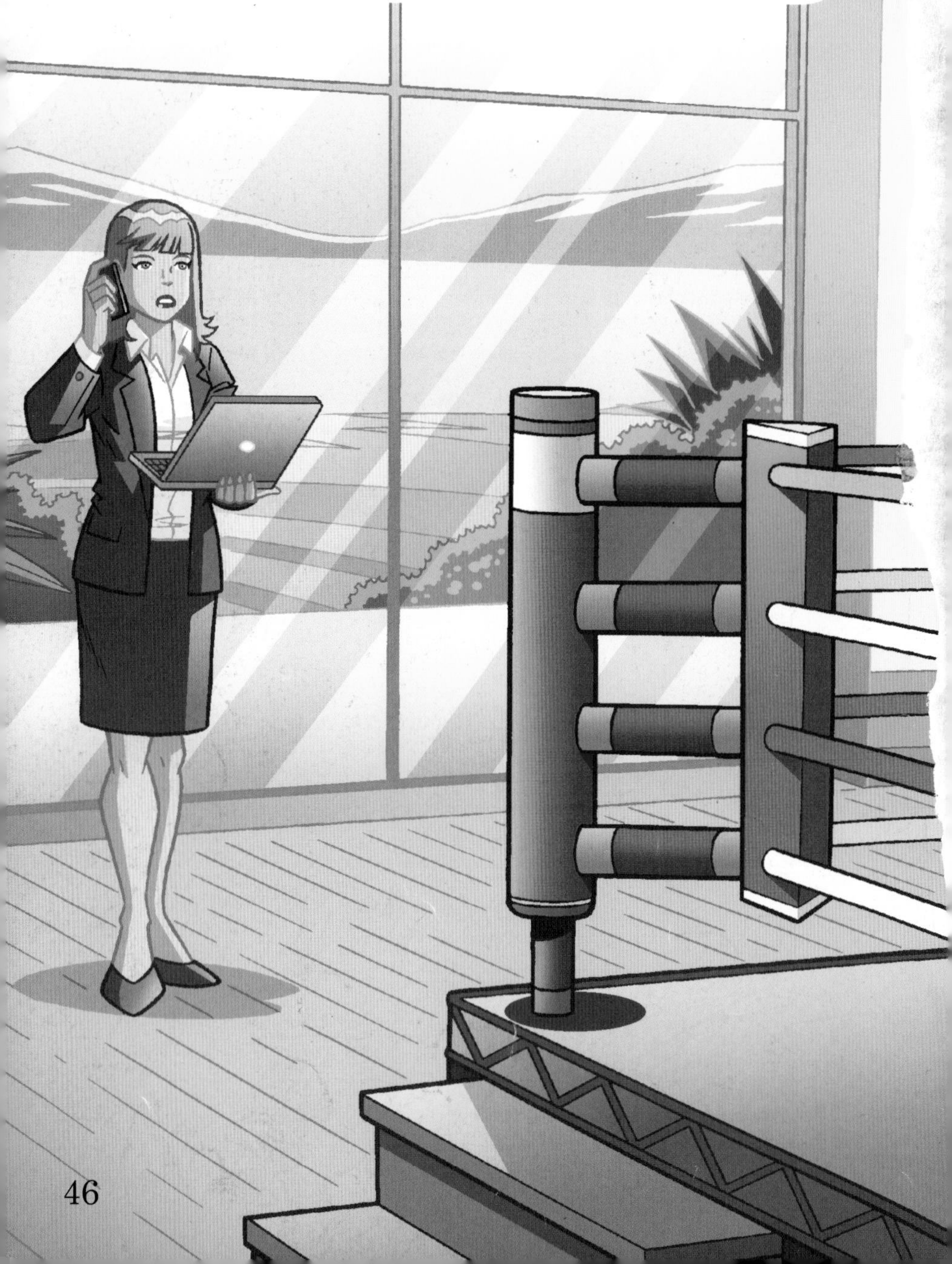

Happy is a bodyguard and limo driver,
and he does anything Tony asks.
He even helps Tony practice boxing!

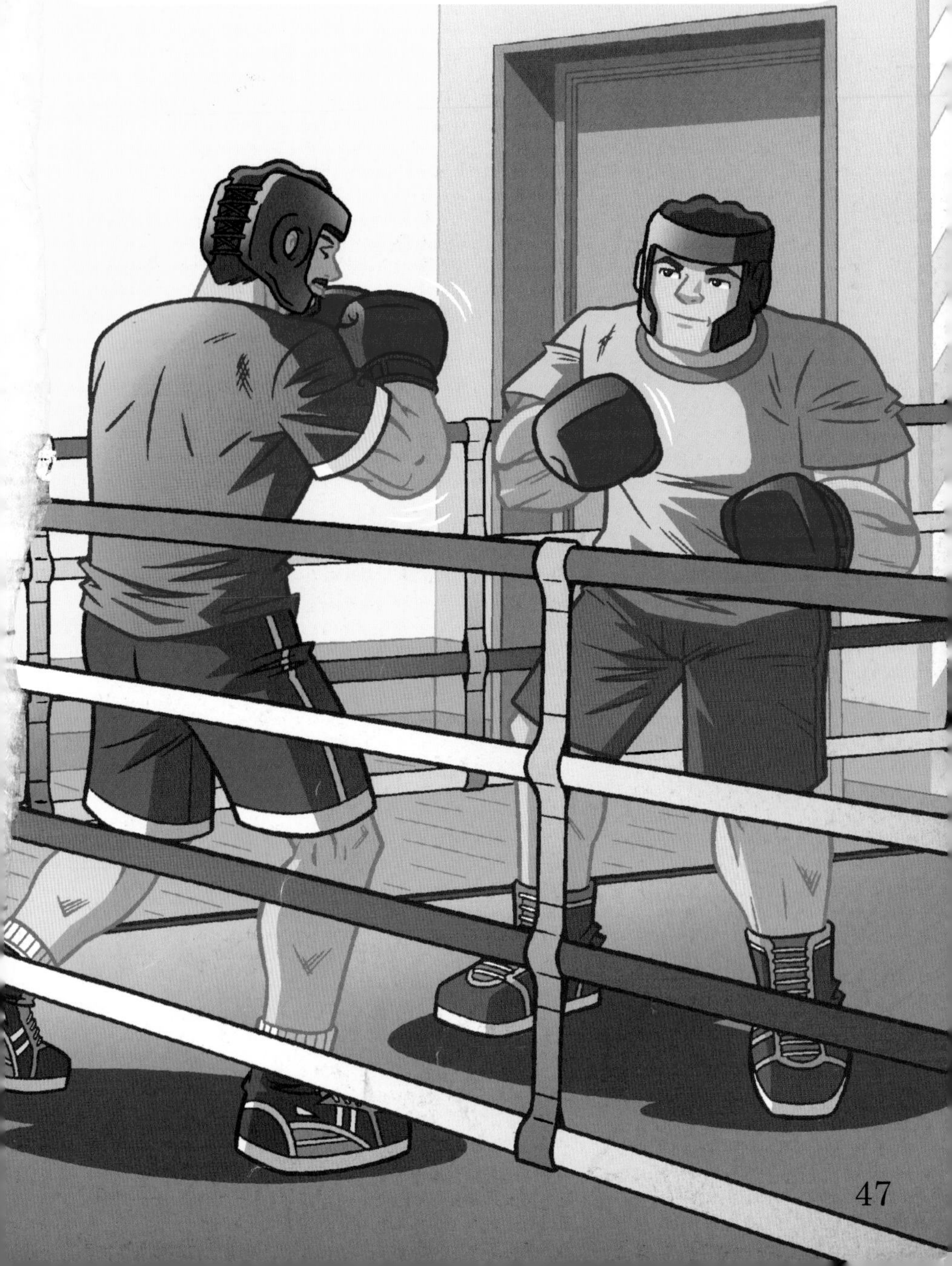

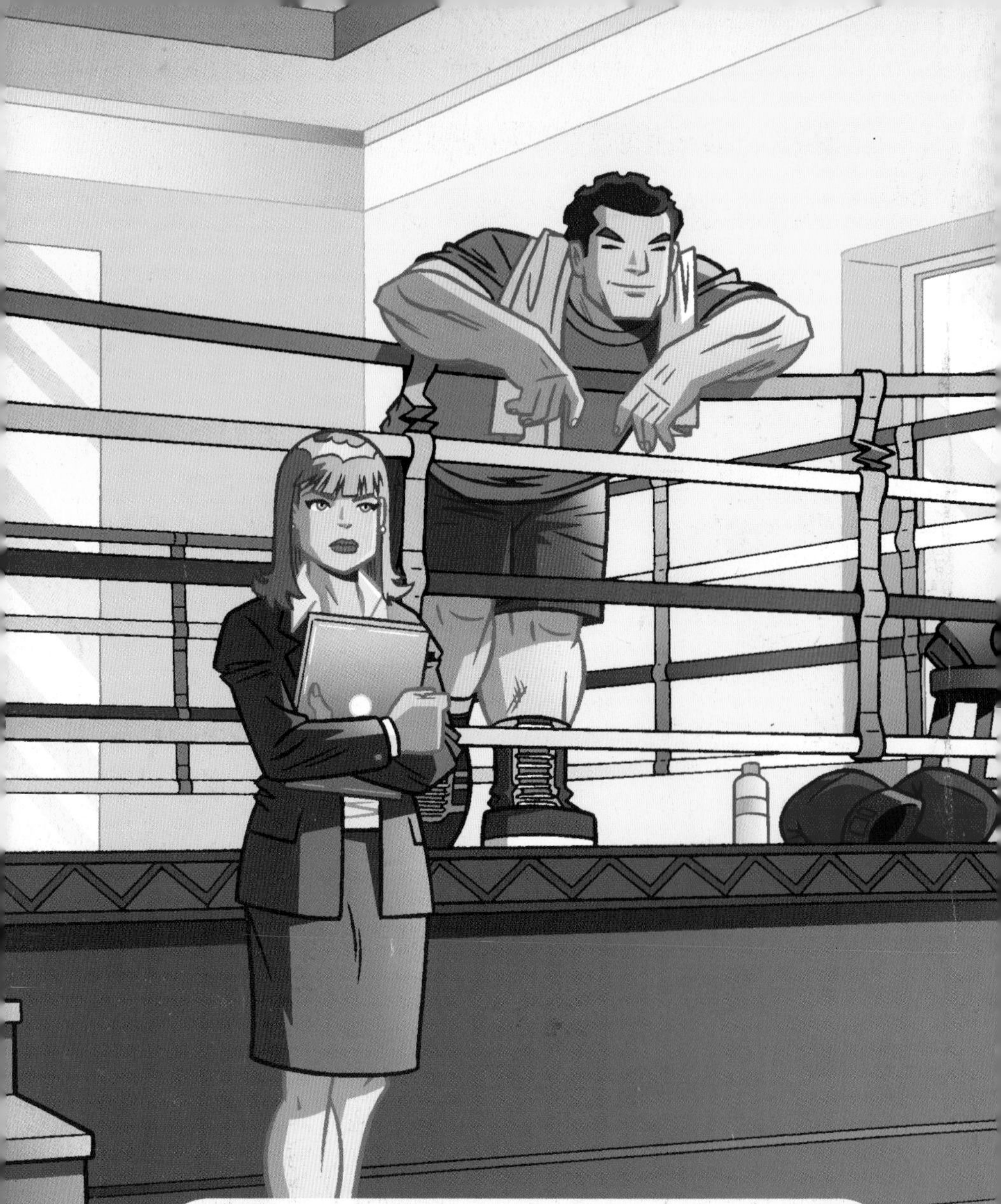

Natalie Rushman is a paralegal.
She works for Tony's company.
Natalie is pretty.
She is smart, too.

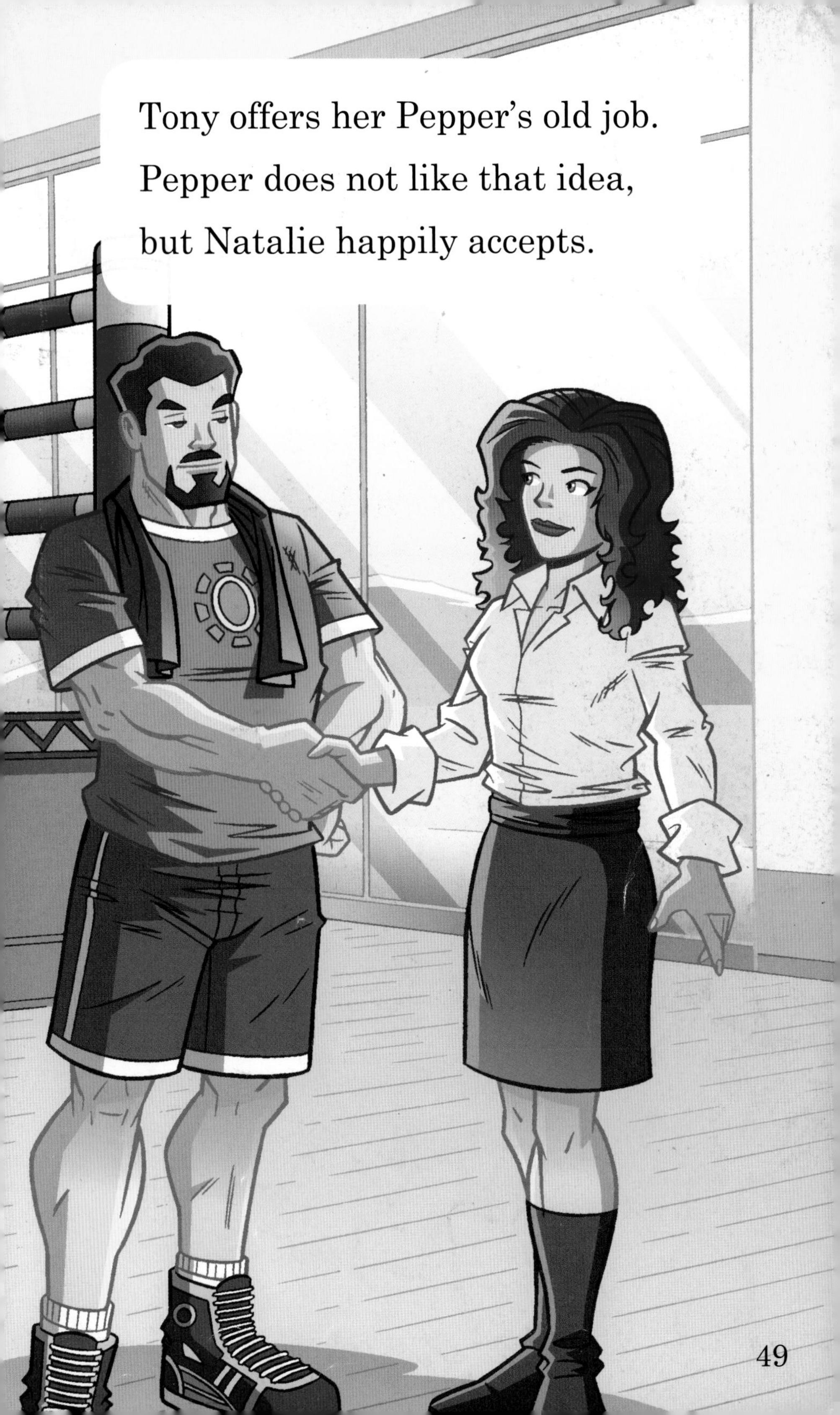
Tony offers her Pepper's old job. Pepper does not like that idea, but Natalie happily accepts.

Tony invites his friends to go to a car race. When they get there, Tony discovers that some of his foes are also there.

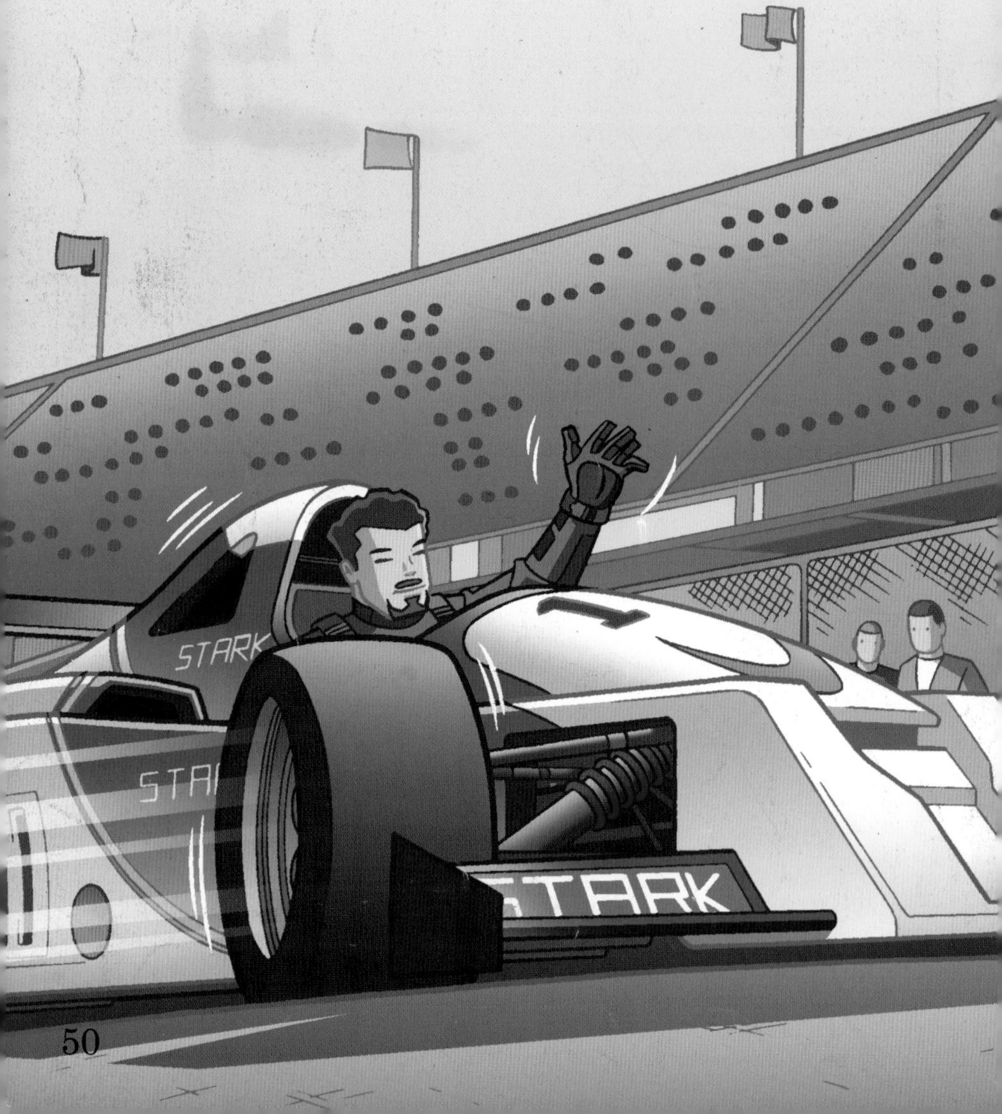
STARK
STARK
STARK

Justin Hammer shows up.

Hammer owns a car, too.

But Tony has a big surprise.

He is one of the race car drivers!

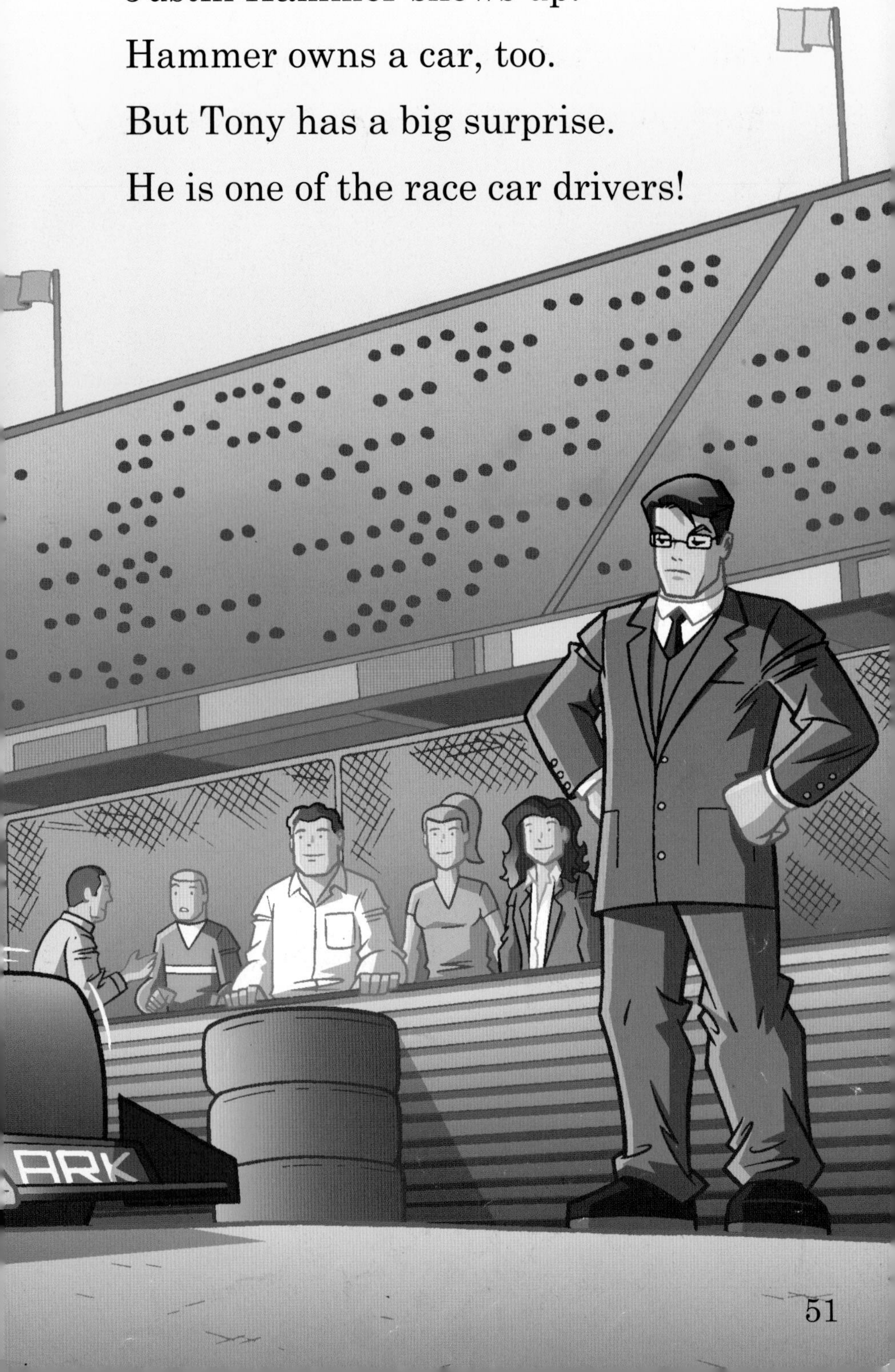
ARK

A strange man walks onto the track during the race.
His name is Ivan Vanko.
Cars crash around him.

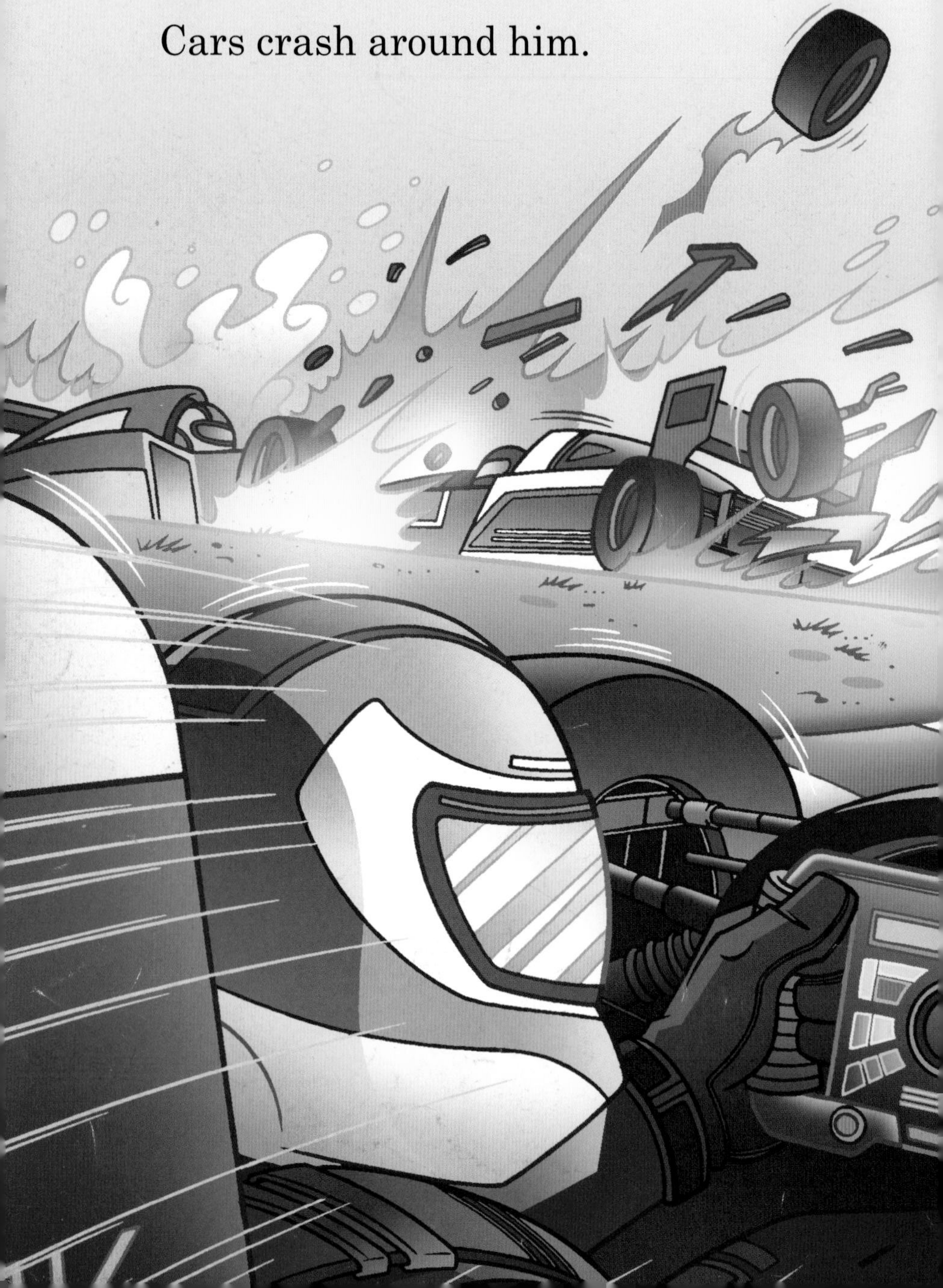

Ivan shouts out loud,
"You come from a family of thieves!"
He wants to hurt Tony!

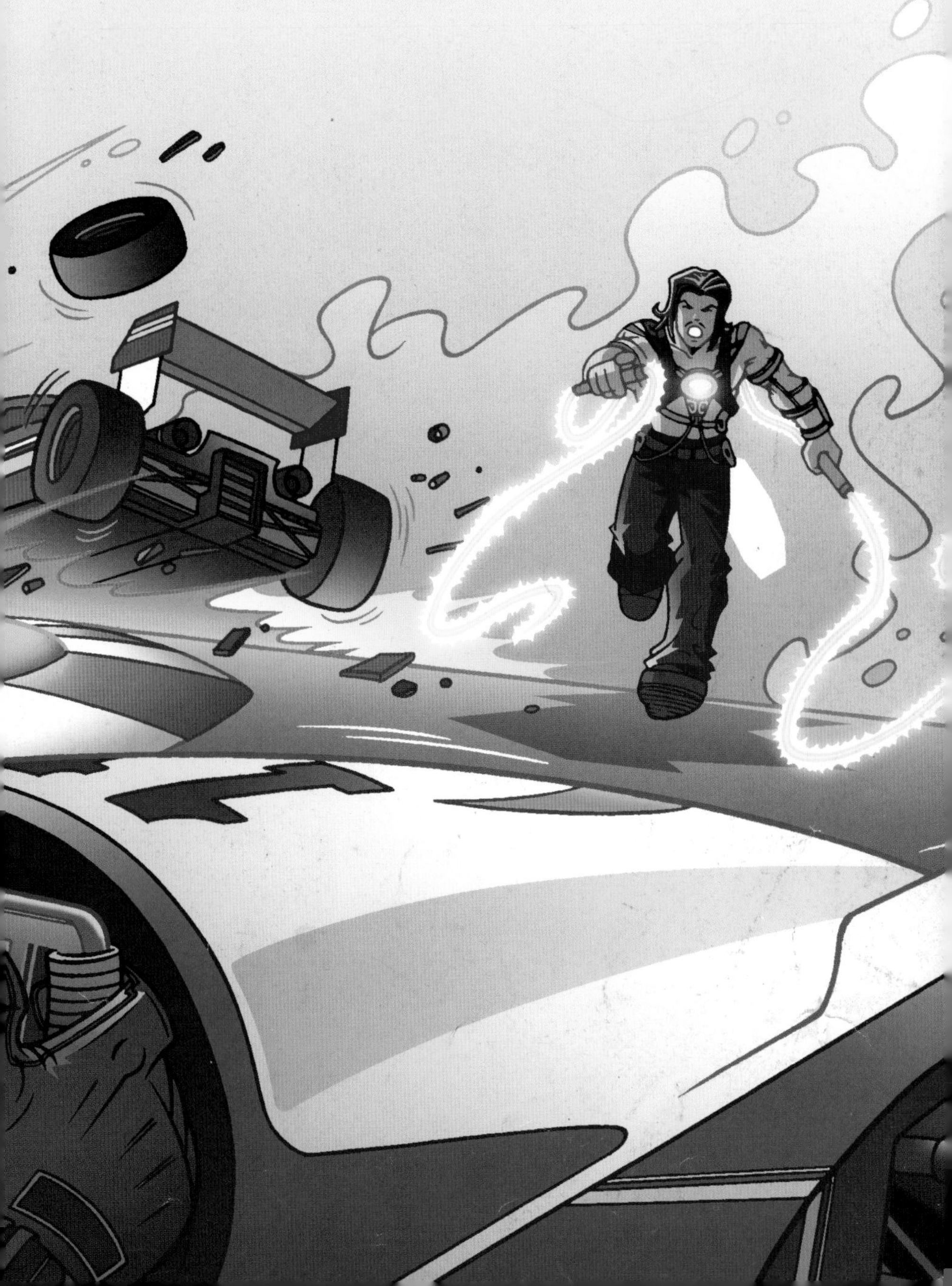

Ivan has a repulsor on his chest.
It is like the one Iron Man wears.
Ivan uses it to power whips on his arms.
He calls himself Whiplash.

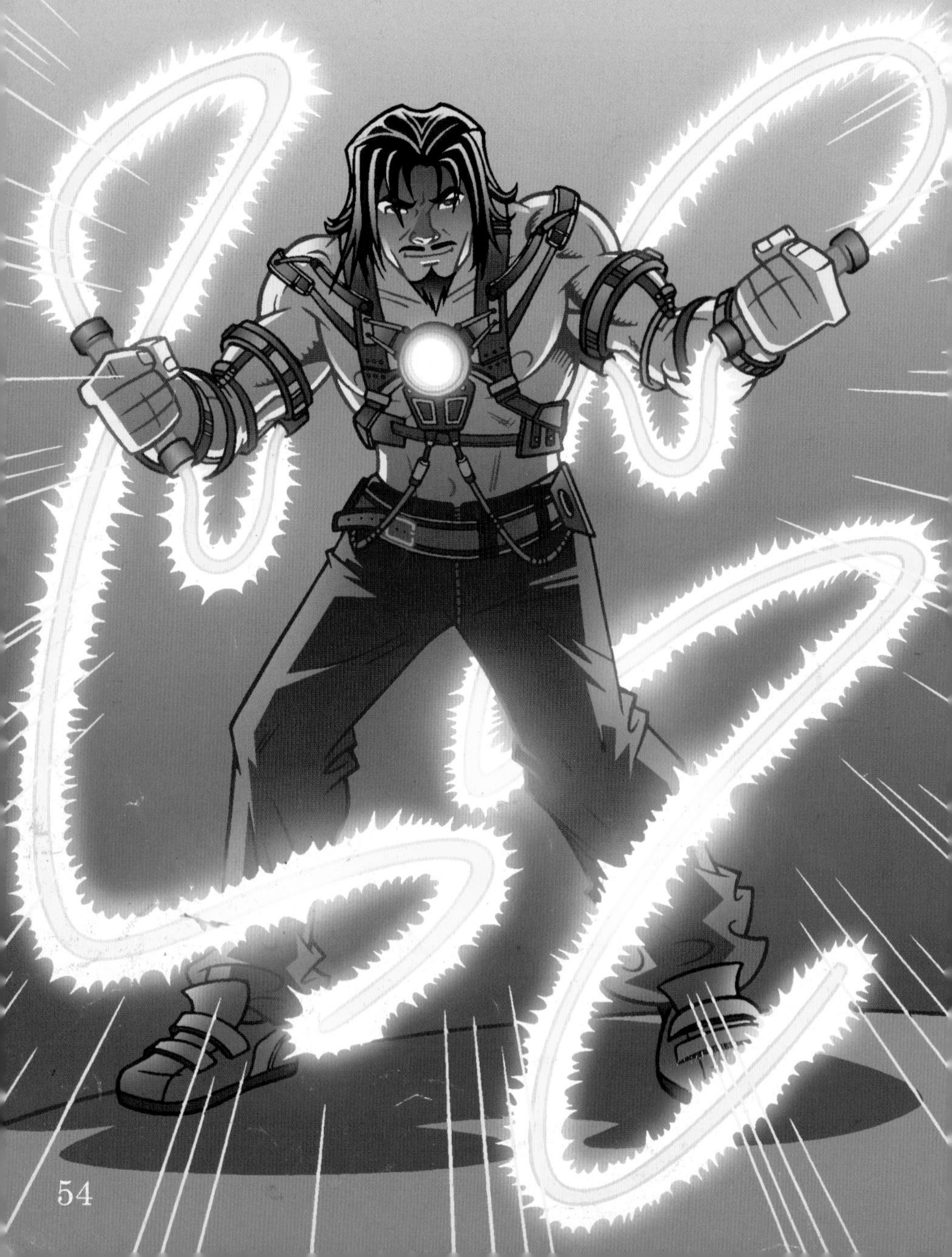

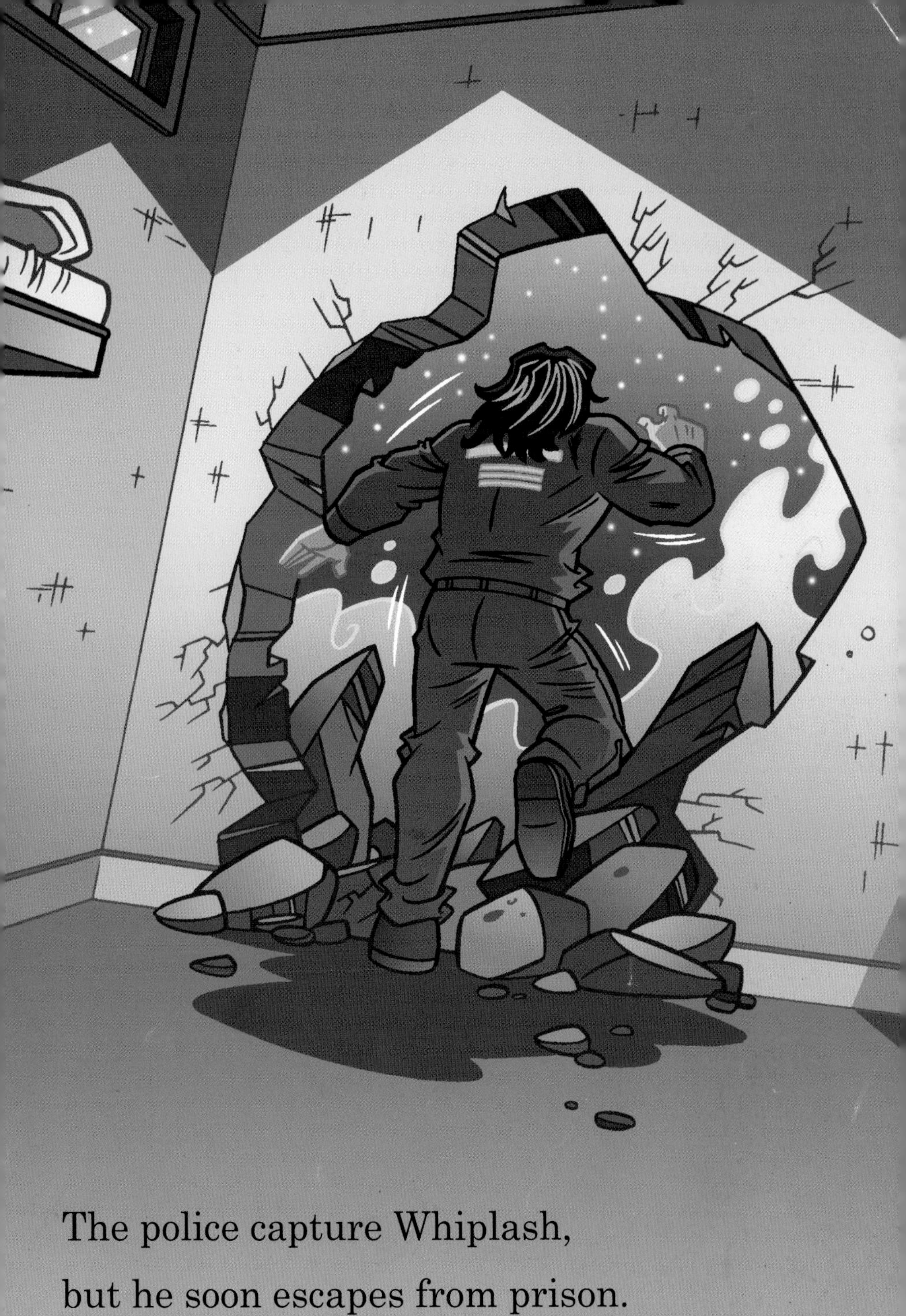

The police capture Whiplash,
but he soon escapes from prison.
He runs off to set his evil plan into motion.

Agent Coulson and Nick Fury talk to Tony about Whiplash. They work for S.H.I.E.L.D. The group fights bad guys, such as Whiplash.

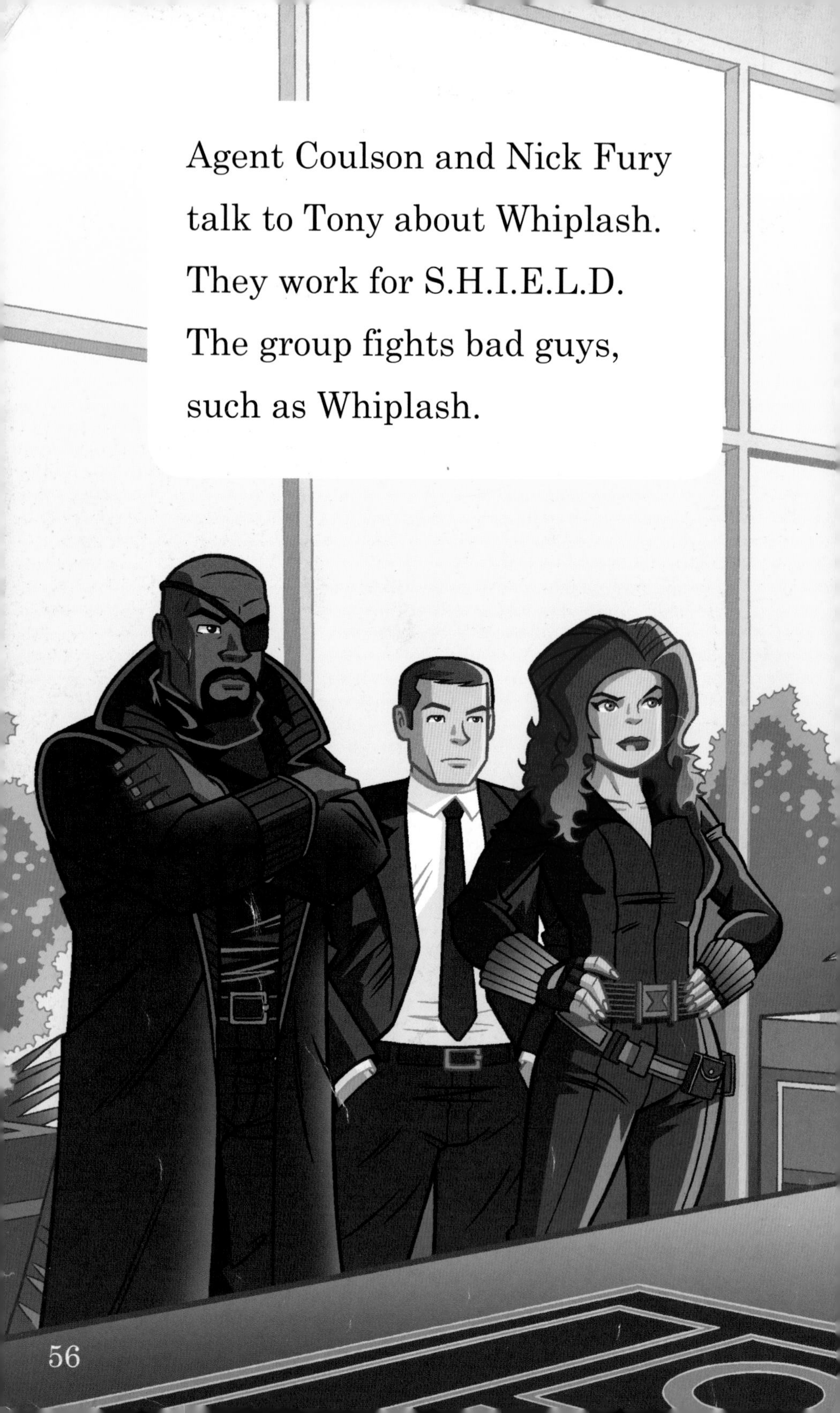

A woman in dark clothes joins Tony and Nick.
Tony cannot believe his eyes—she is Natalie!
Her real name is Natasha Romanoff.
She works for S.H.I.E.L.D., too.

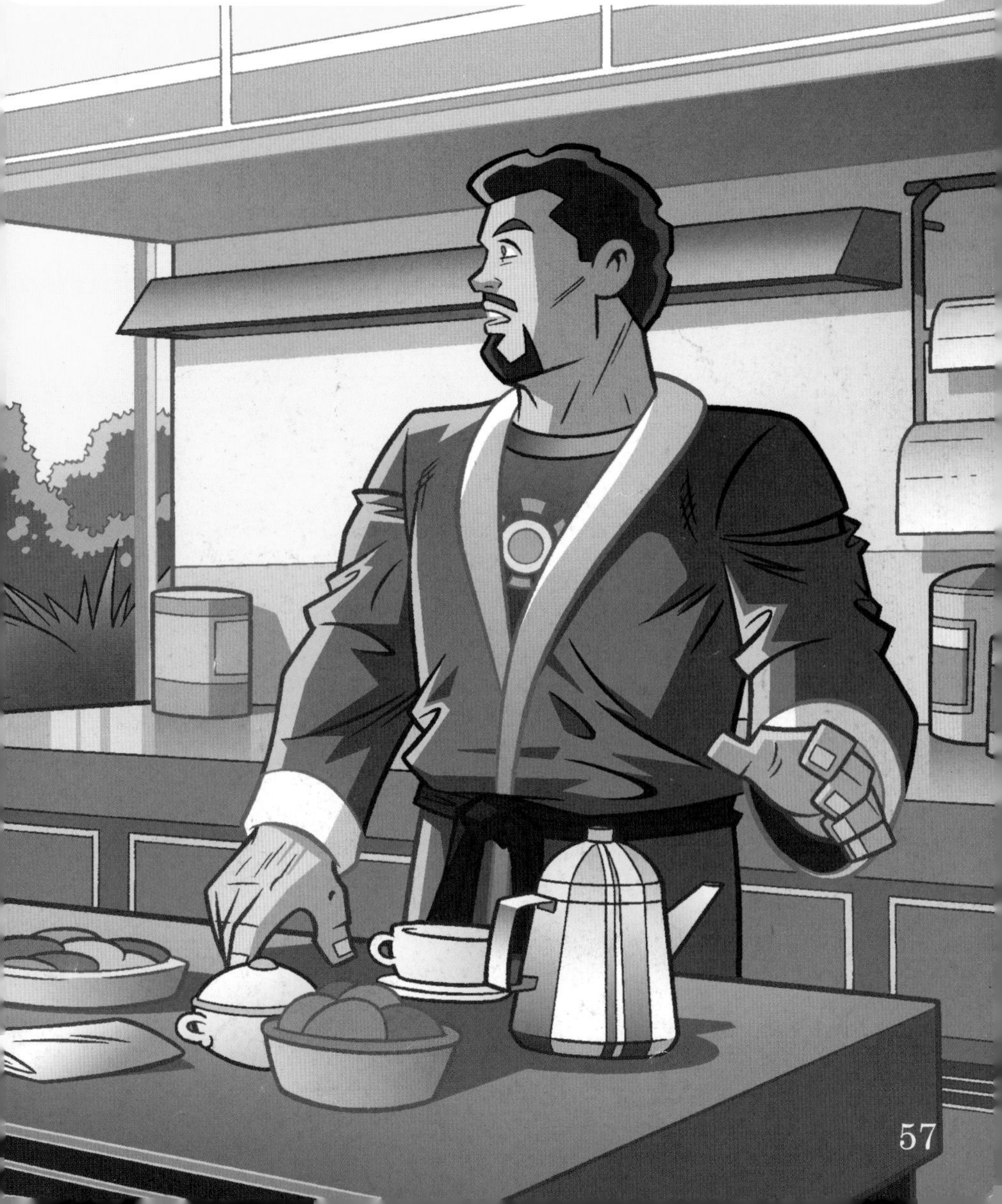

Rhodey sneaks an old Iron Man suit onto an air force base.
Weapons are added to the suit, turning it into a War Machine.

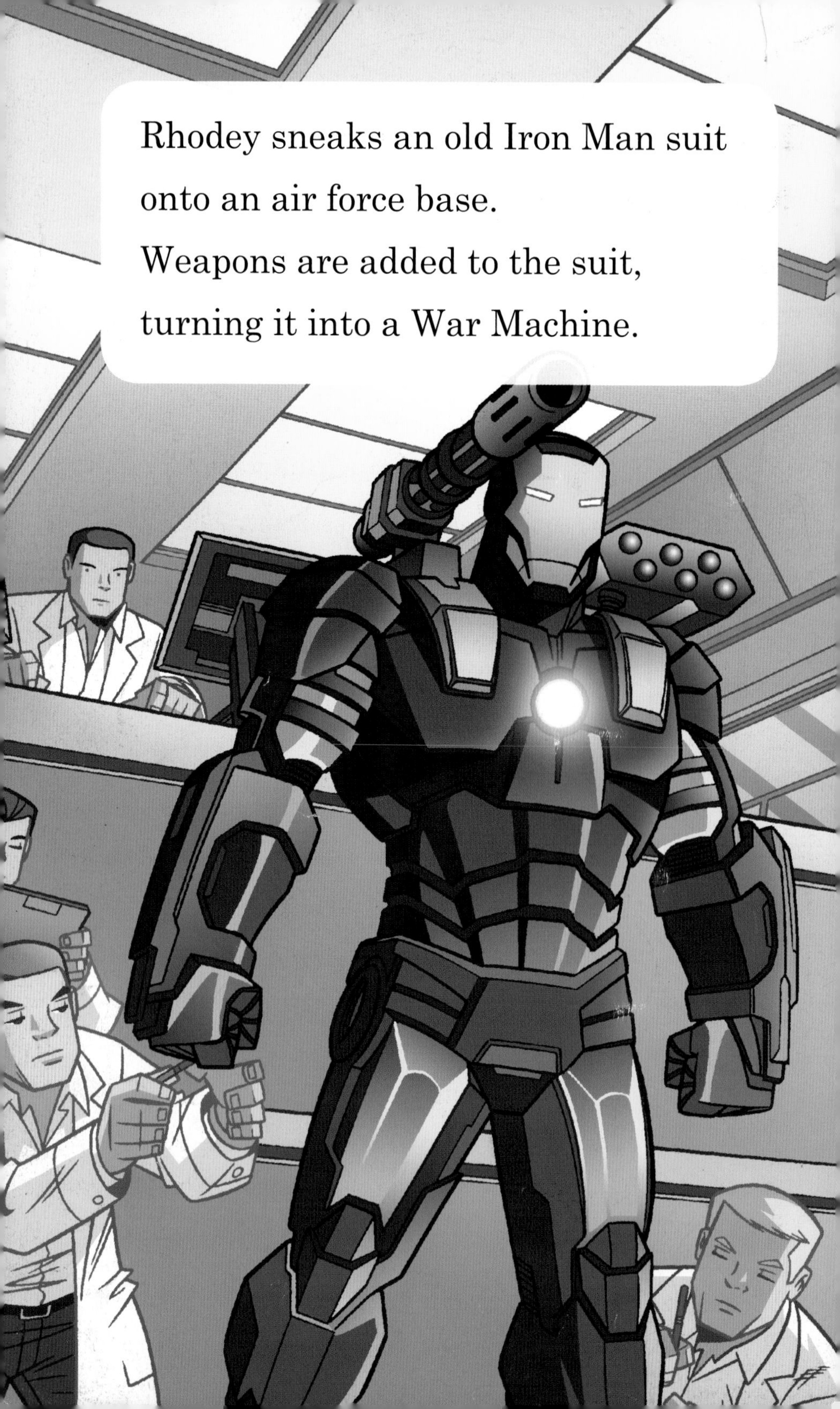

Rhodey says the suit is top secret.
It should be used only in an emergency.
But a general issues an order.
He wants the new suit shown to the public.

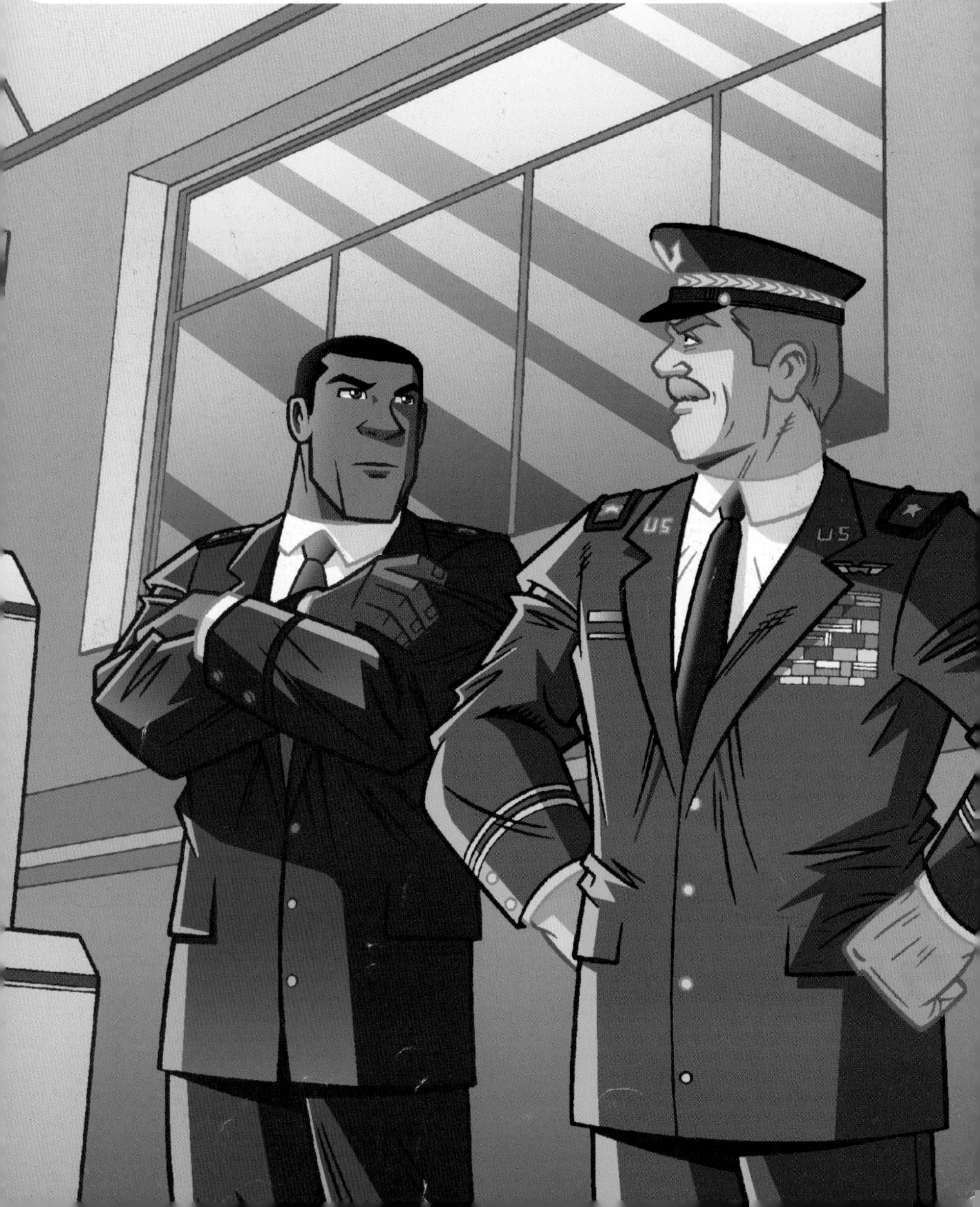
US
US

Pepper and Happy attend an expo. People show off their new inventions. They see Rhodey in the War Machine suit.

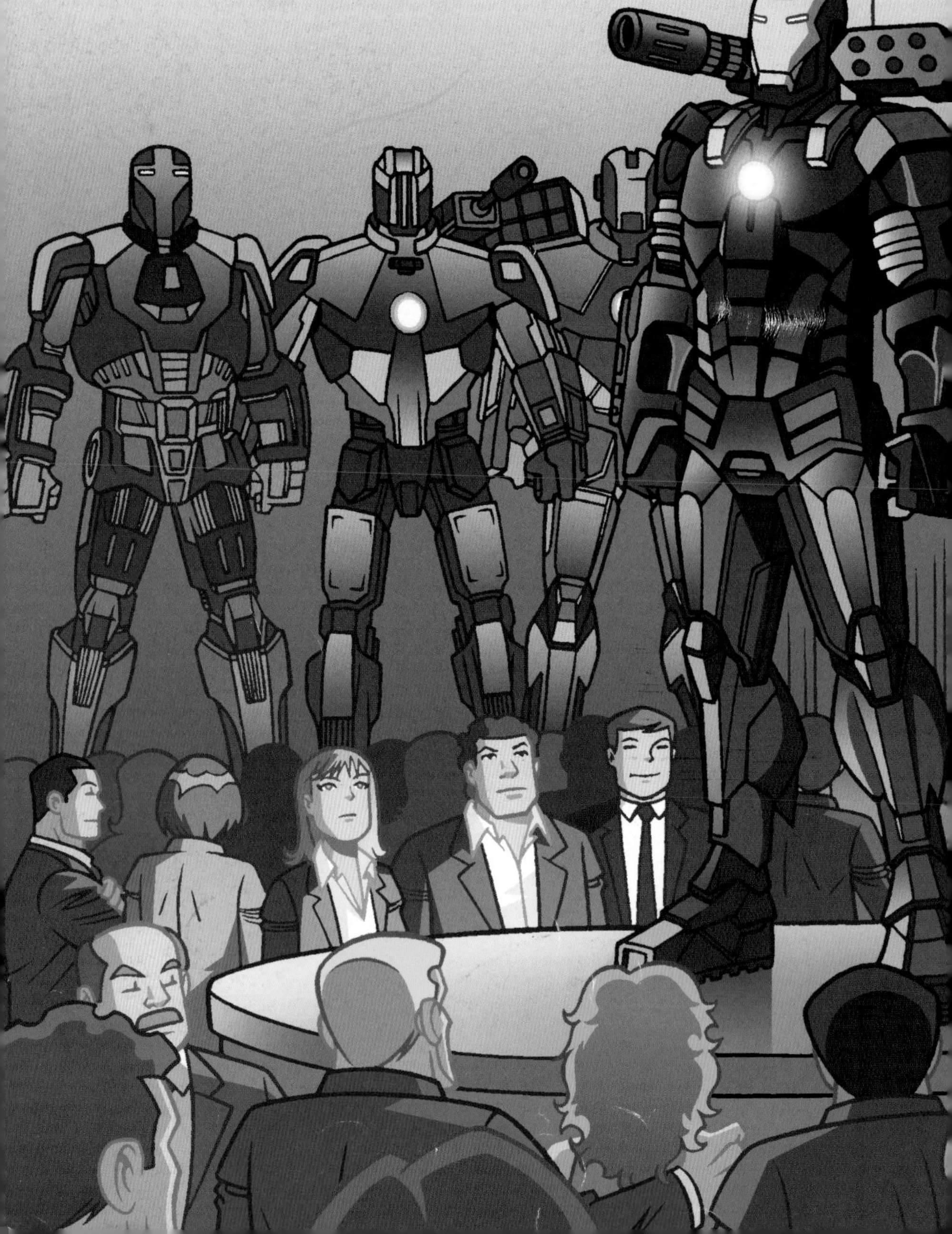

There are some new robots on display.
No one knows where they came from—
no one except Whiplash.
He built them to start trouble.

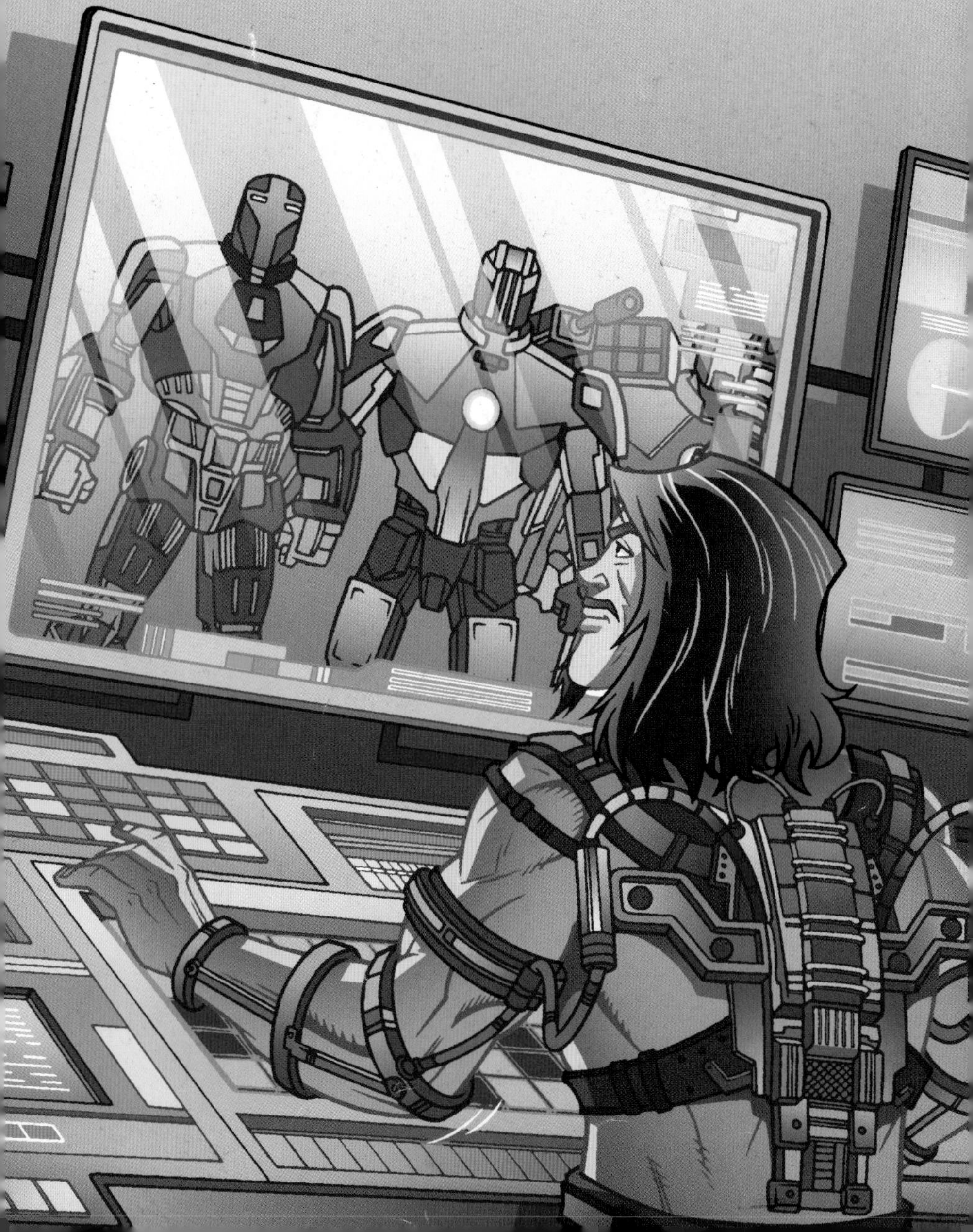

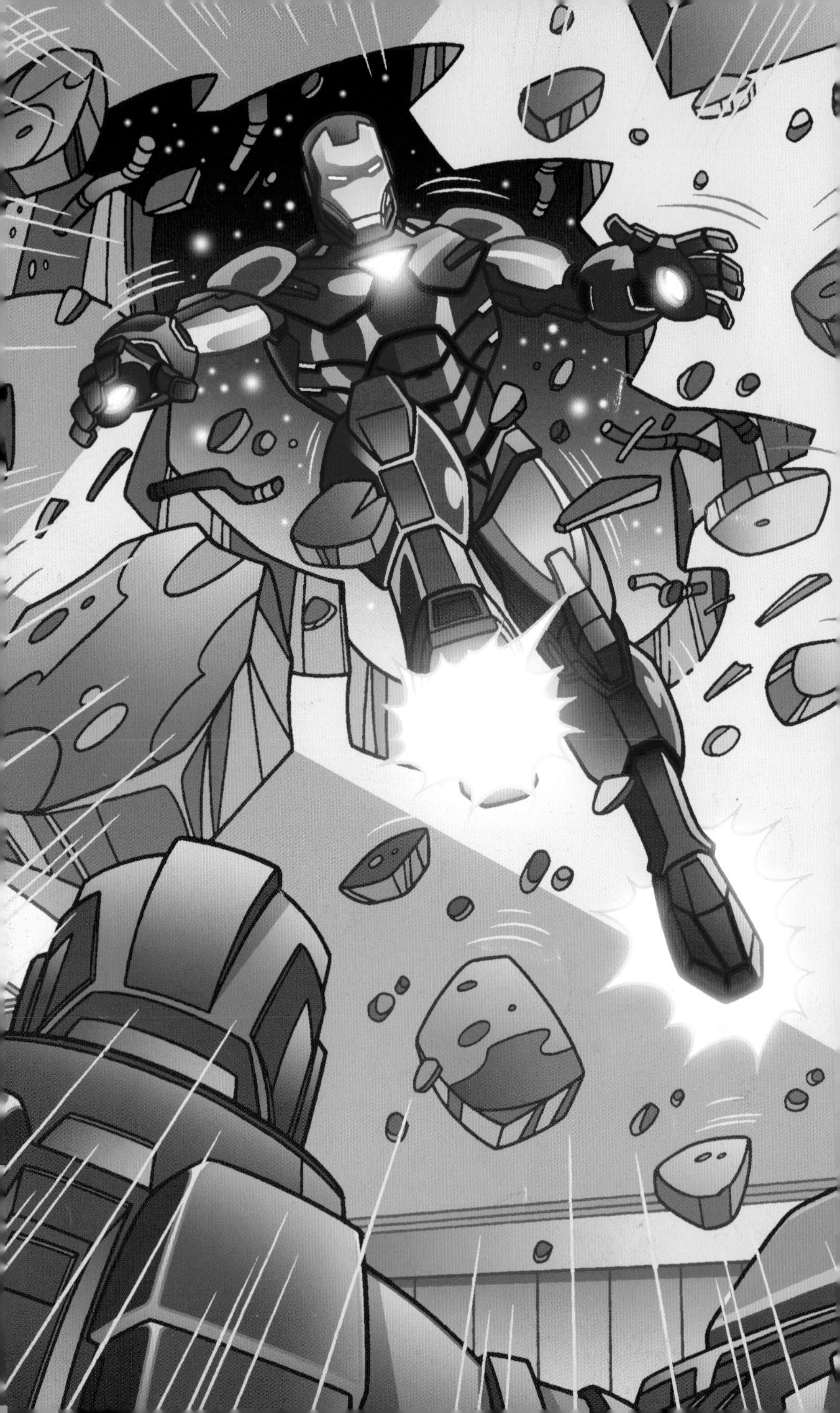

Surprise!

Iron Man drops in.

Iron Man was tracking Whiplash.

He knows that the villain built the robots.

He knows that the robots are dangerous.

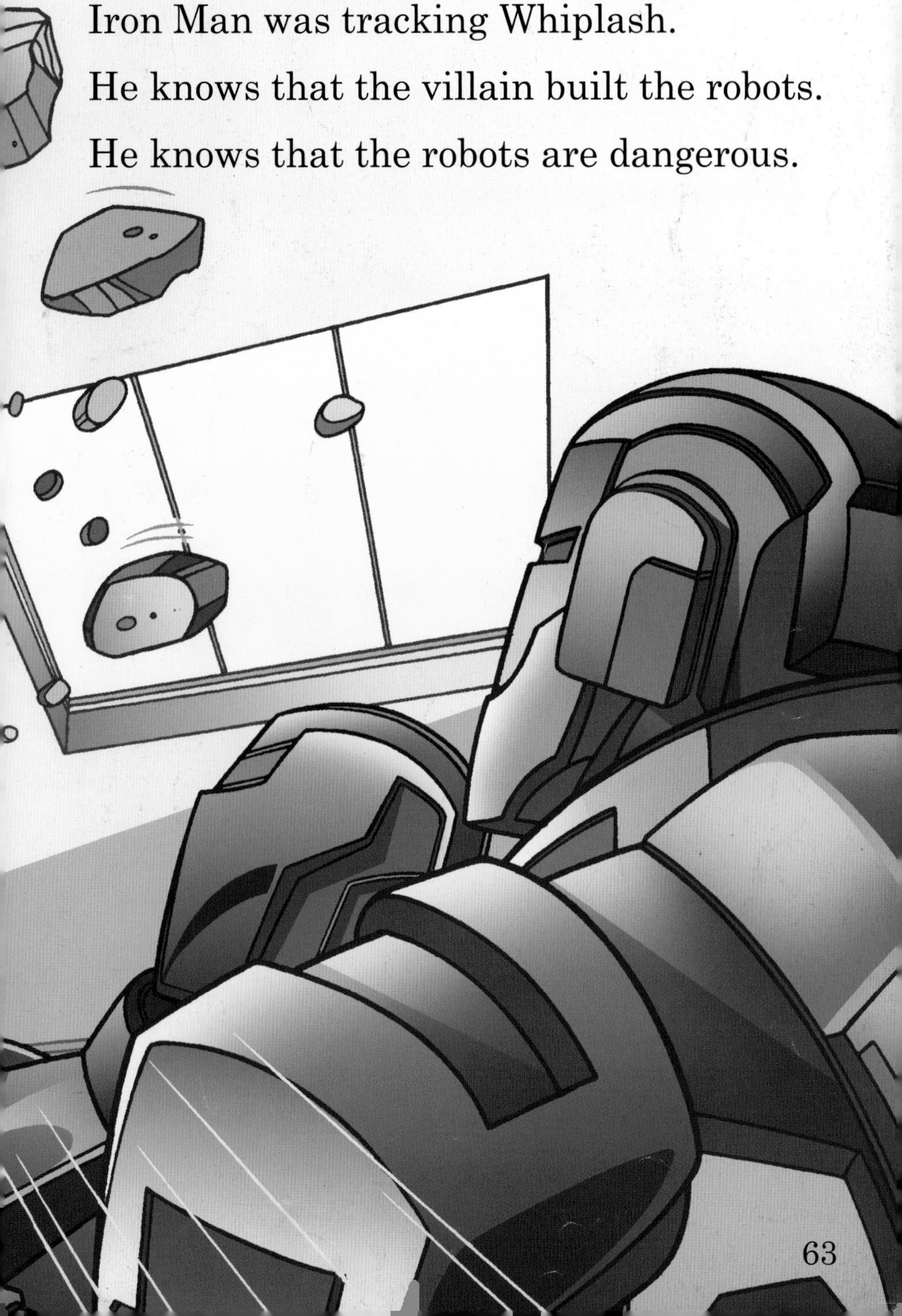

He is right—the robots start to fire!
Even the War Machine suit
takes aim at Iron Man!
Rhodey cannot control it!
He warns his friend
to watch out.

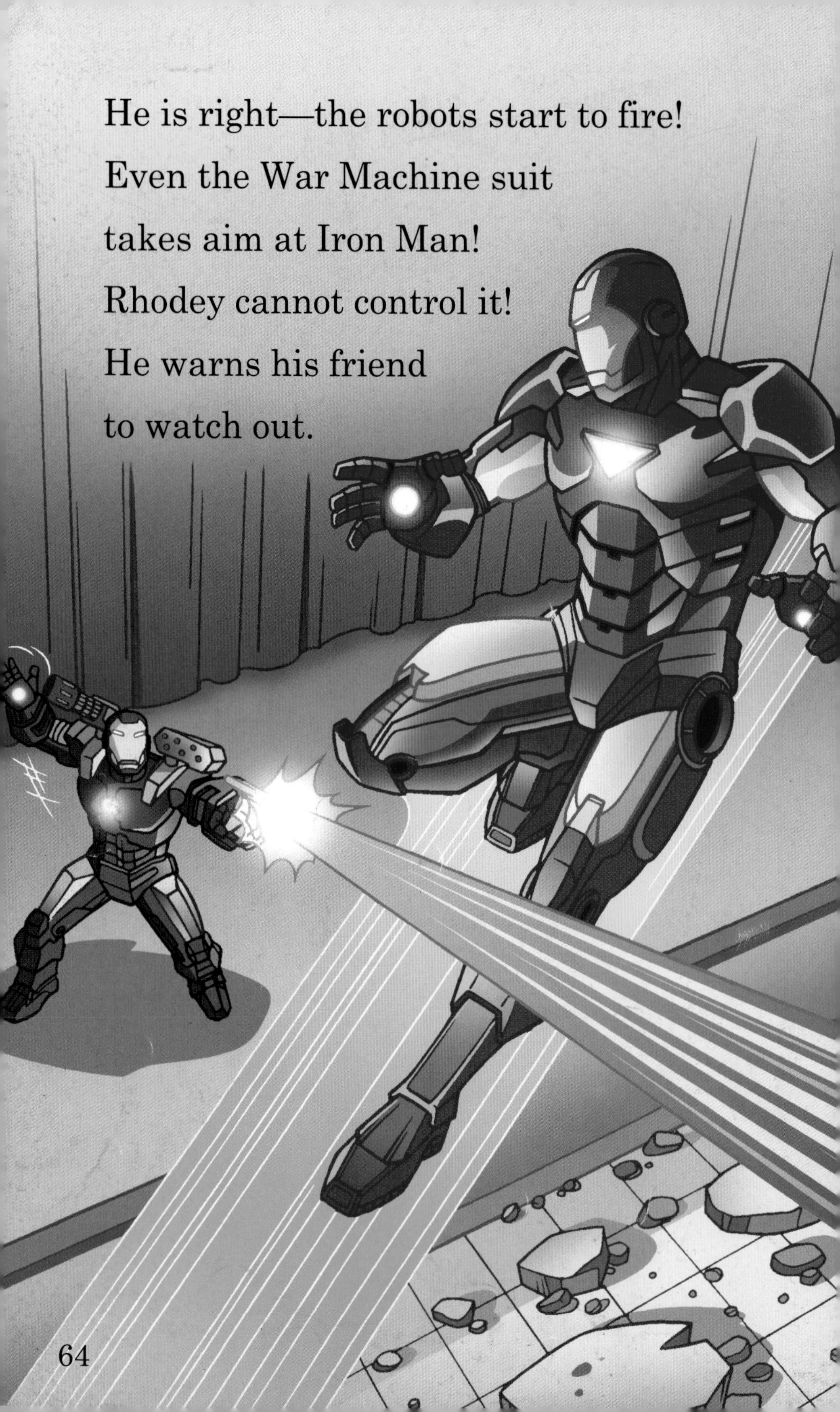

There are too many robots
for Tony to handle alone.
Even in his Iron Man suit,
Tony needs help from his friends.

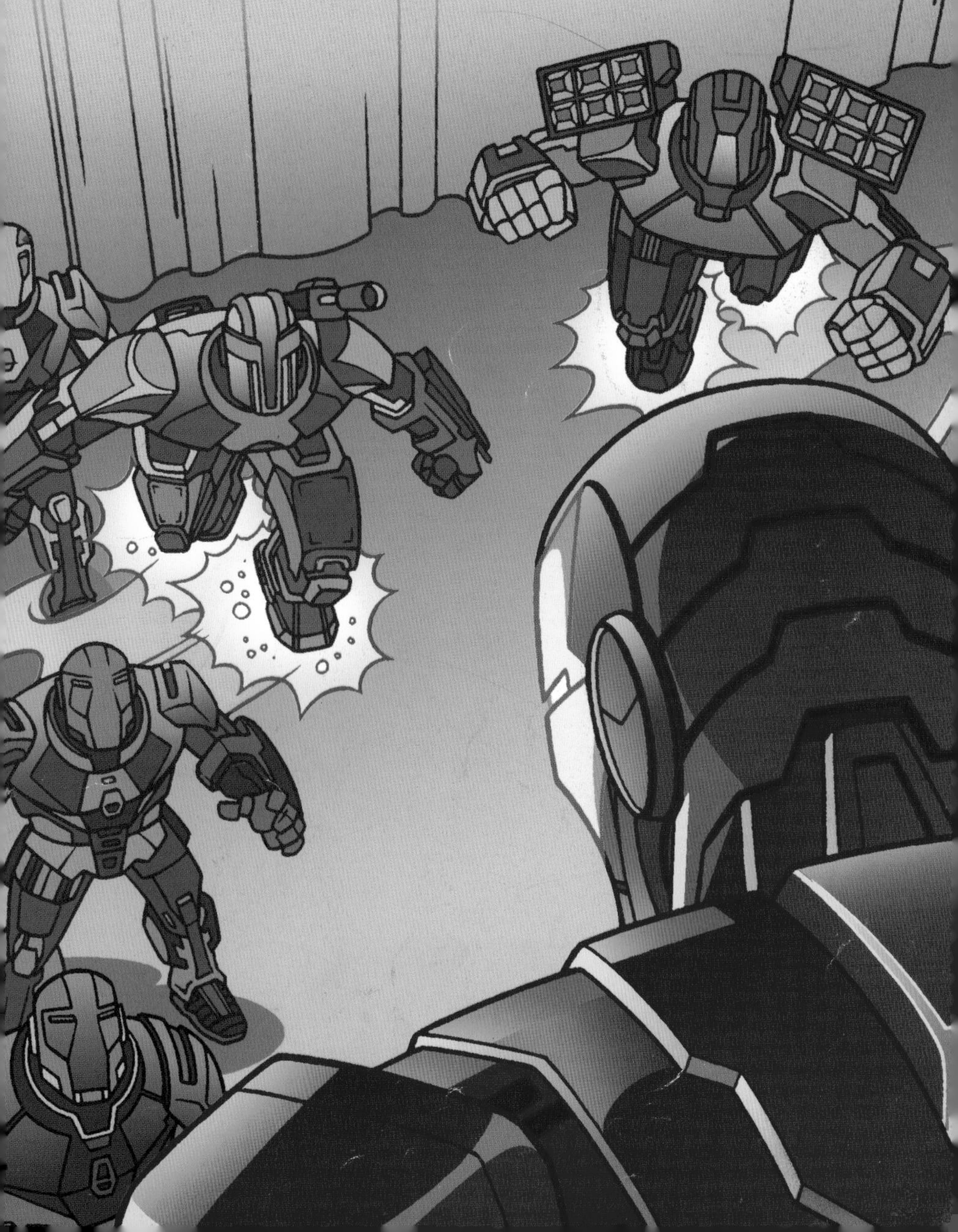

Pepper and Happy are there to help.
The S.H.I.E.L.D. agents show up
just in time to join the battle, too.
Iron Man knows that with friends
like these, he will always win.

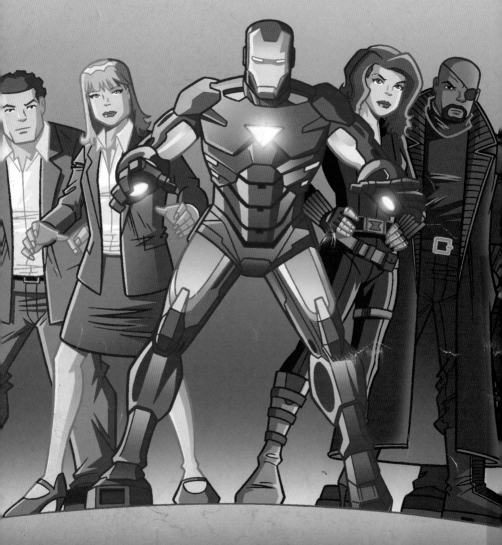

MARVEL

IRON MAN 2

MEET THE BLACK WIDOW

100% POWER

Adapted by LISA SHEA

Screenplay by JUSTIN THEROUX

Produced by KEVIN FEIGE

Directed by JON FAVREAU

Pictures by GUIDO GUIDI

When he is not saving the day
as the Super Hero named Iron Man,
Tony Stark runs a company
called Stark Industries.

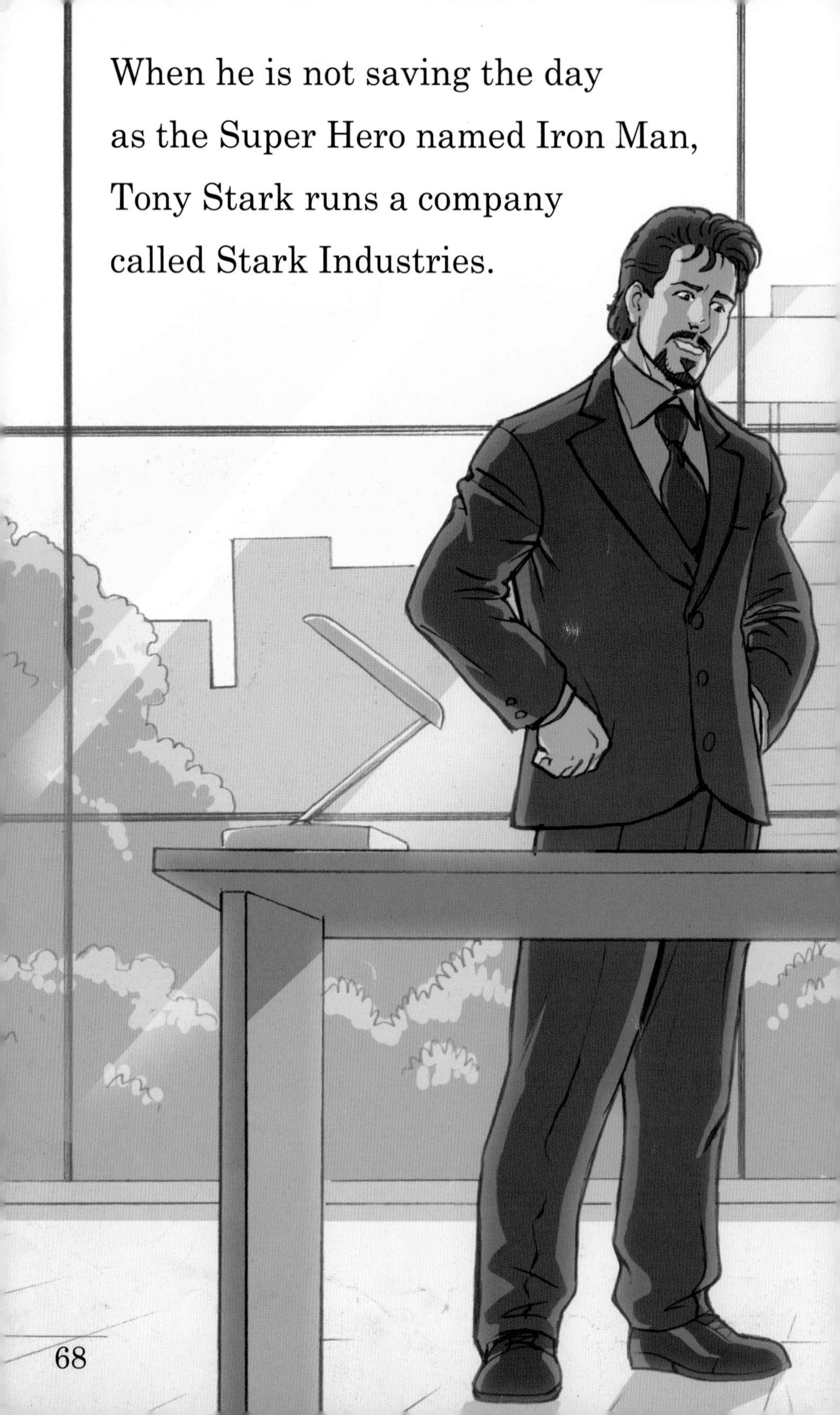

Pepper Potts works for Tony.
She used to be his assistant.
Tony was so happy with Pepper,
he gave her a promotion.

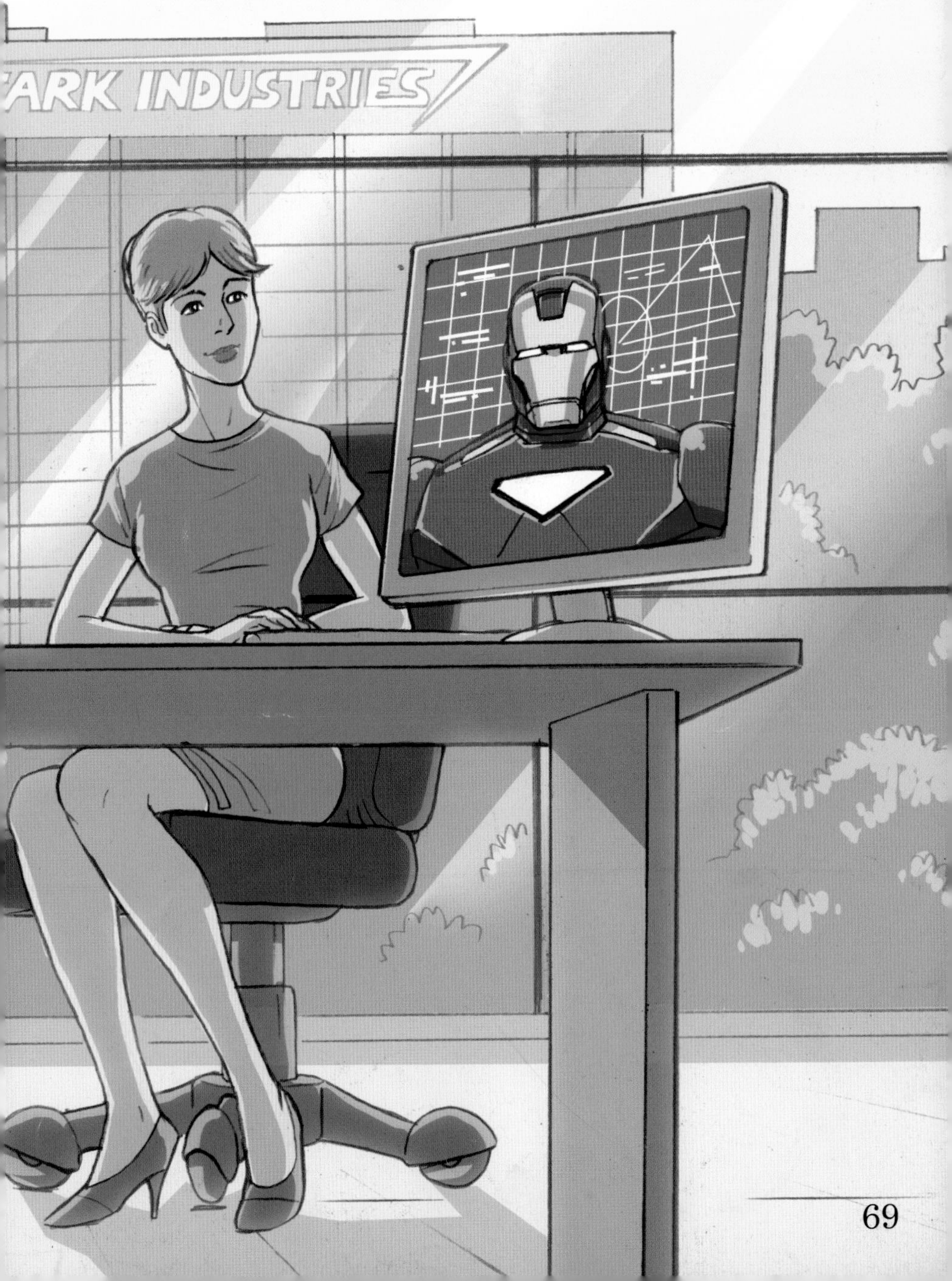
ARK INDUSTRIES

Now Tony needs a new assistant.

What about Happy?

He is a good friend.

But Happy already has a lot of jobs.

He is Tony's bodyguard and driver.

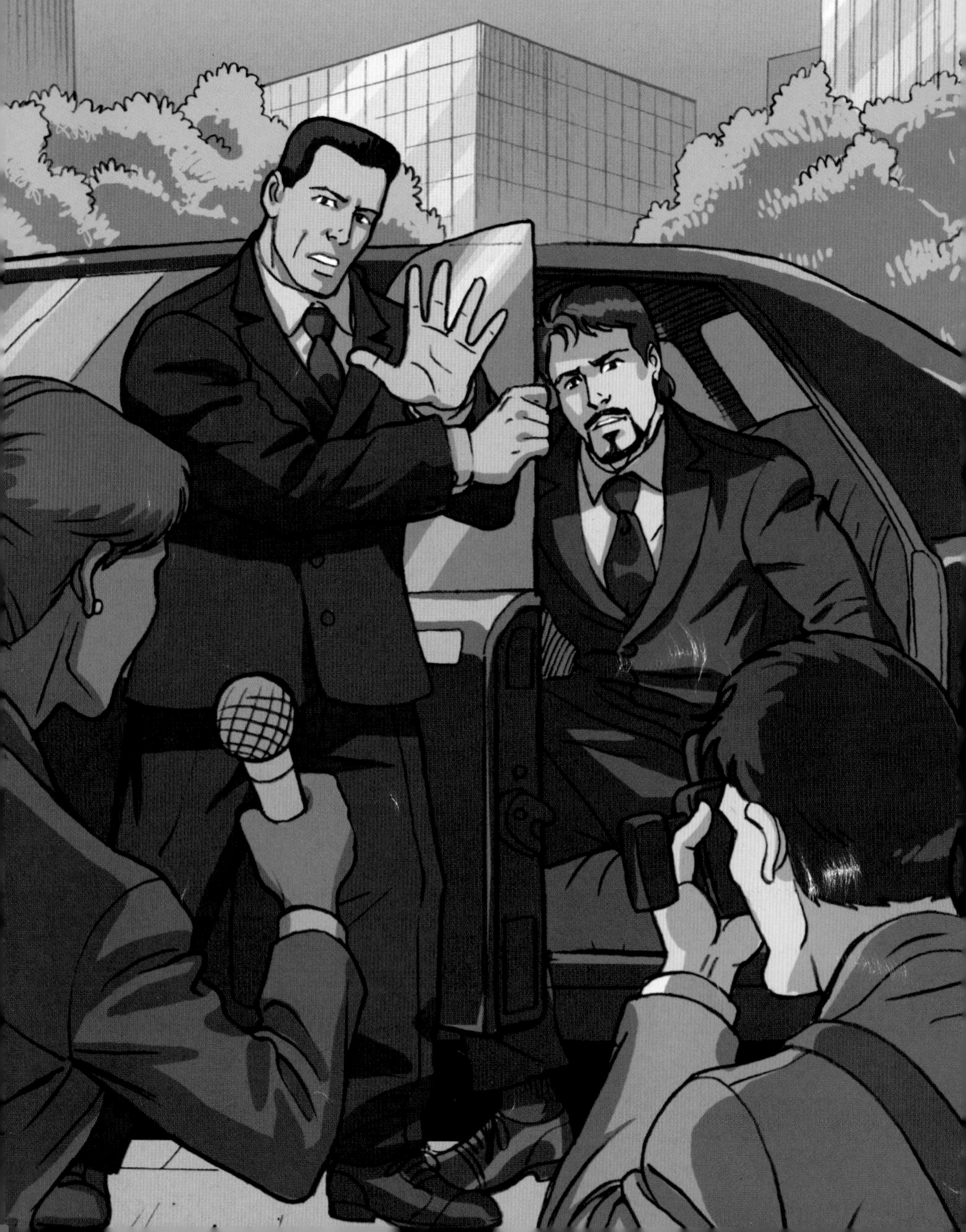

Happy also works as Tony's trainer
and throws punches in a boxing ring.
Being Iron Man is hard work.
Tony needs to stay in shape.

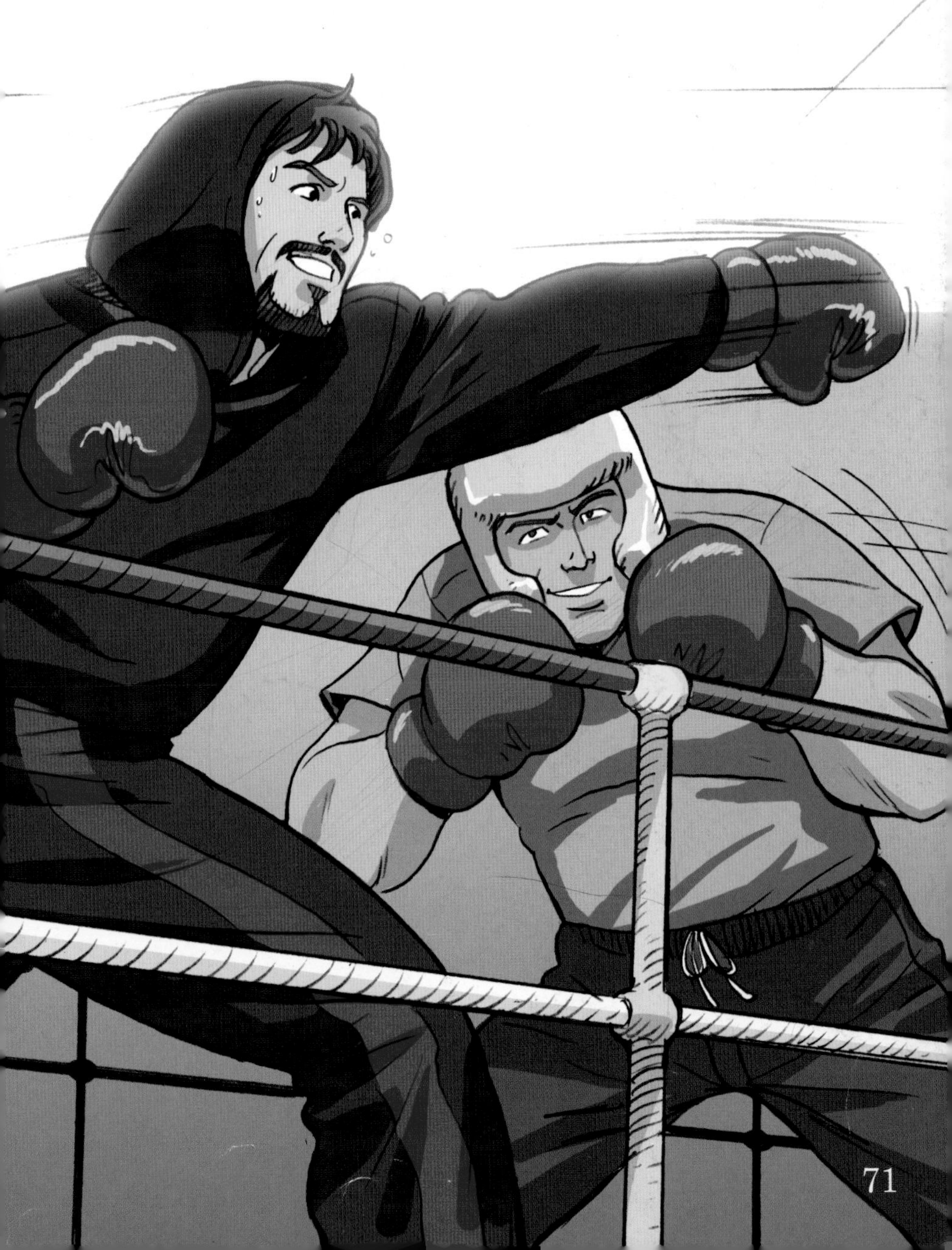

Natalie Rushman shows up at the gym.
She is new at Stark Industries
and has a contract for Tony to sign.
Natalie watches Tony and Happy box.

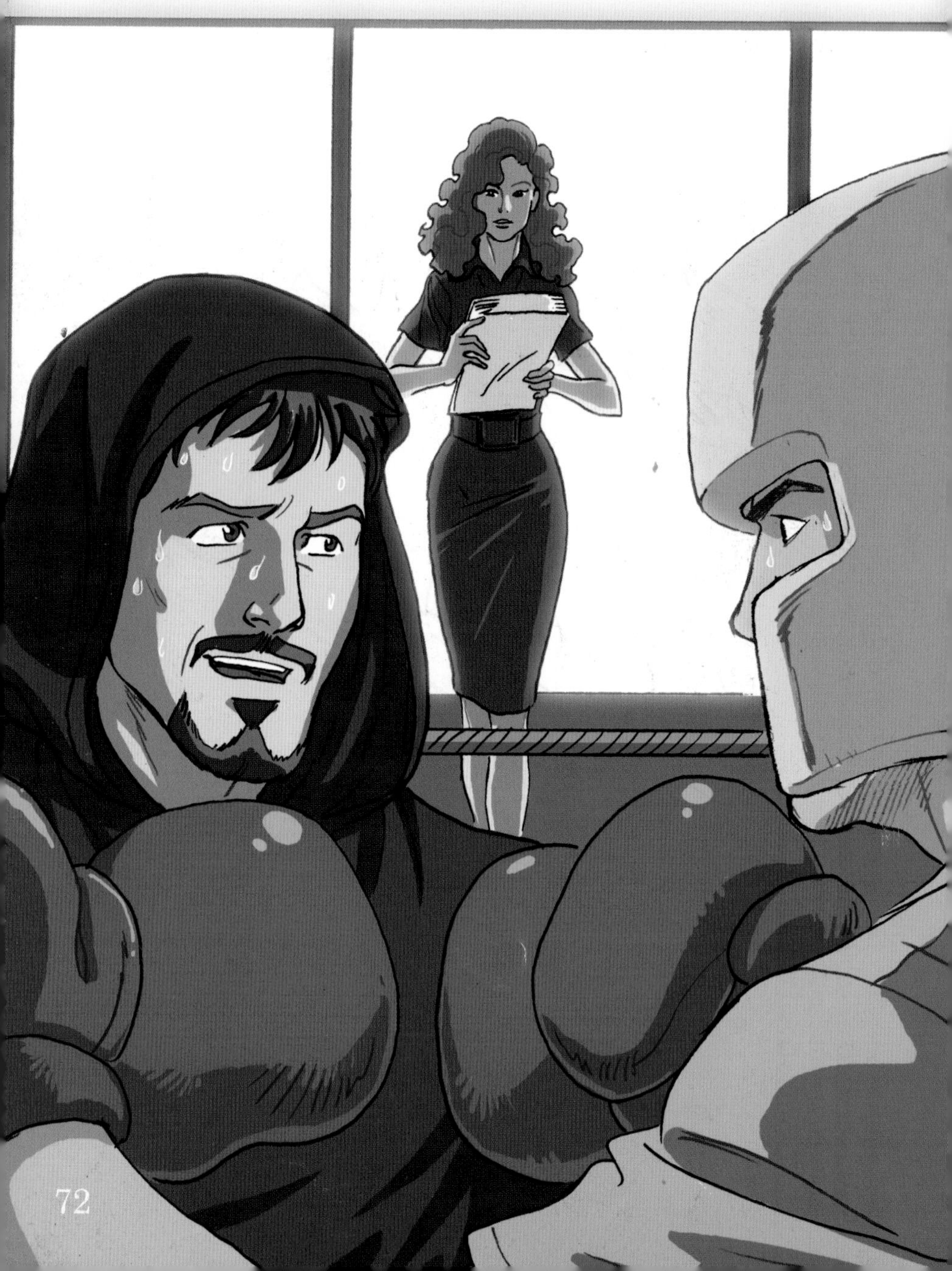

Tony stops boxing to meet Natalie.
Tony asks about her work experience
and is impressed with her answers.
"Will you be my new assistant?" he asks.
Natalie says yes!

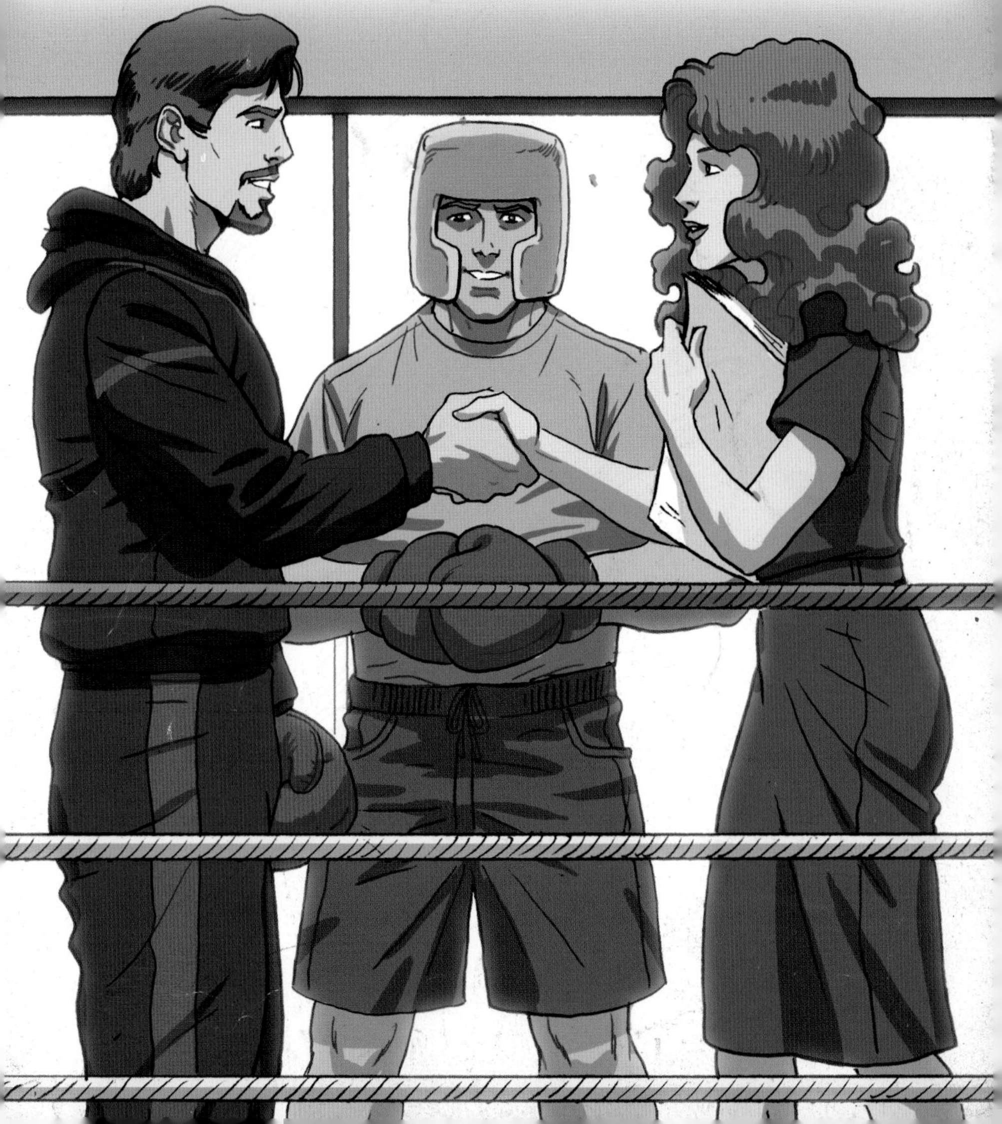

Tony takes everyone to Monaco so they can watch a car race. At a restaurant, Tony and Pepper try to order water, but the waiter only speaks French.

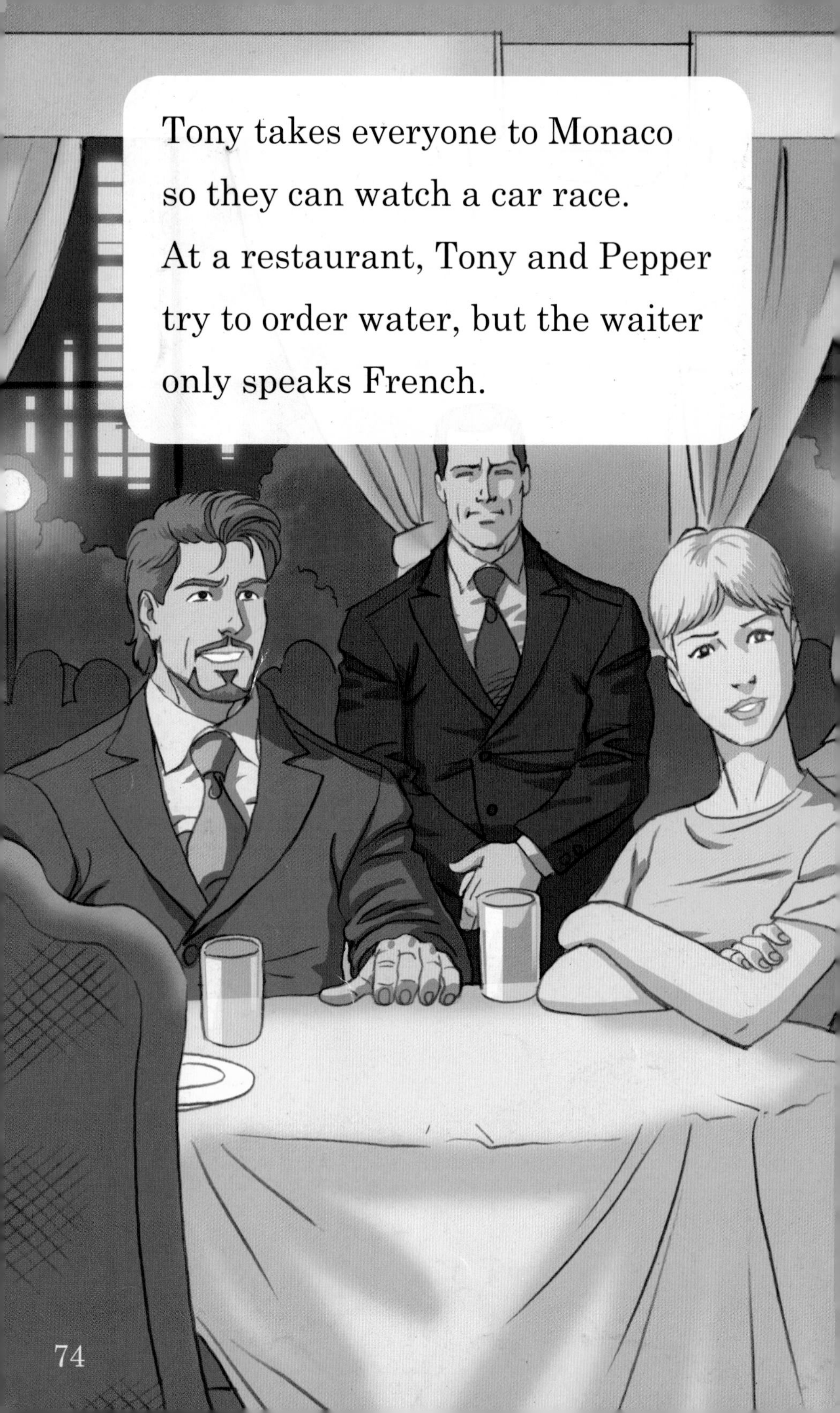

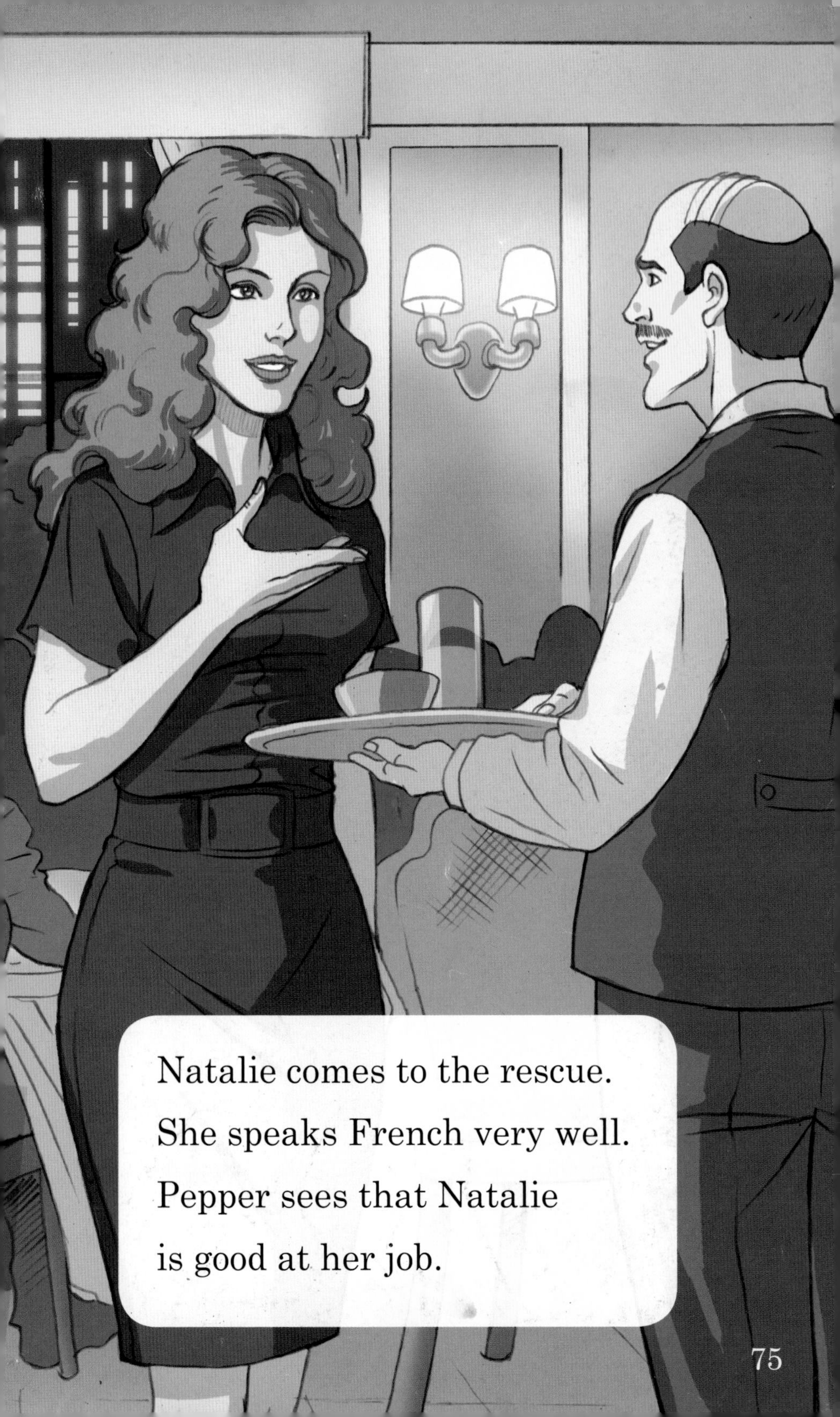

Natalie comes to the rescue.
She speaks French very well.
Pepper sees that Natalie
is good at her job.

As Pepper watches Natalie,
she notices some strange things.
When Natalie's phone rings,
she walks away to answer it.

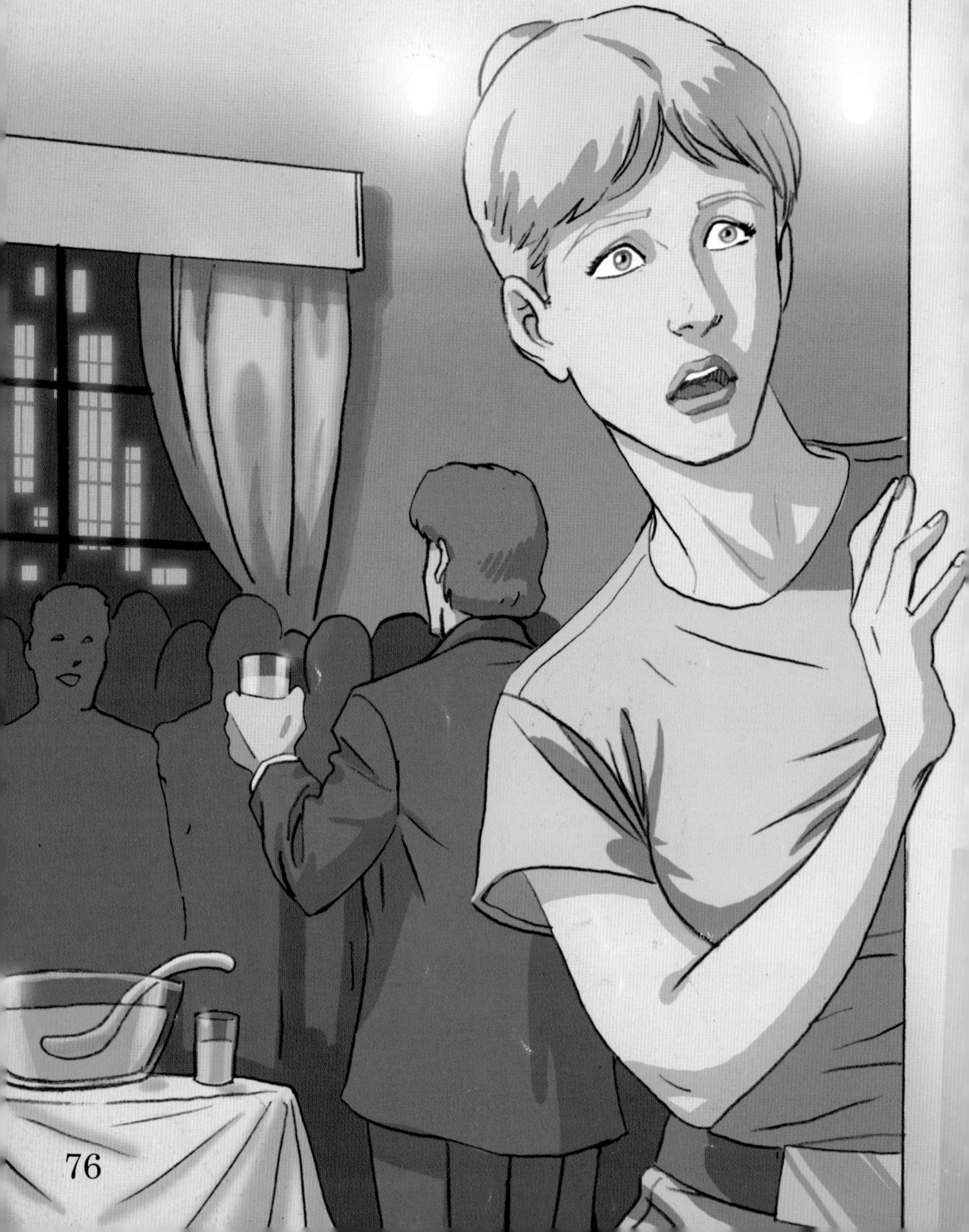

Pepper follows her.
She hears Natalie say,
"Tony Stark just arrived."

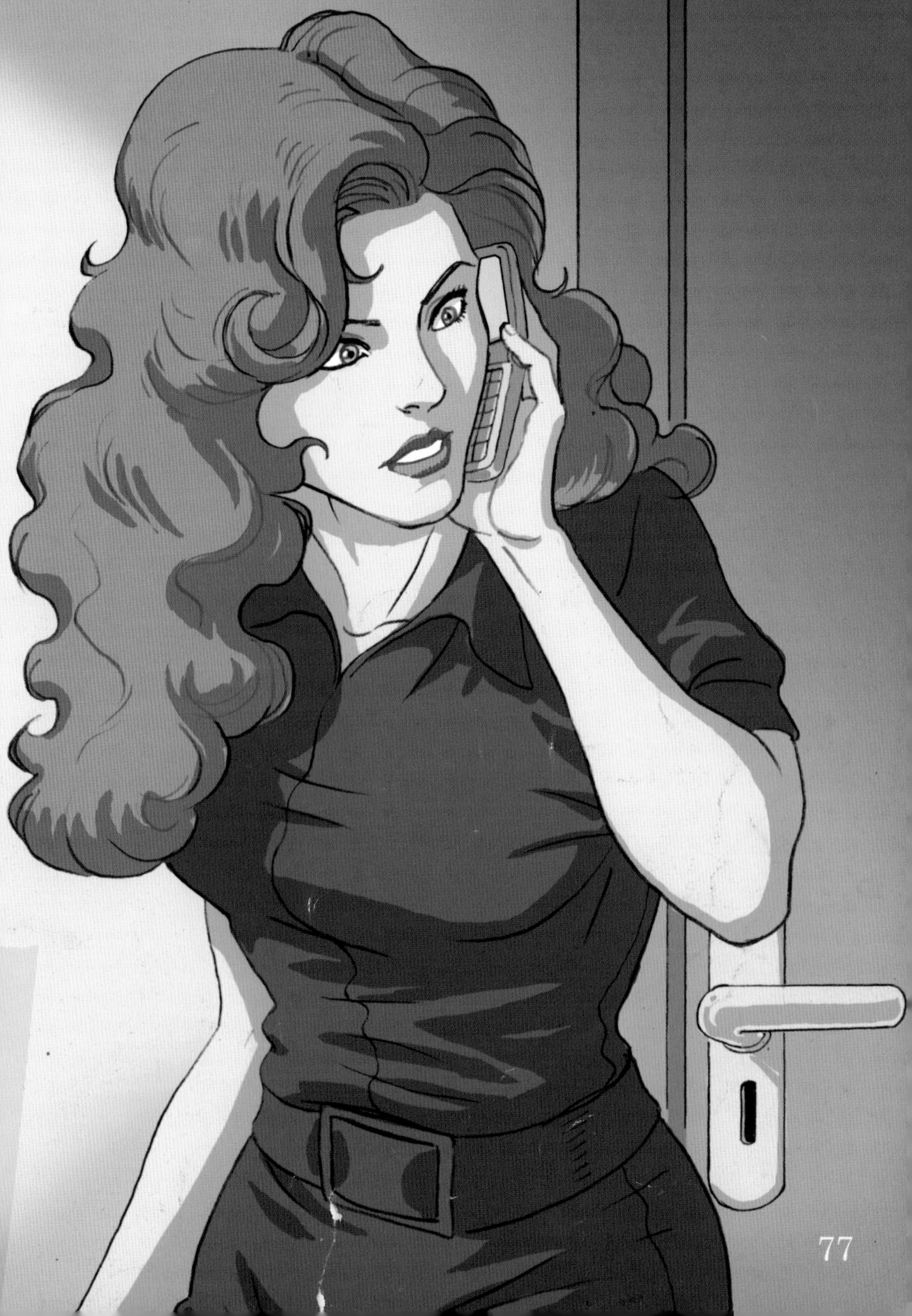

Pepper steps forward in anger.

"Who are you talking to?" she asks.

Natalie says it is her dad,

but Pepper does not think that is the truth

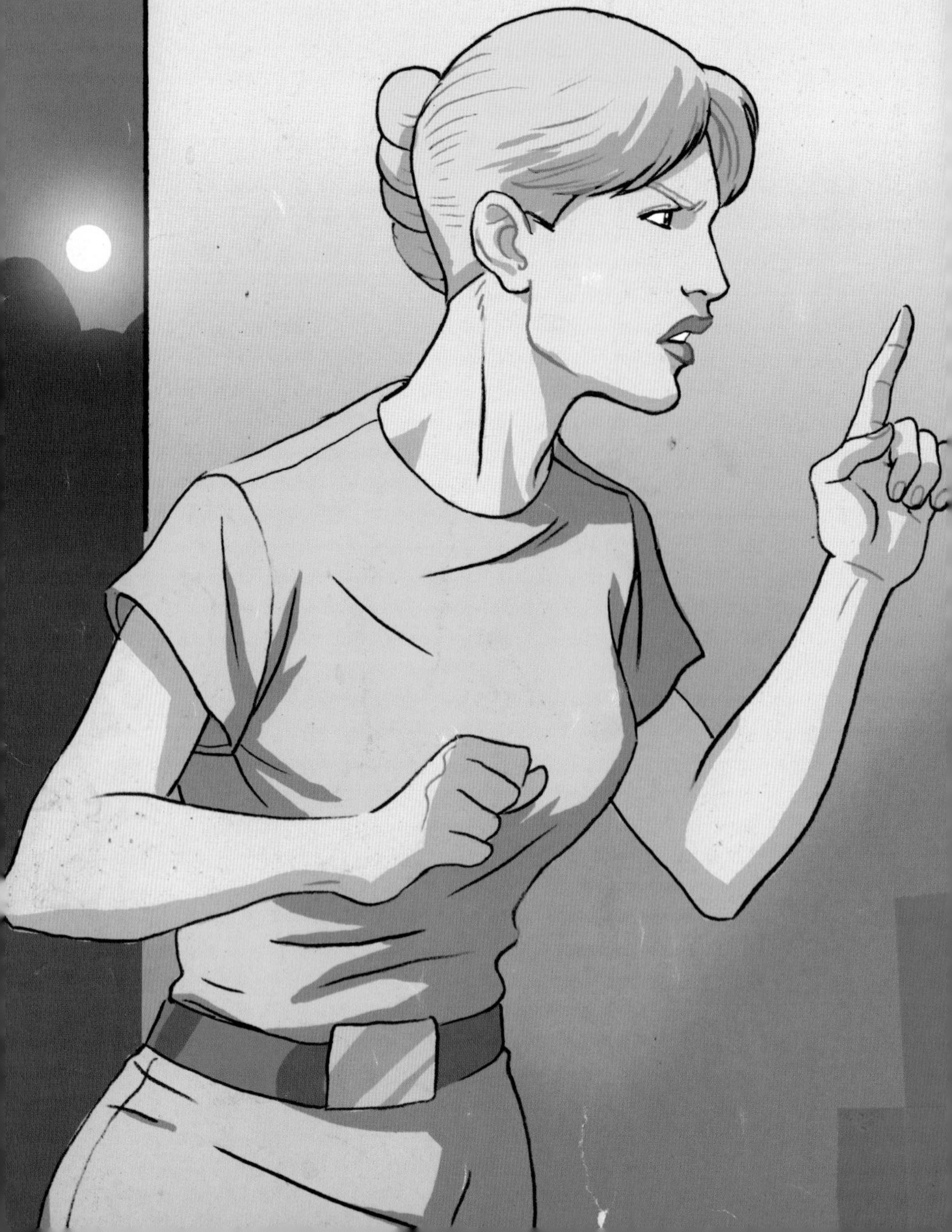

"Your job is to protect Tony,"
Pepper scolds her.
"Do not tell people where he is."

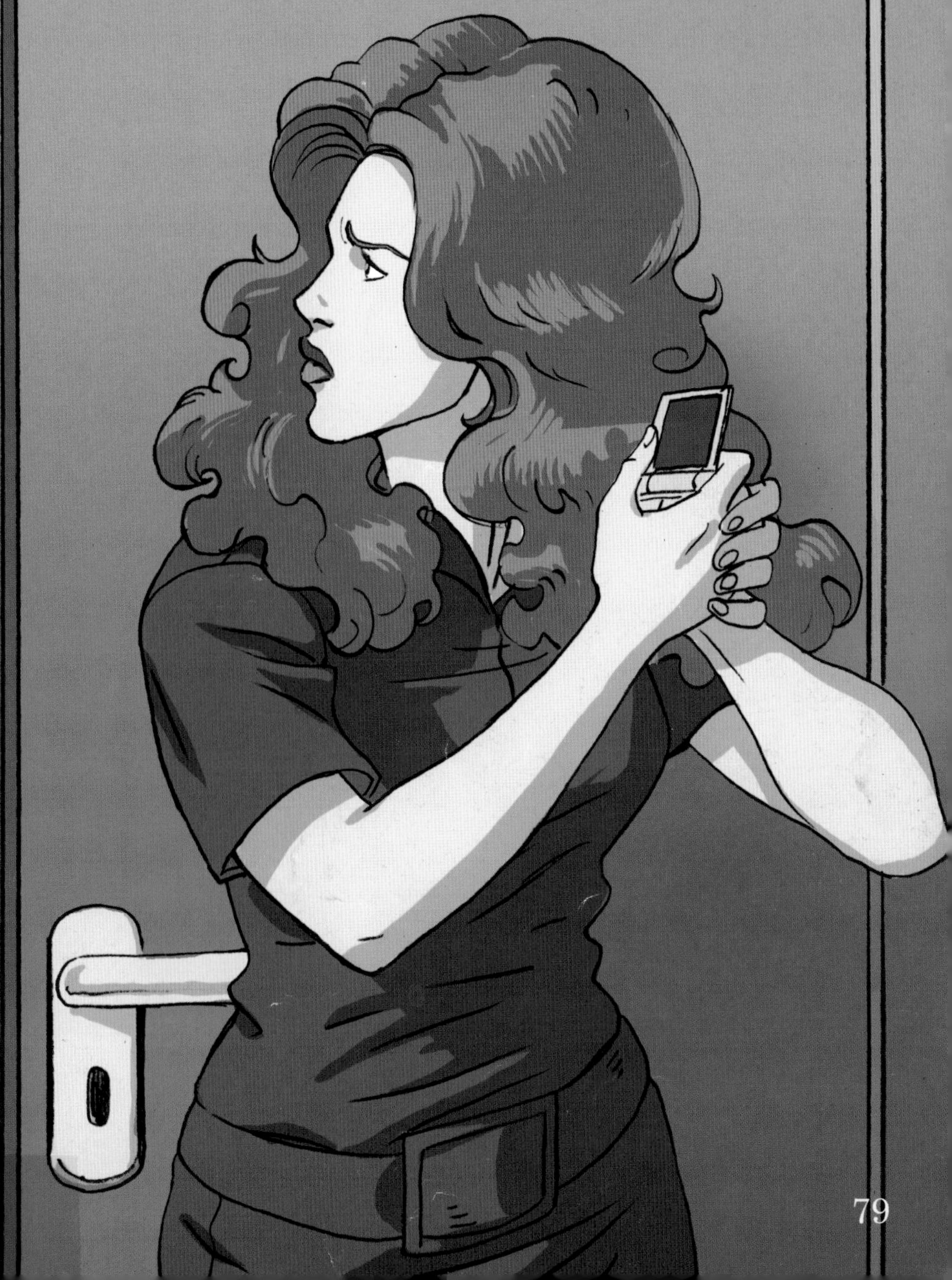

The women walk back to Happy.
Tony has a surprise for everyone:
He is going to drive one of the race cars!
Natalie slips away again.

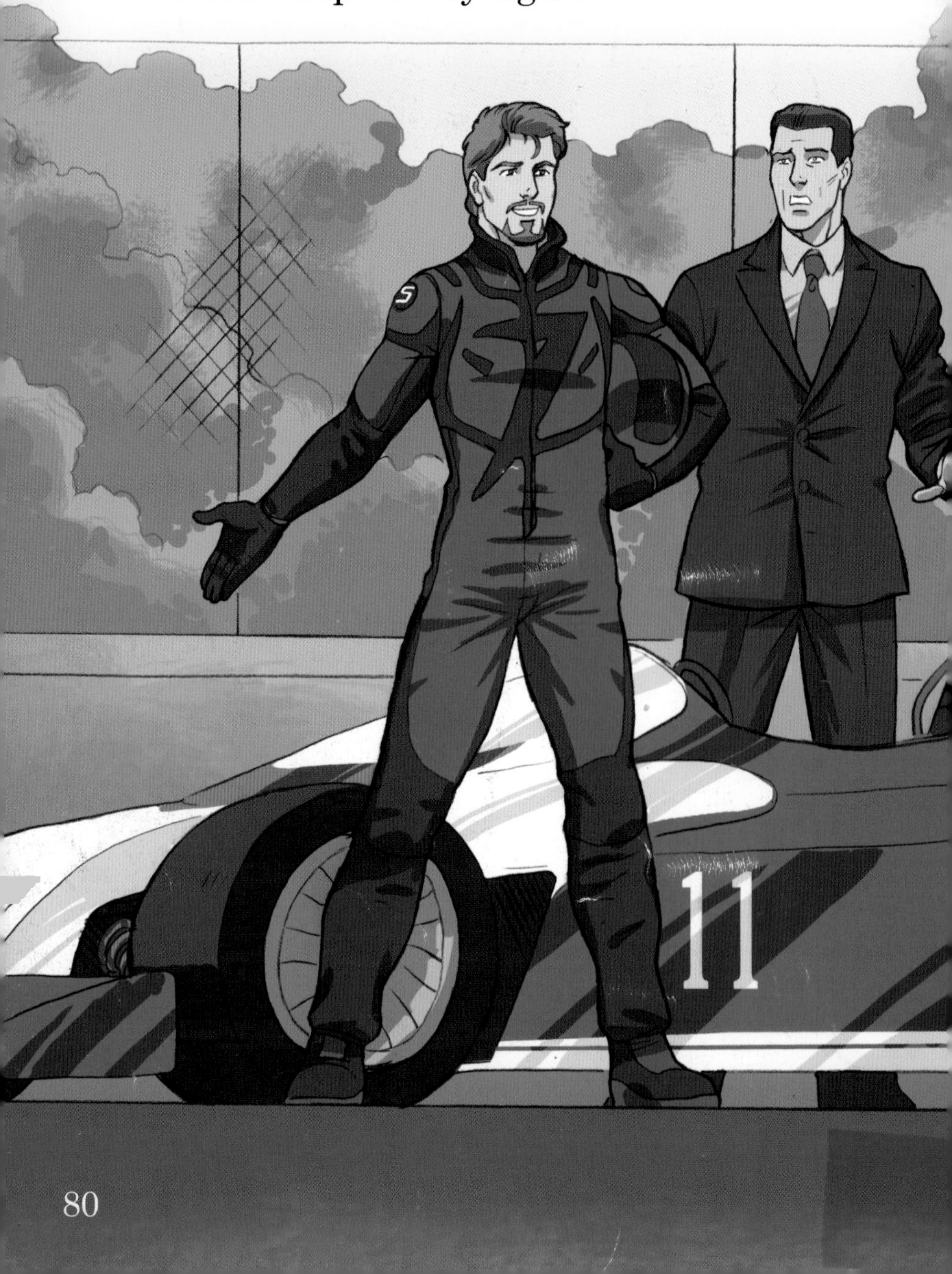
11

She makes another secret phone call.

"I did not know.

He told no one," Natalie whispers.

Who is she calling?

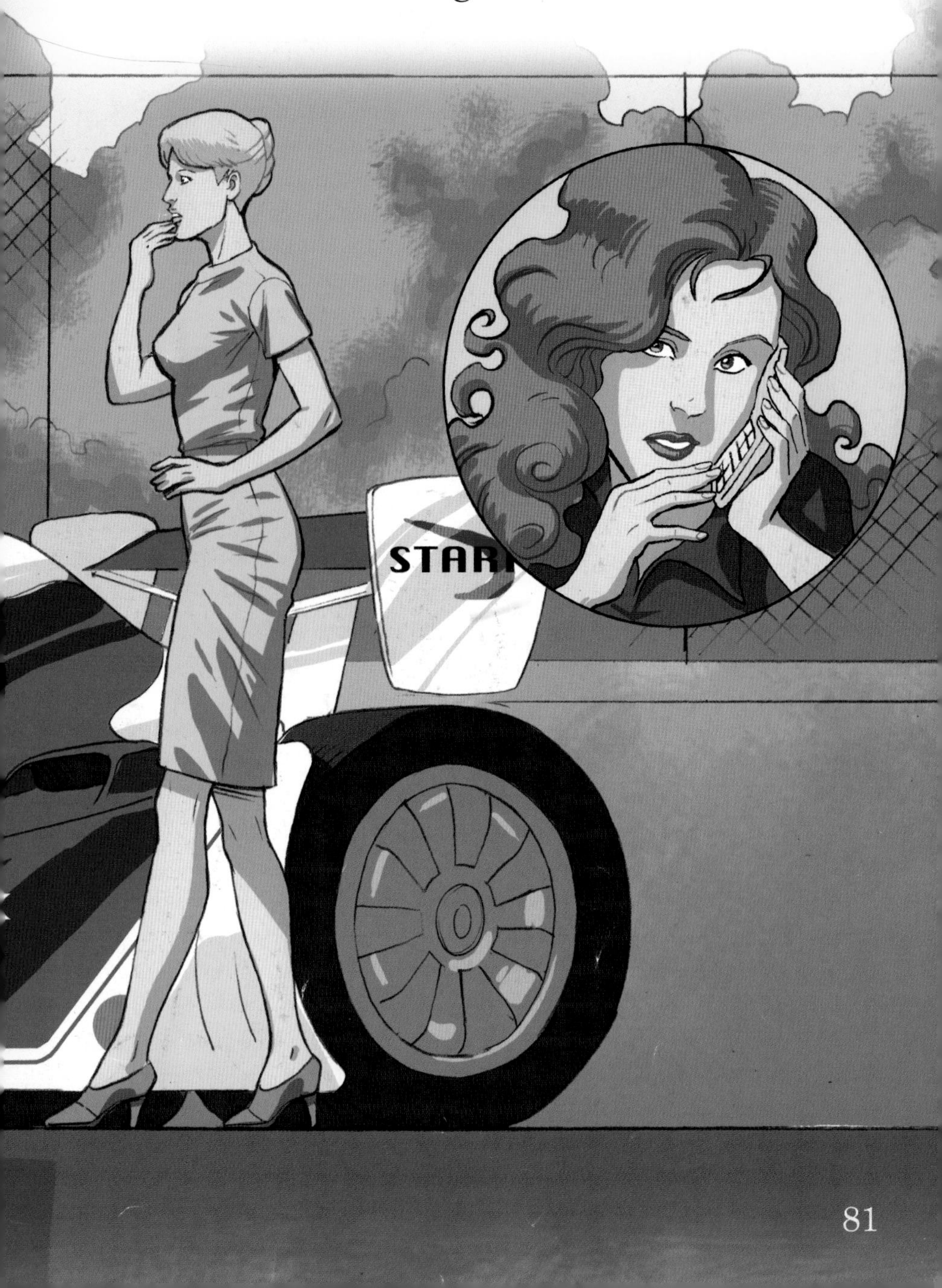
STAR

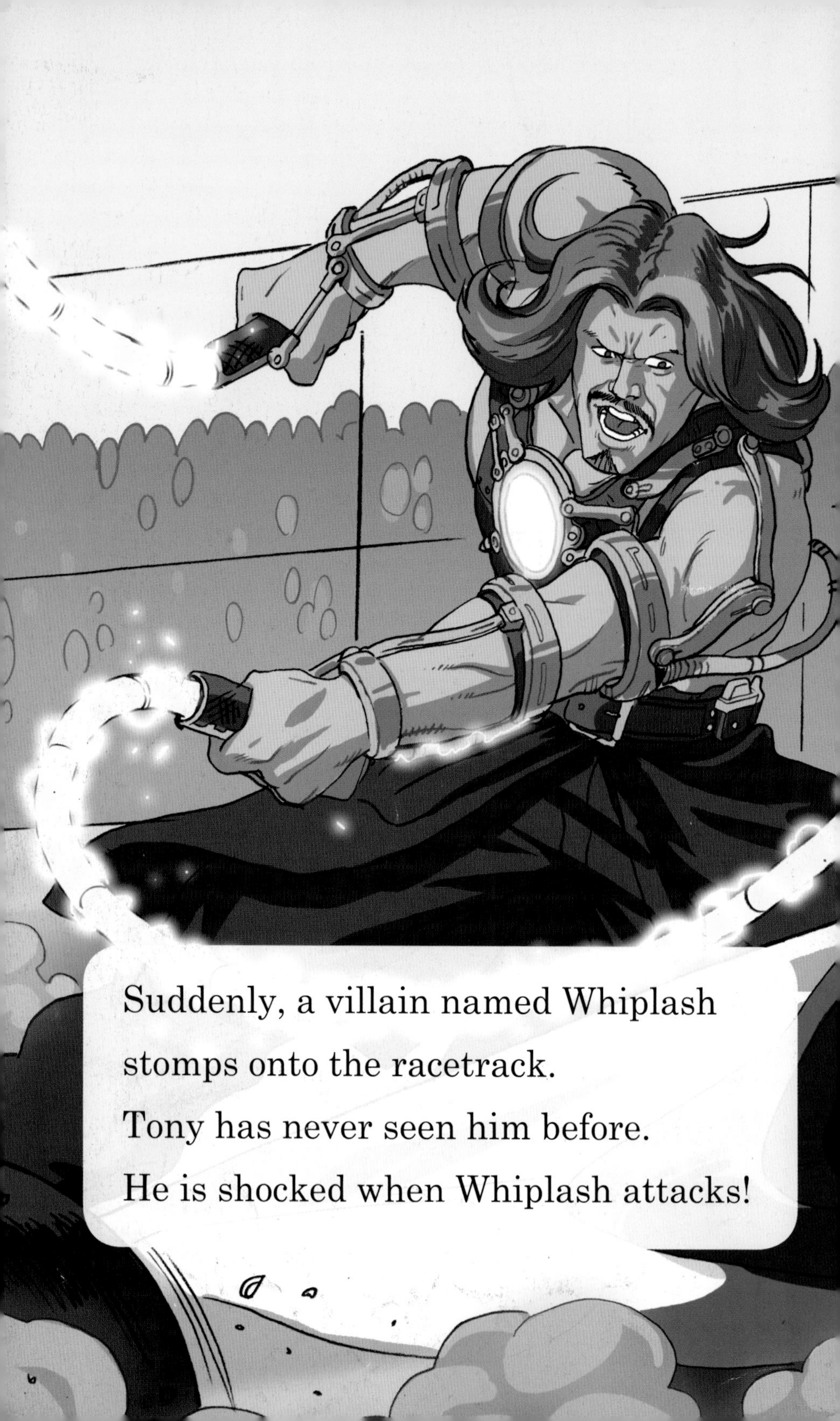

Suddenly, a villain named Whiplash stomps onto the racetrack.
Tony has never seen him before.
He is shocked when Whiplash attacks!

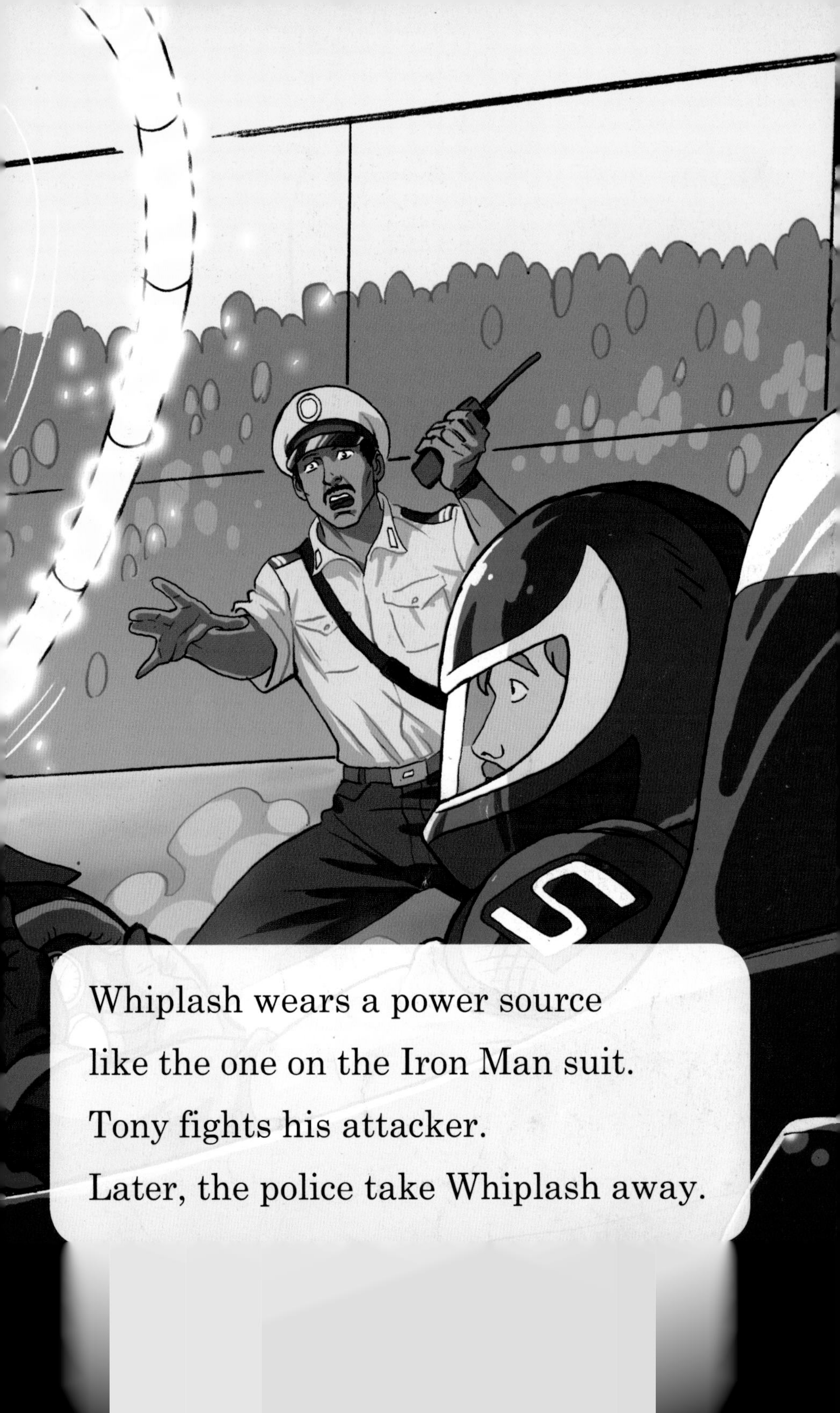

Whiplash wears a power source
like the one on the Iron Man suit.
Tony fights his attacker.
Later, the police take Whiplash away.

Tony goes home to rest,
but soon a friend comes to visit.
Nick Fury works for S.H.I.E.L.D.,
a group that tries to keep people safe.

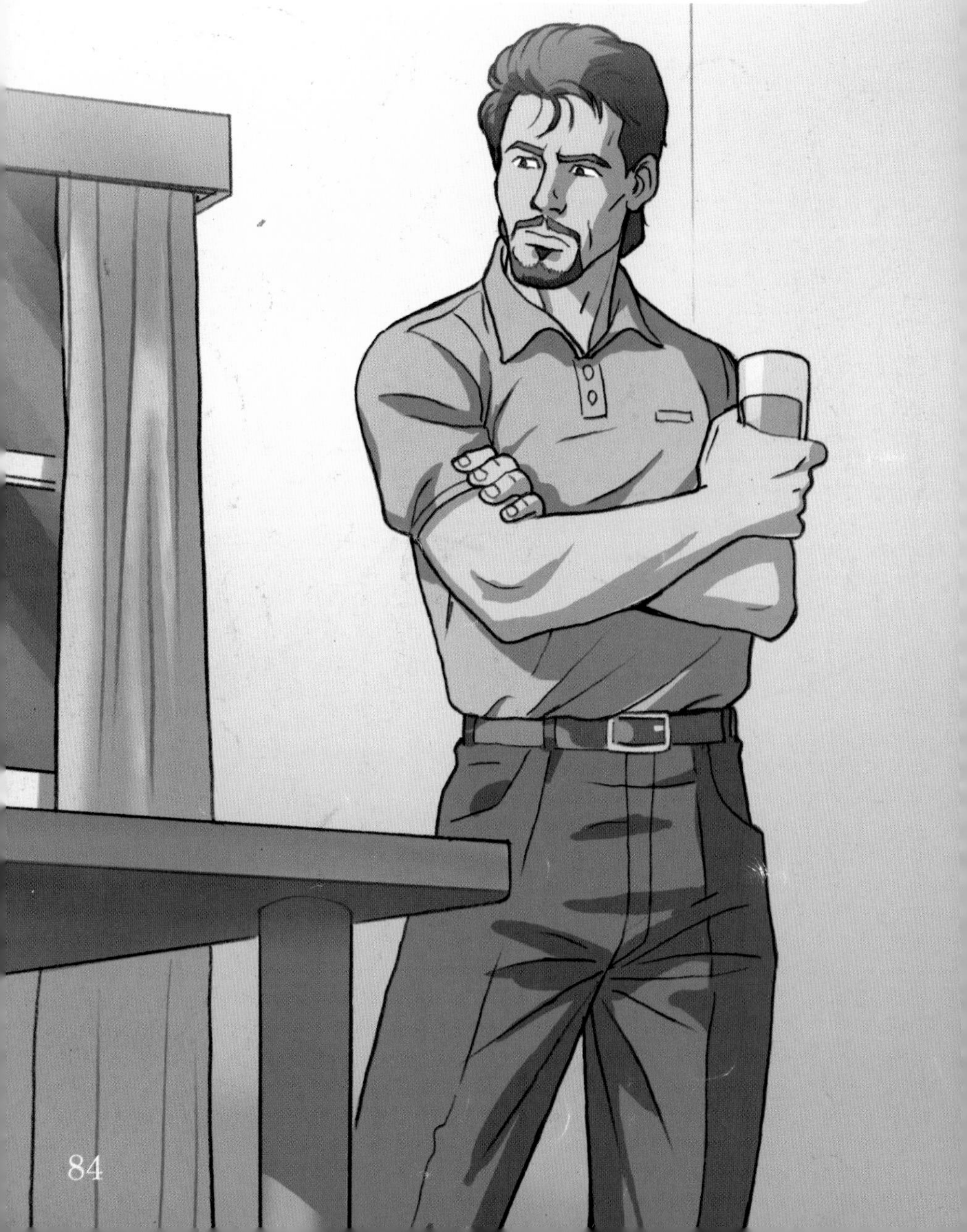

Nick tells Tony to be careful.

Tony has many enemies, such as Whiplash.

"I have someone I want you to meet," Nick says.

"She can help you."

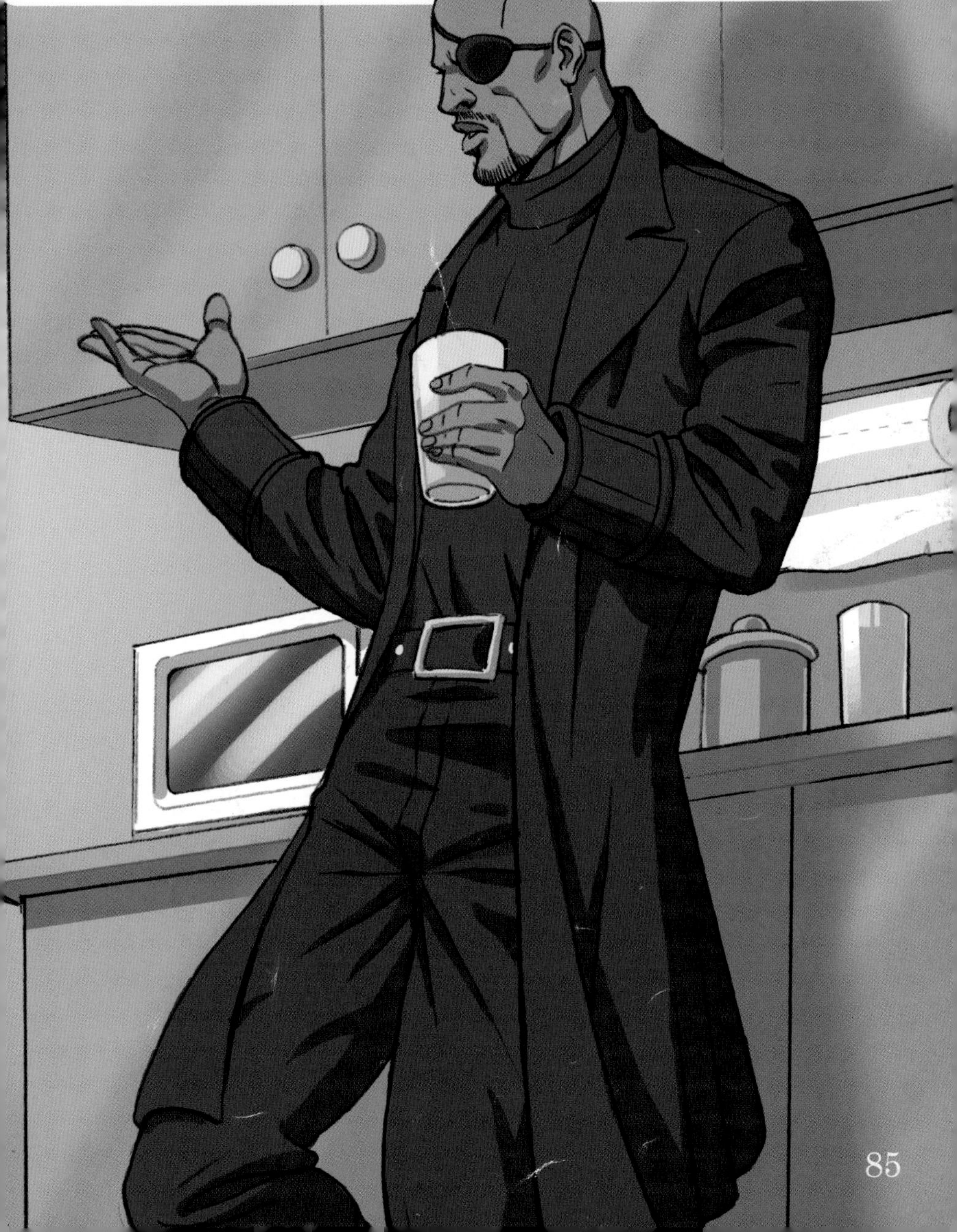

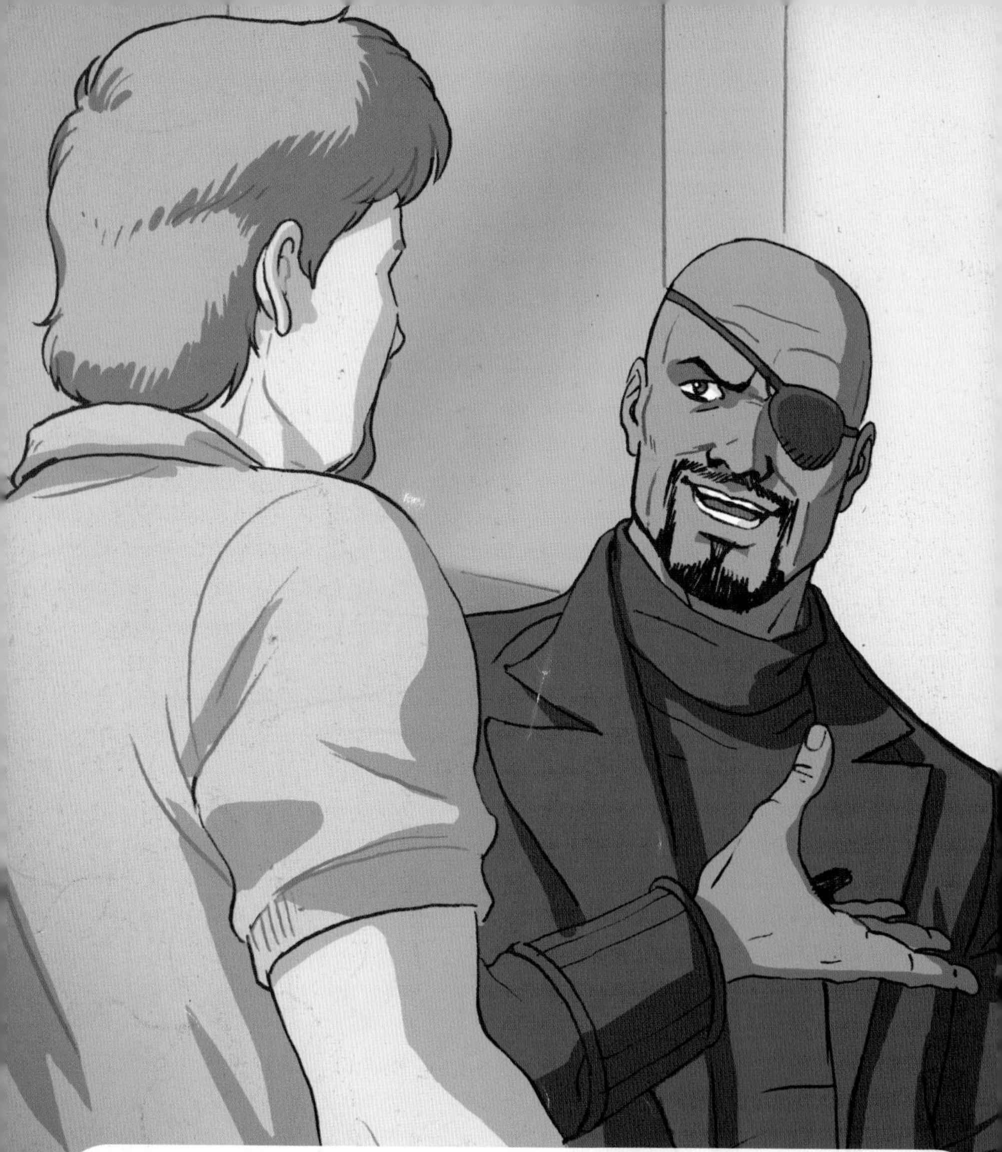

A woman wearing dark clothes
enters the room.
Nick introduces her as Natasha Romanoff.
But she is Tony's assistant, Natalie!
"Natalie is not my real name," she says.

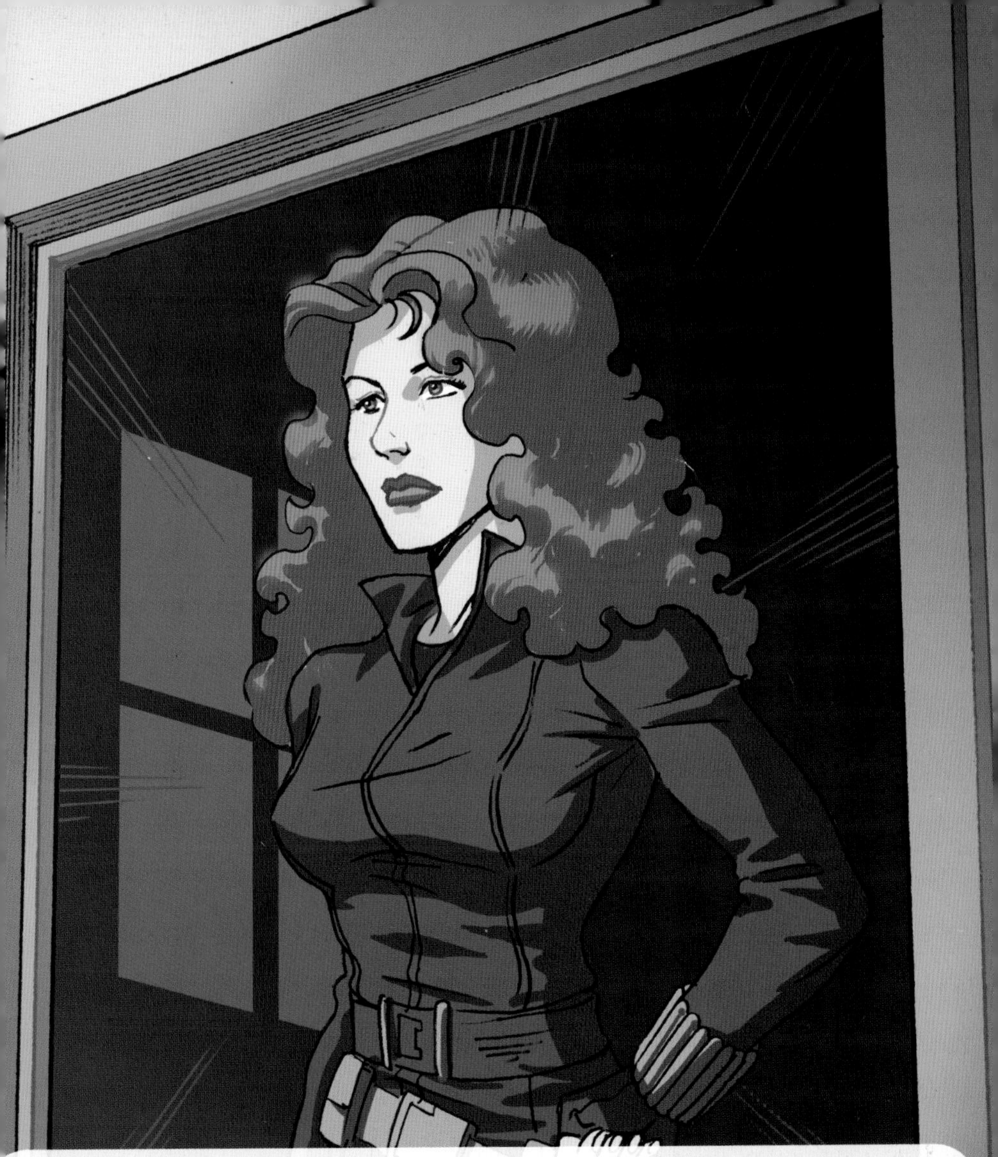

She works undercover for S.H.I.E.L.D.
Just as Tony fights as Iron Man,
she goes by the name Black Widow!
Earlier, Black Widow had been making phone
calls to help S.H.I.E.L.D. keep Tony safe.

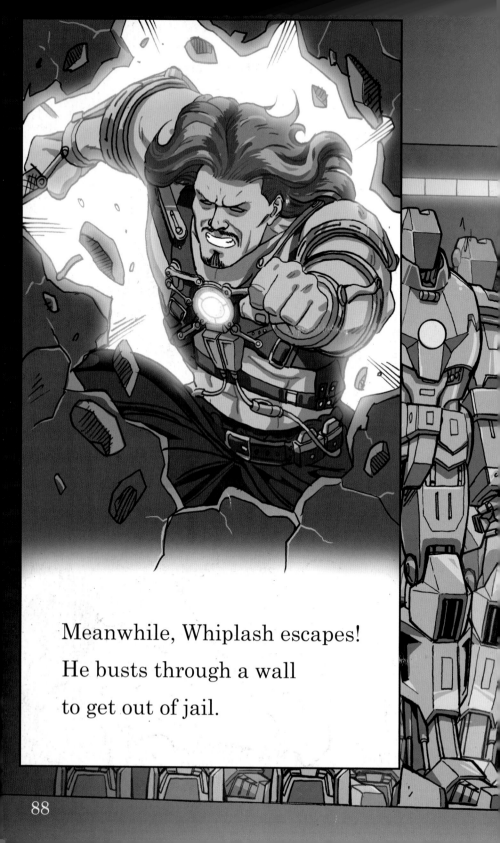

Meanwhile, Whiplash escapes!
He busts through a wall
to get out of jail.

Whiplash sets up a workshop
in an abandoned warehouse.
There, he builds powerful attack robots.
Who is his first target?
Iron Man!

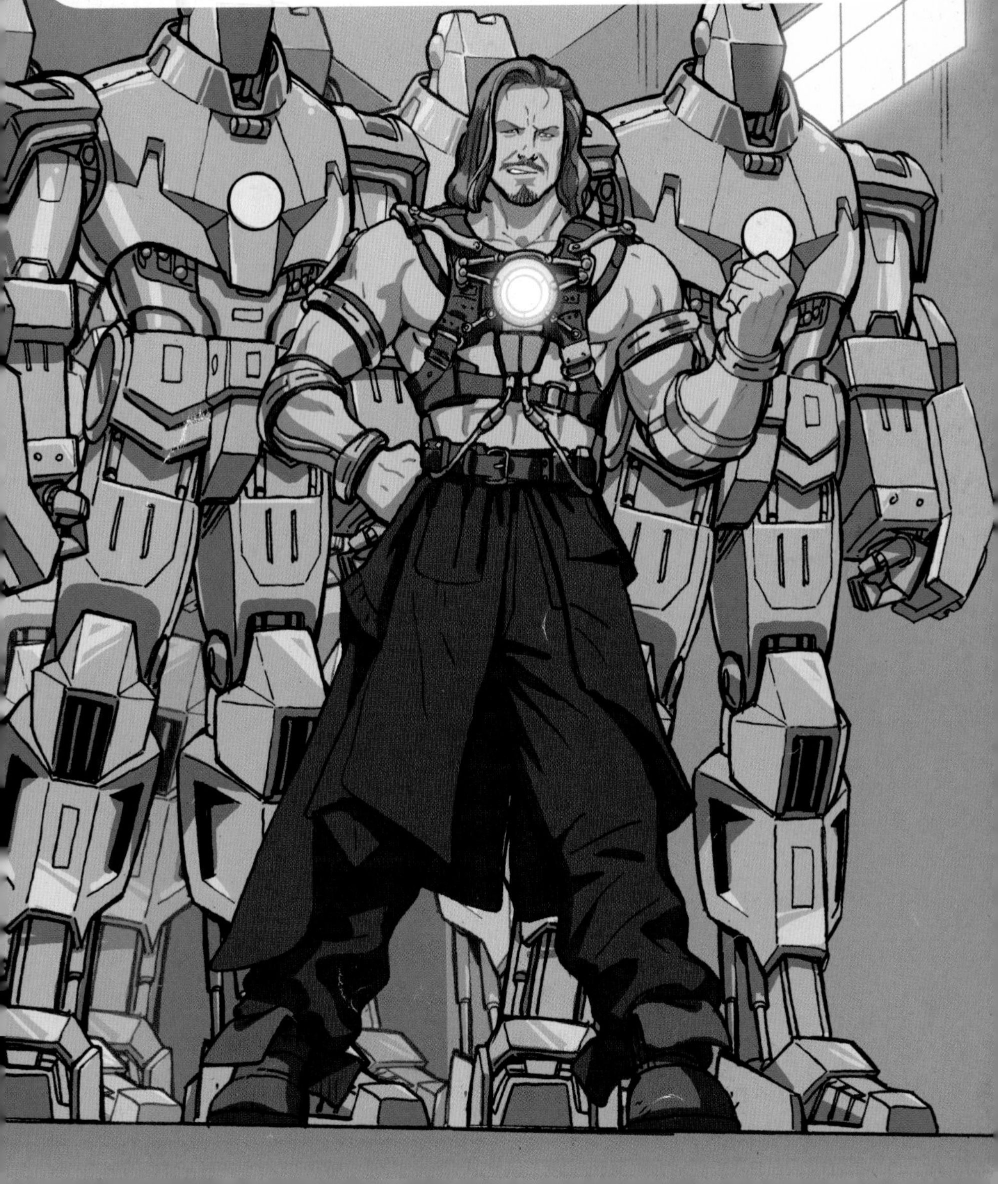

A few days later, Whiplash sneaks his robots into a show of new inventions.
Pepper, Happy, and Black Widow are there.

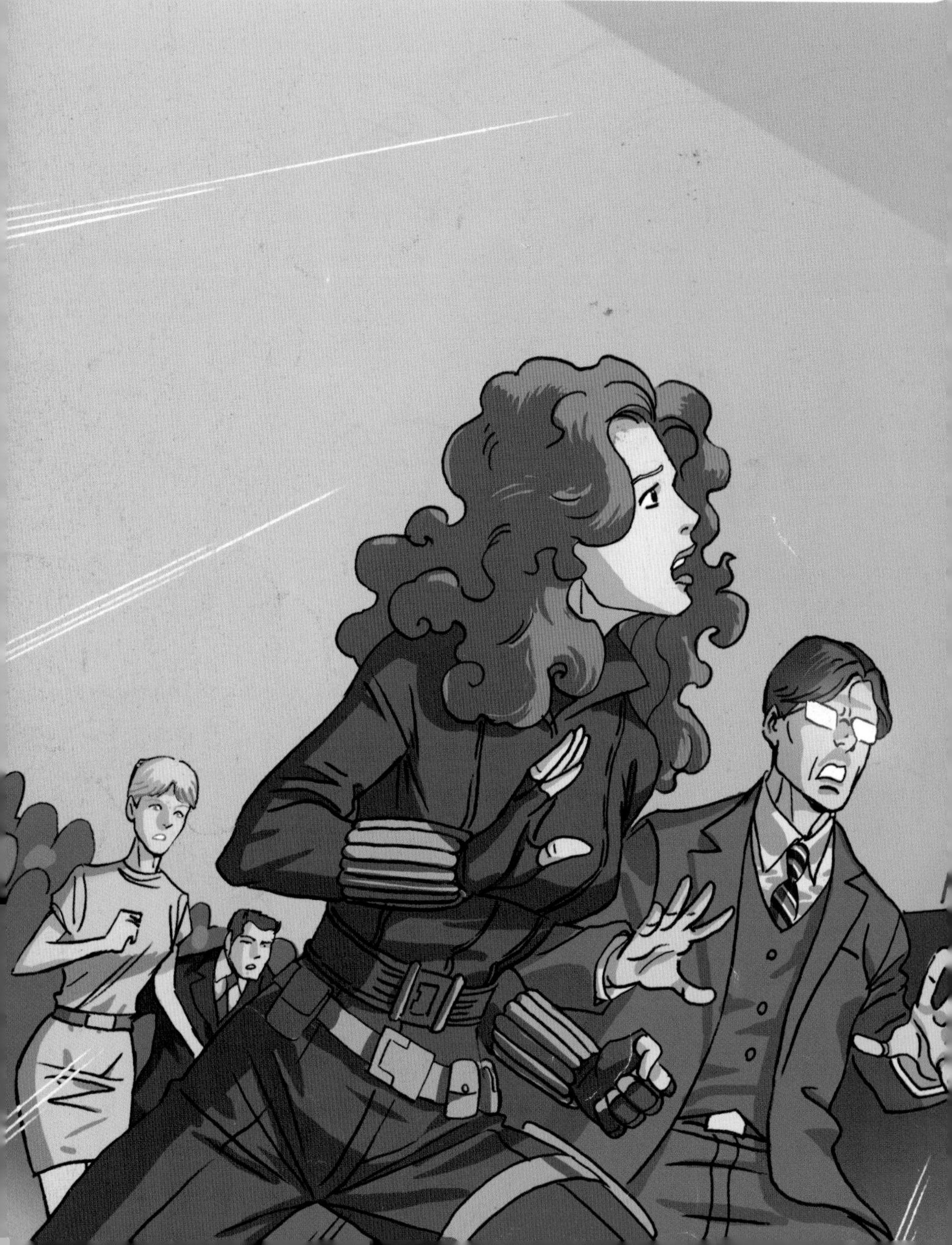

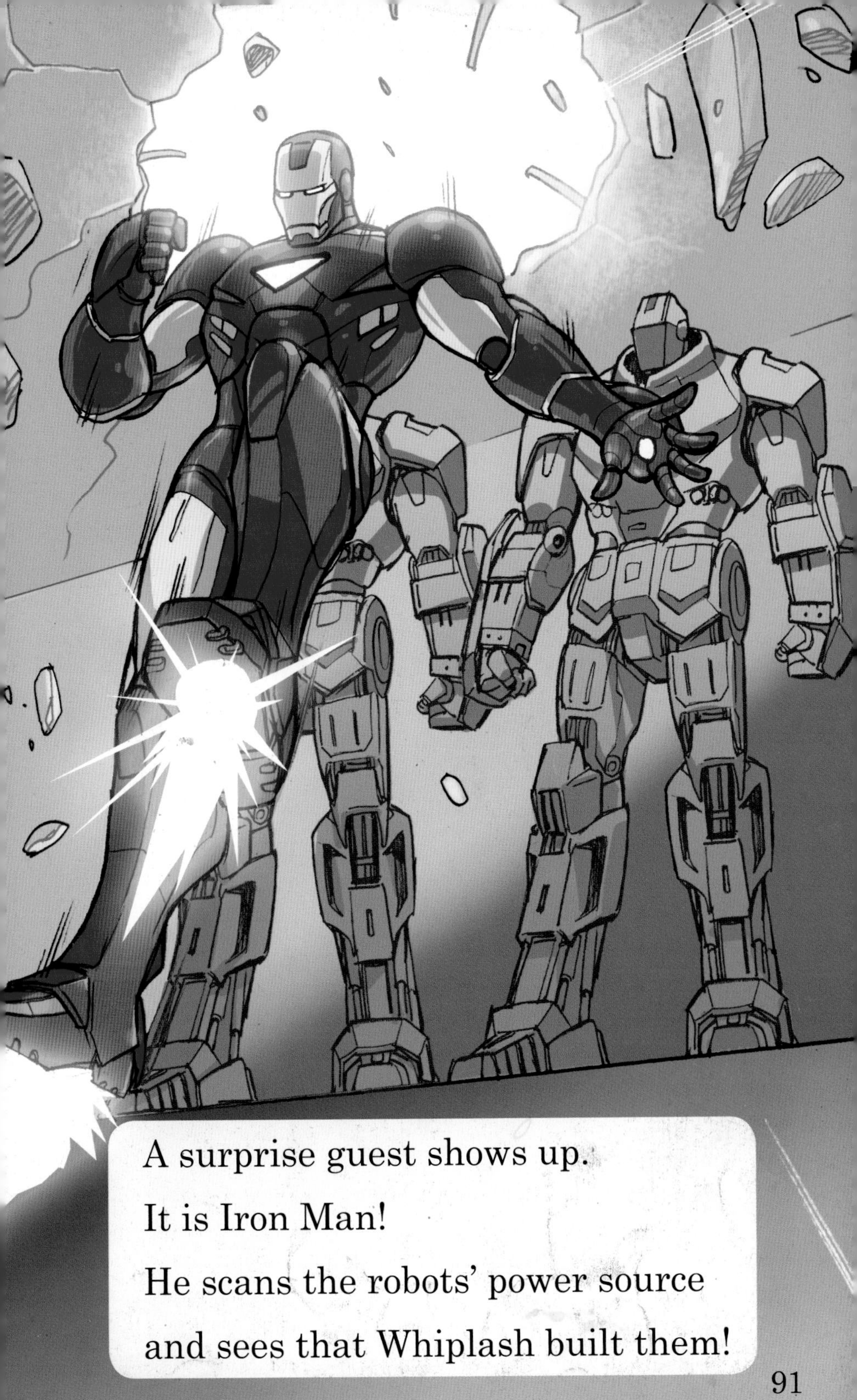

A surprise guest shows up.
It is Iron Man!
He scans the robots' power source
and sees that Whiplash built them!

The robots fire at Iron Man!
The hero is strong, but he needs help—
there are just too many enemies.

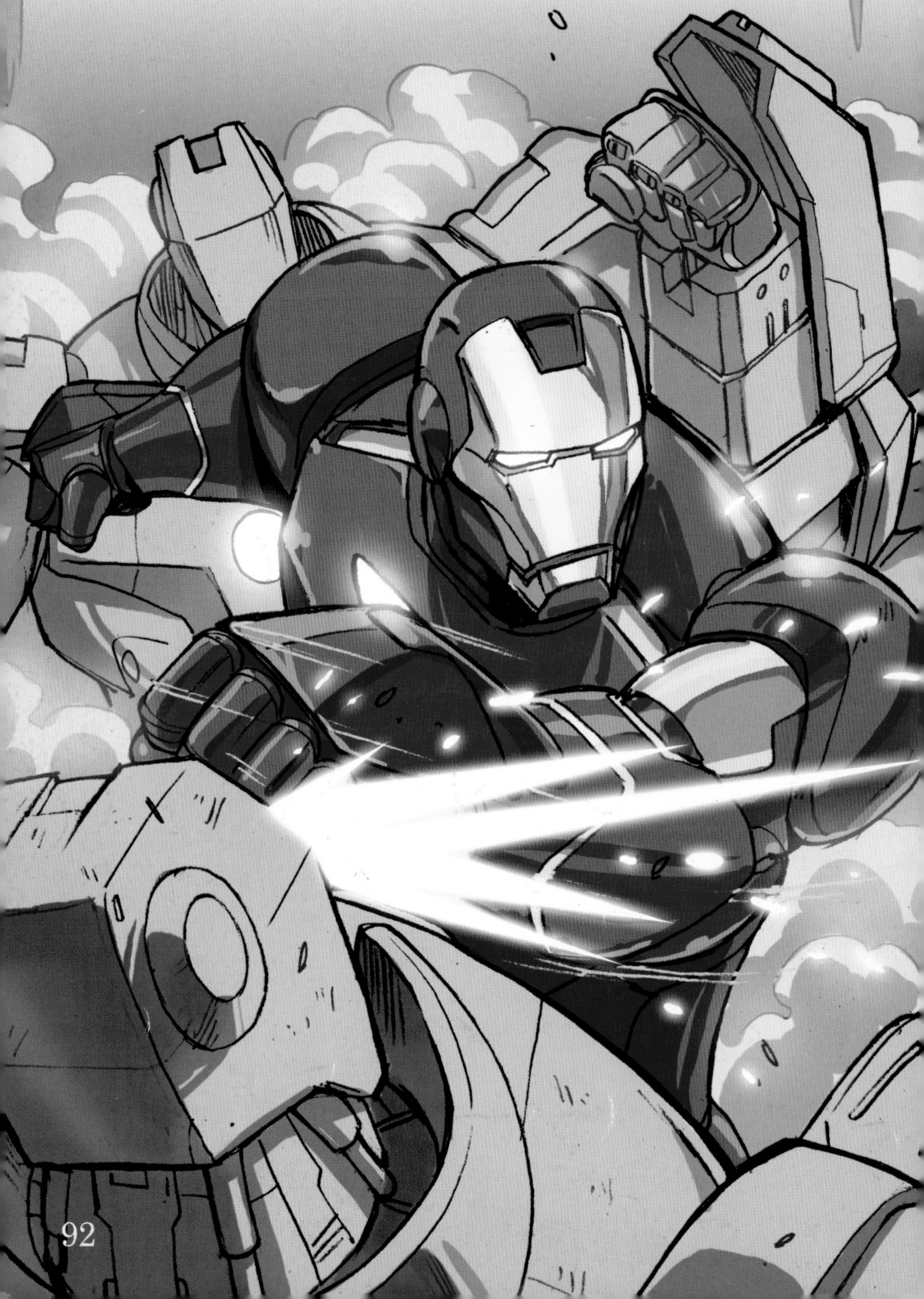

Where is Whiplash?

He might arrive for a fight, too.

“Find his hideout!” says Iron Man.

Black Widow and Happy go to look.

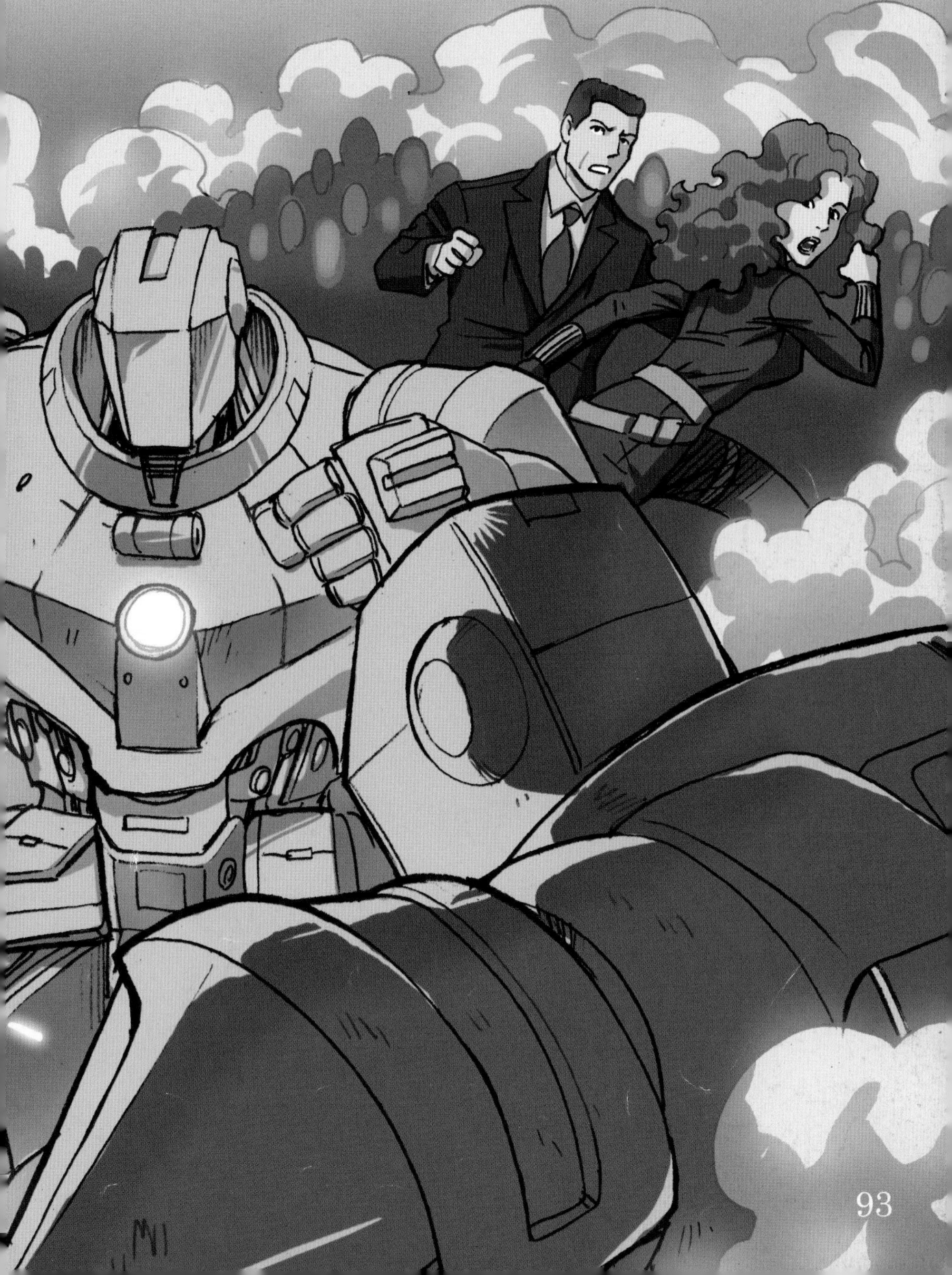

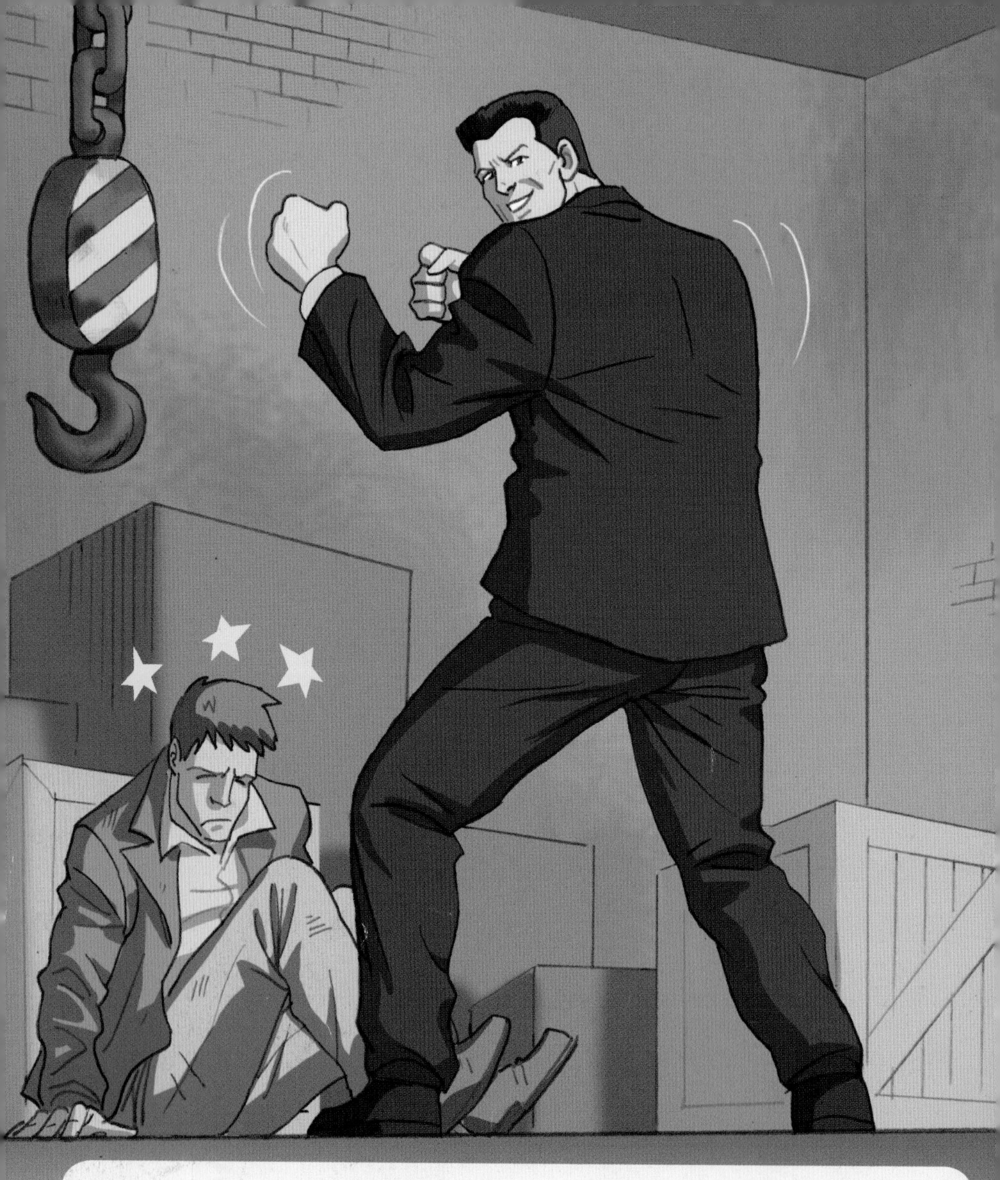

They soon find Whiplash's workshop.
They break in, but guards try to stop them.
Happy knocks out a guard with one punch.
"Look, I got one!" he yells.

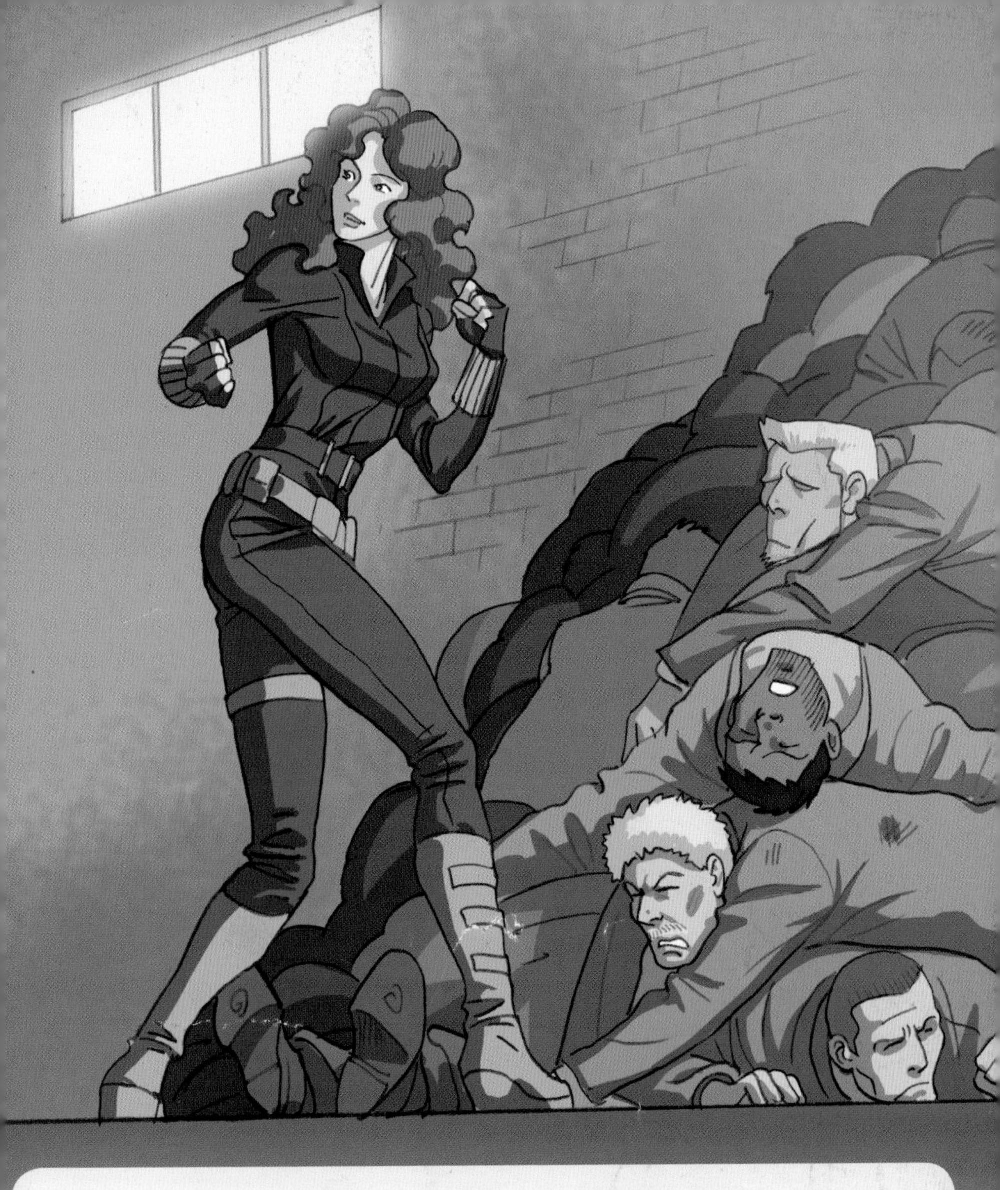

But Black Widow is not impressed.
She already knocked out twelve guards
and checked the building for Whiplash.
“Whiplash must have left already,” she says.
“Let’s go help Iron Man.”

Black Widow arrives just in time to help Iron Man fight his enemies. She is now on Iron Man's team and ready to save the day!

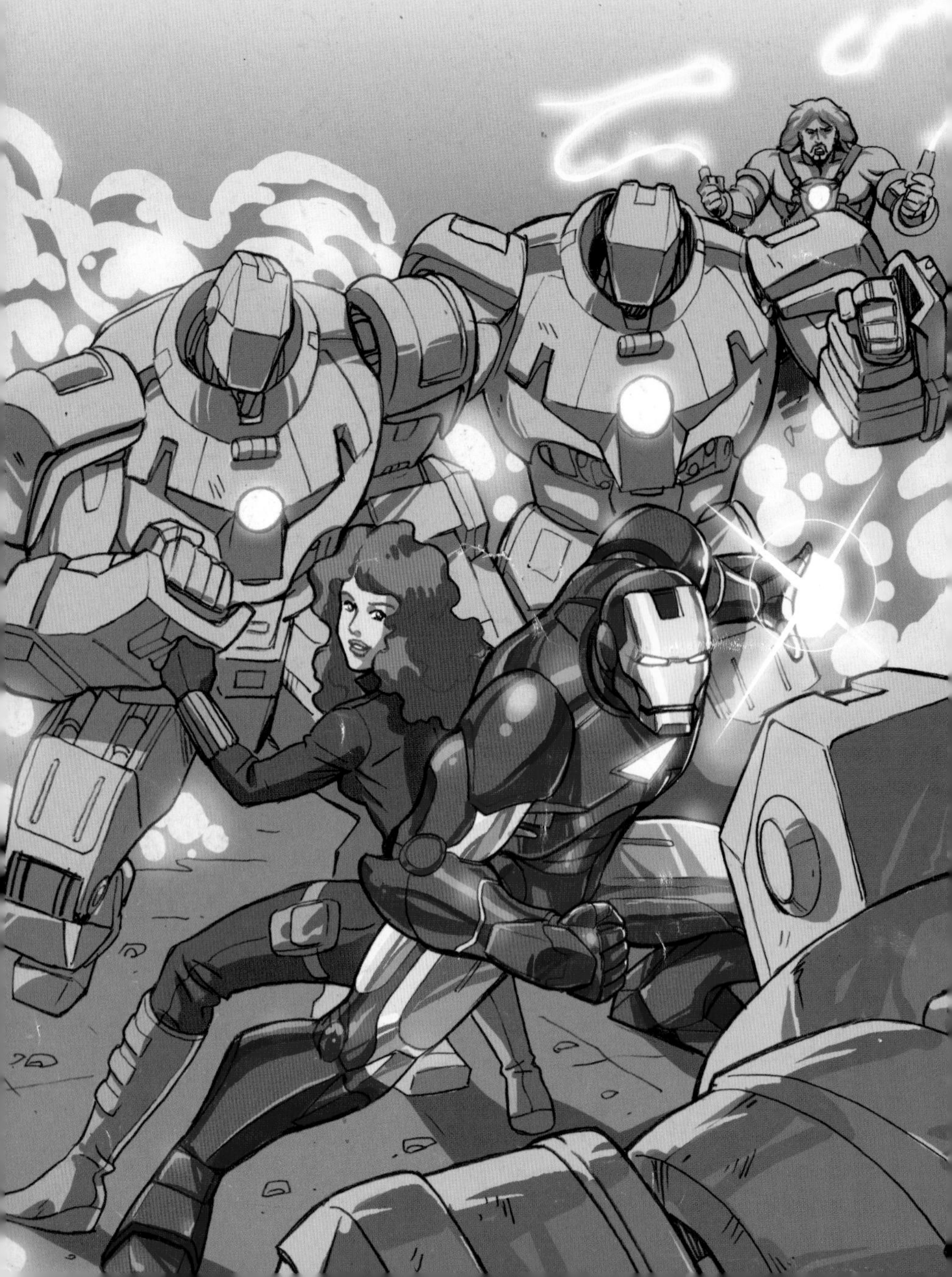

MARVEL
IRON MAN 3

IRON MAN FIGHTS BACK

WRITTEN BY THOMAS MACRI

BASED ON A SCREENPLAY BY DREW PEARCE & SHANE BLACK

PRODUCED BY KEVIN FEIGE

DIRECTED BY SHANE BLACK

ILLUSTRATED BY RON LIM, CAM SMITH, & LEE DUHIG

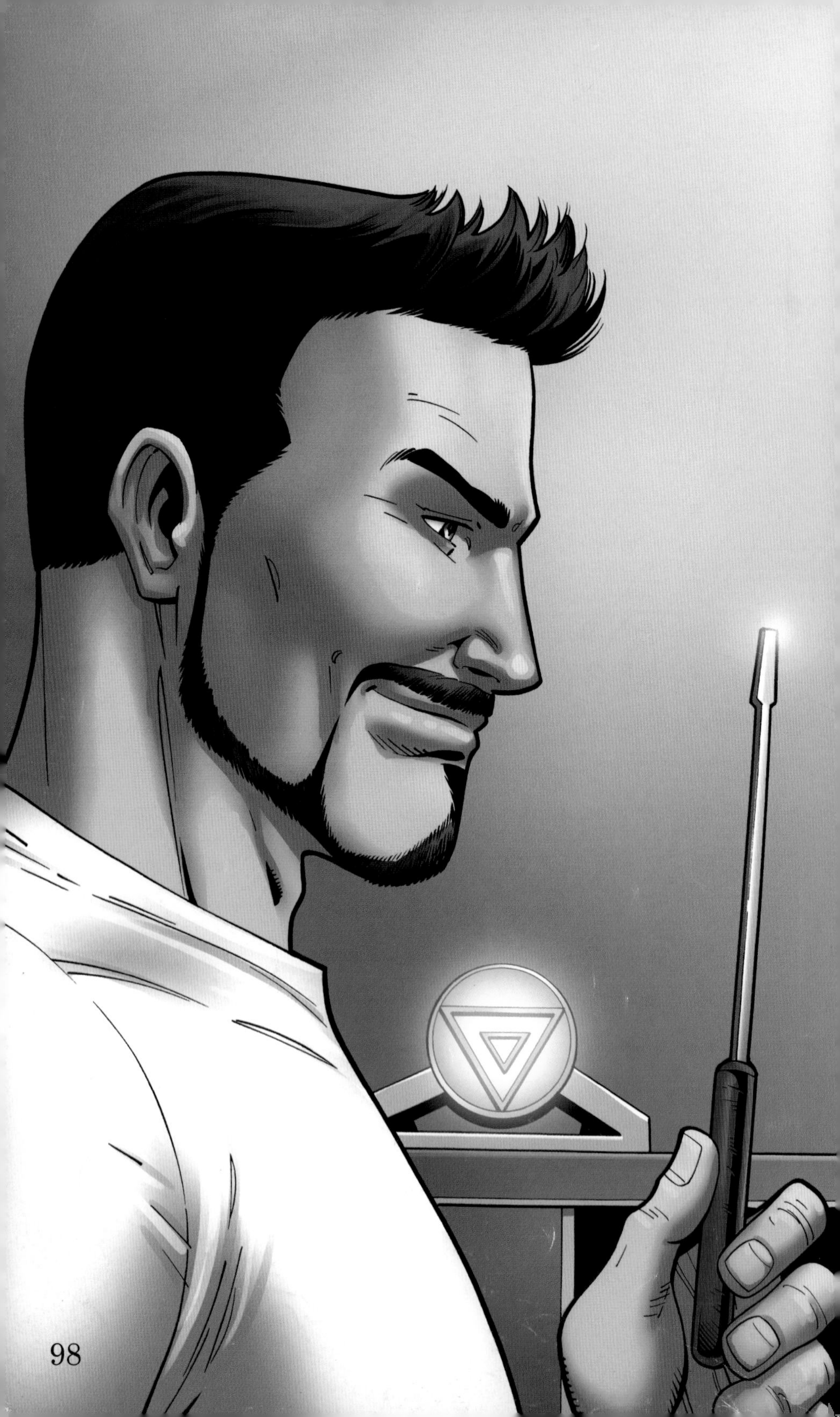

This is Tony Stark.

Tony was having
a really bad day.

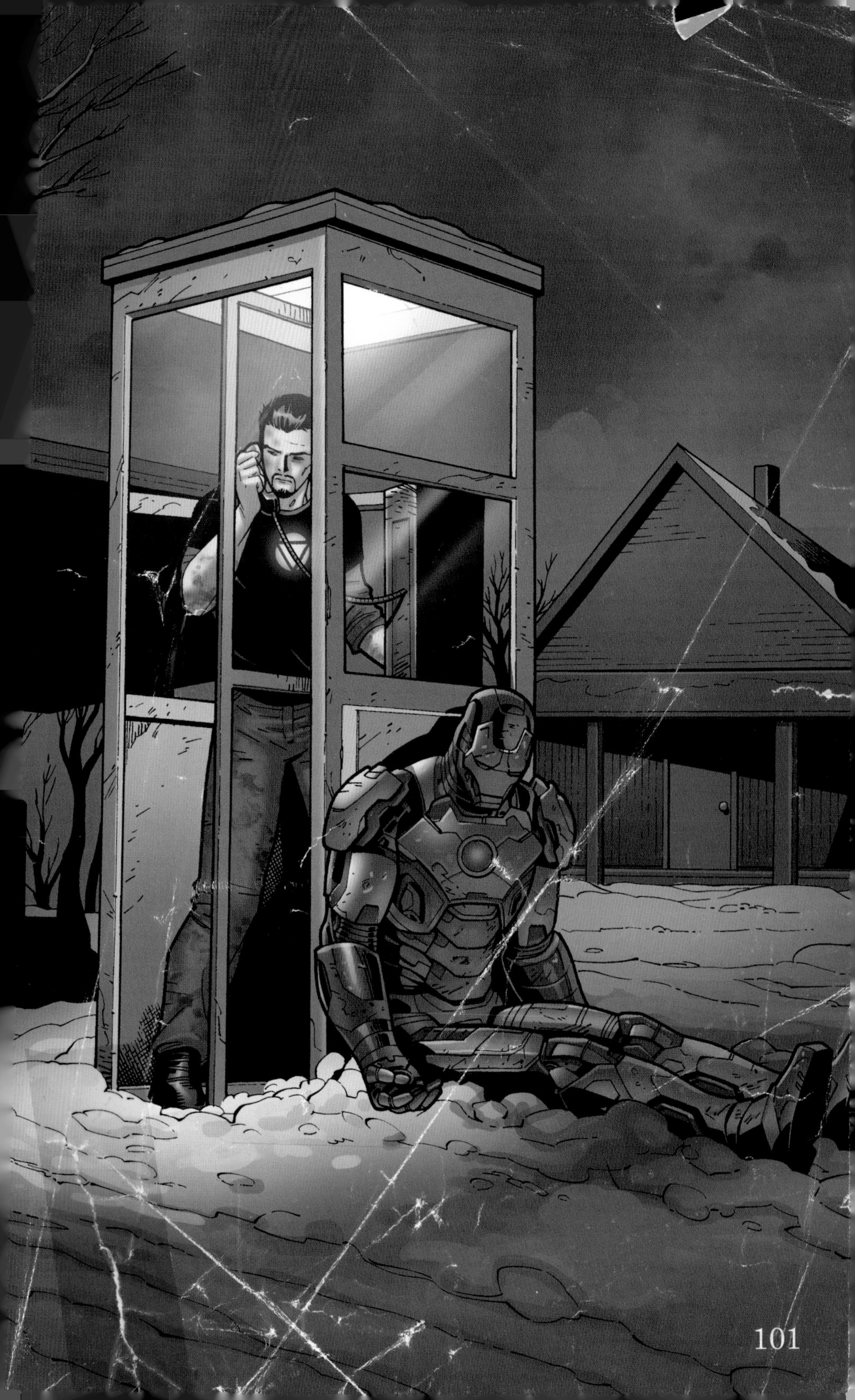

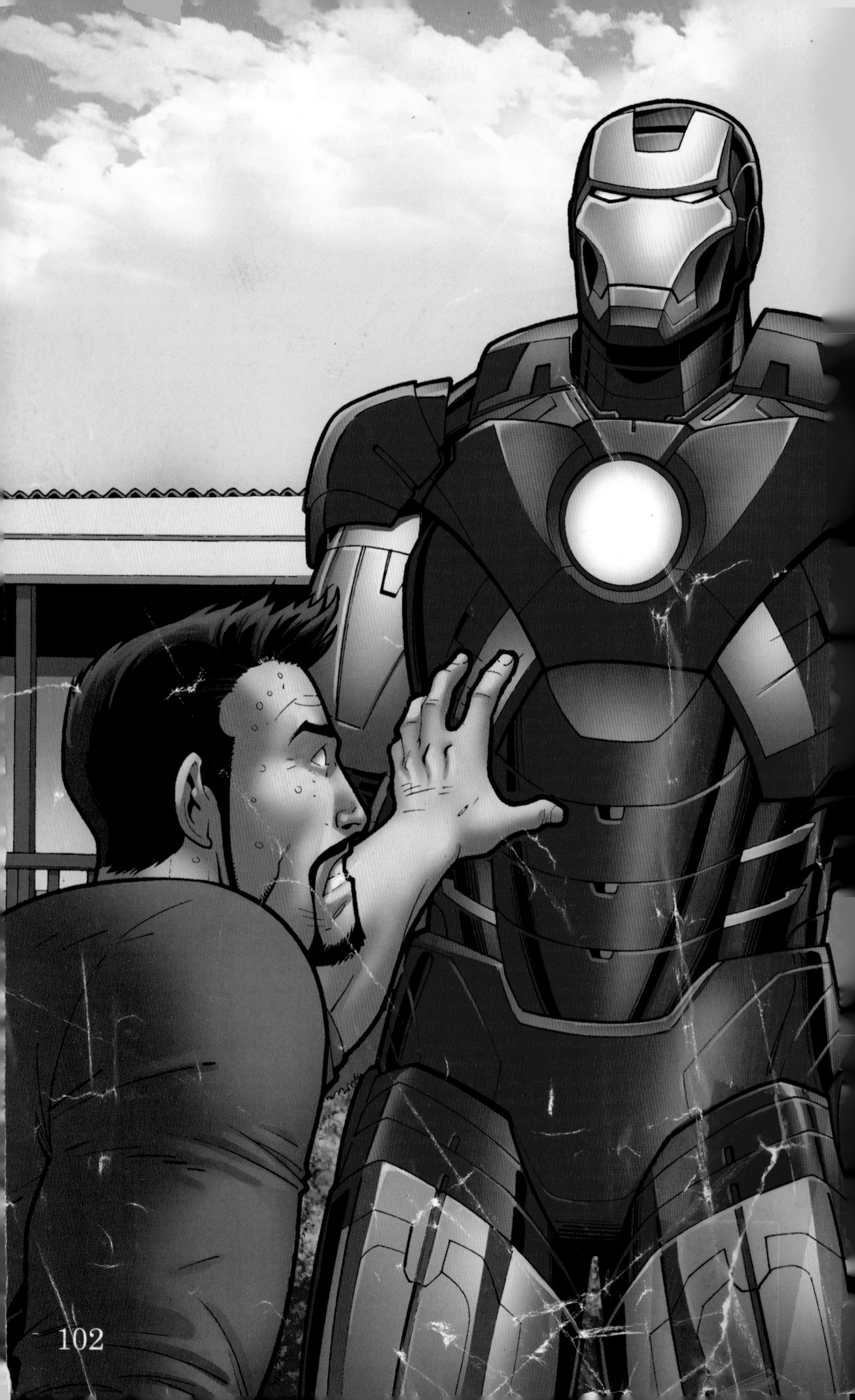

You see, Tony was not feeling very well.

His girlfriend had become friends with someone he did not like.

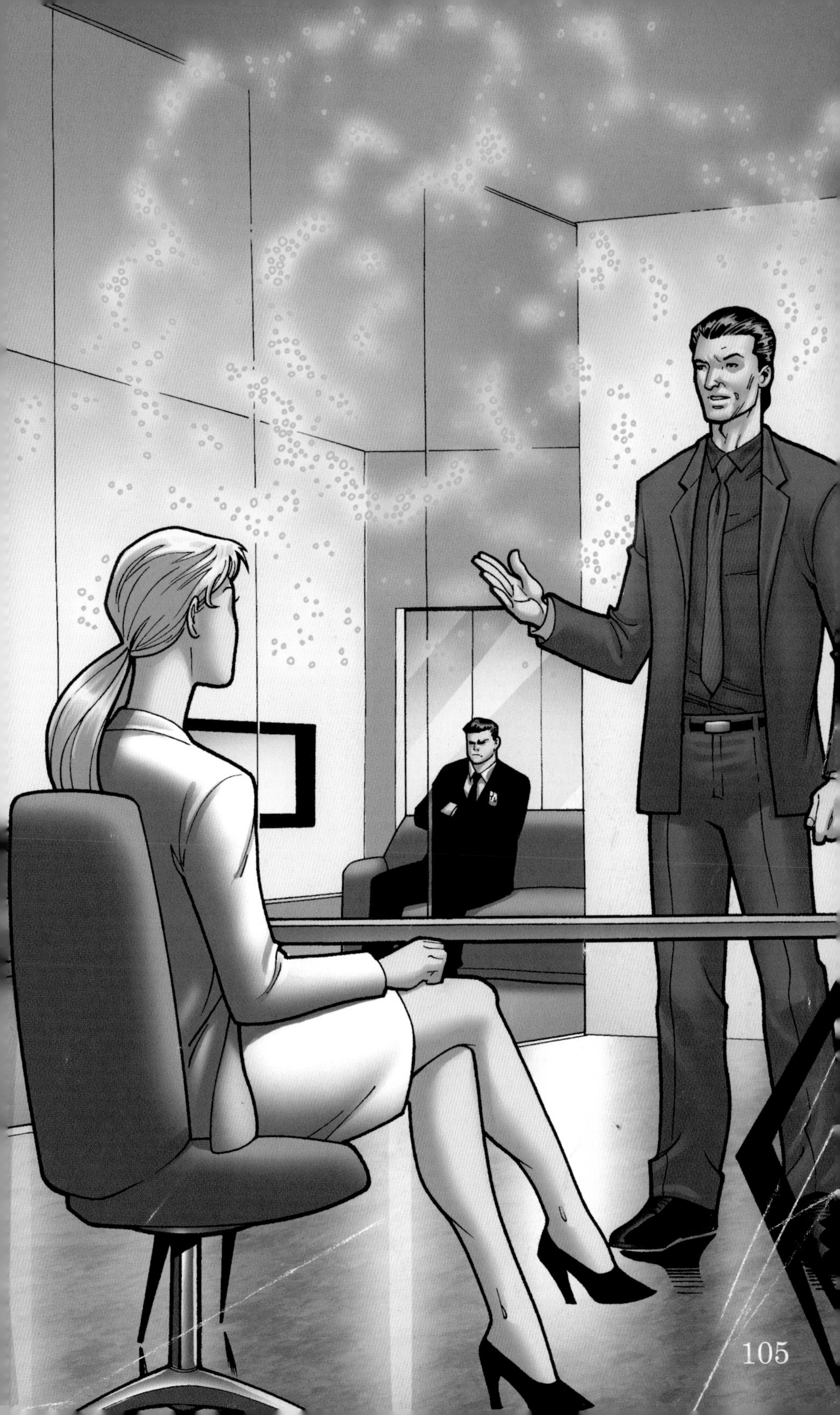

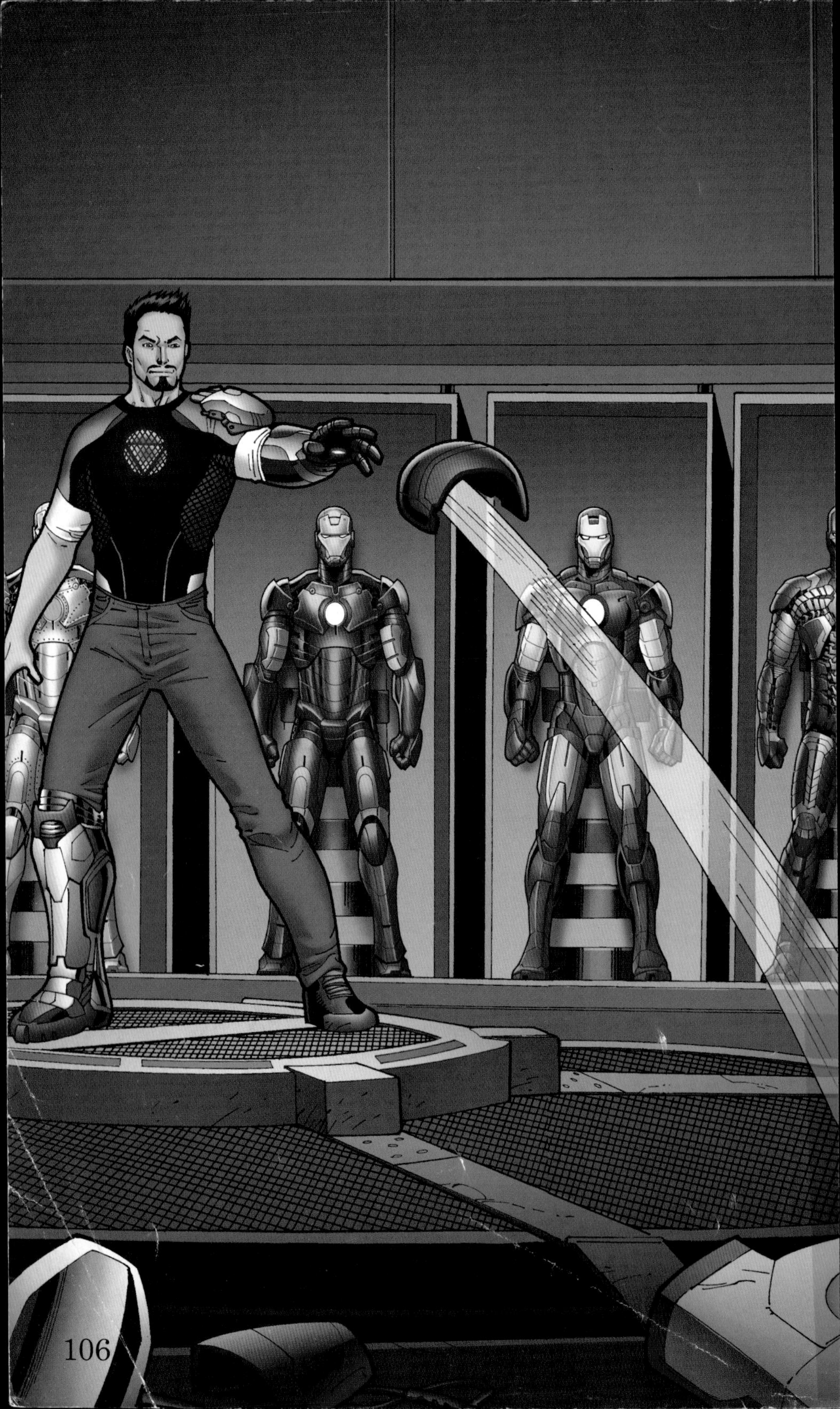

He had also been working too hard.
Tony was trying to make
the perfect Iron Man suit.

Sure, Tony was still Iron Man.

But he could not solve every problem.

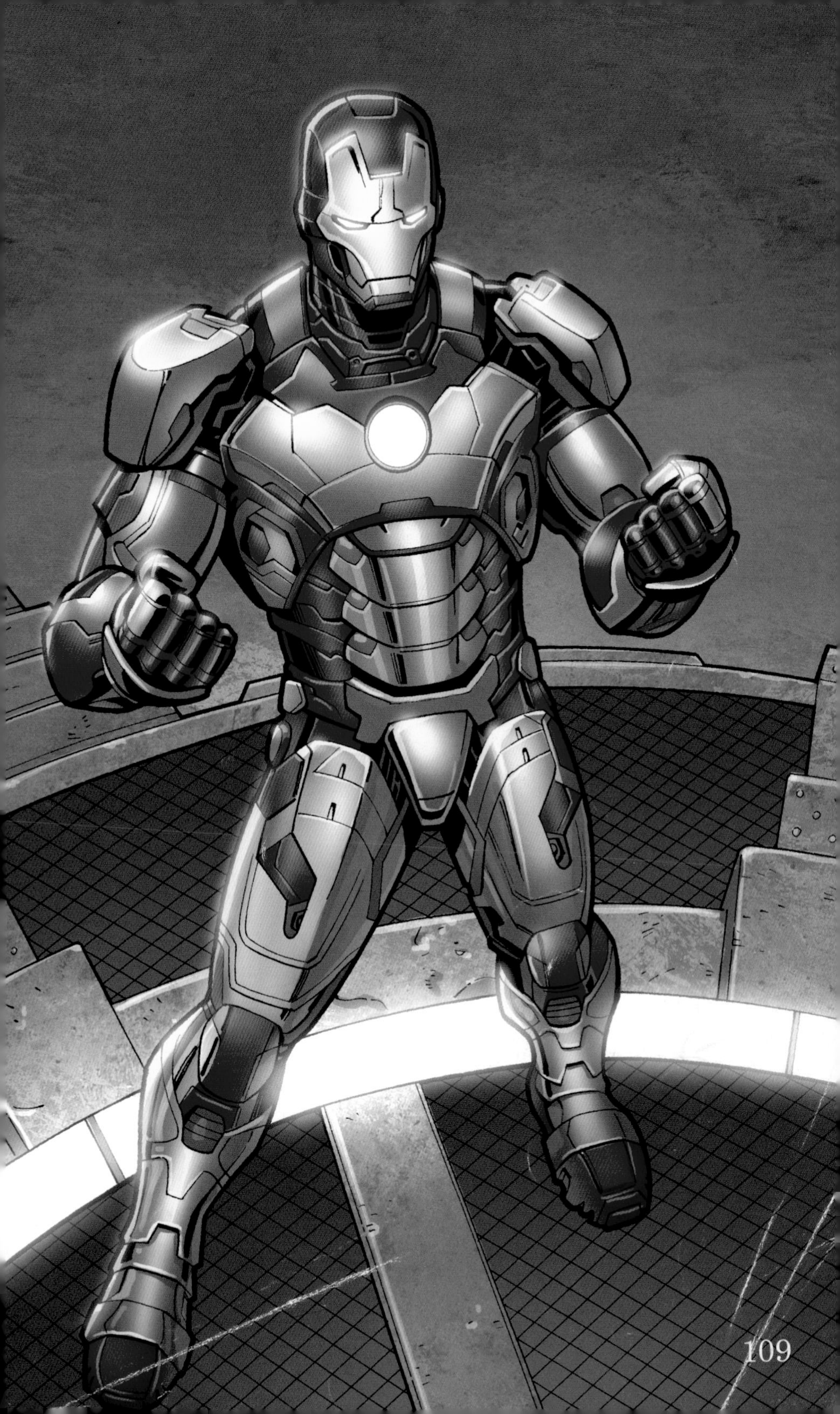

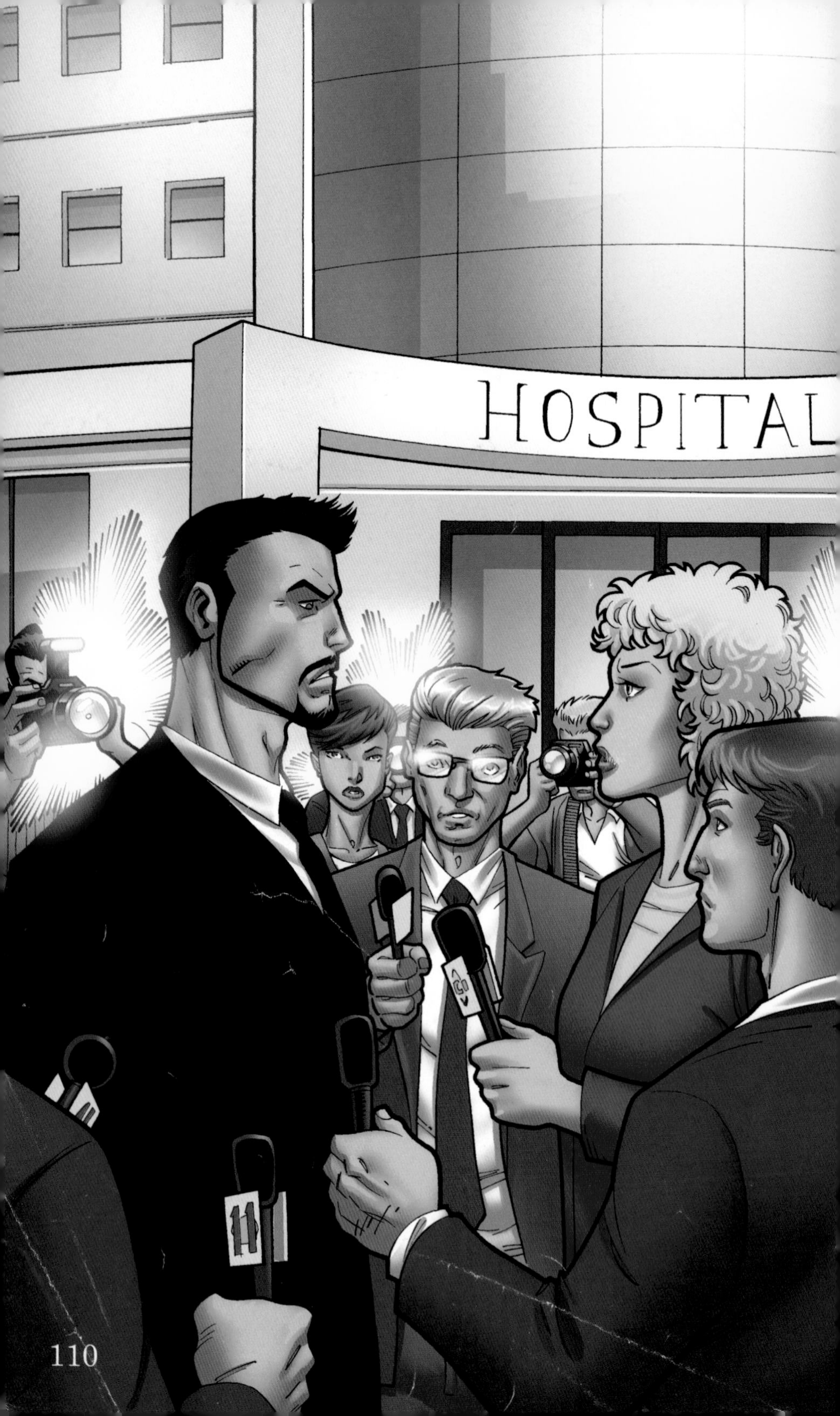
HOSPITAL
11

His enemies hurt people.

They wound up in the hospital.

This made Tony angry.

Then the day got even worse.

His house was attacked!

It was the villain known

as the Mandarin.

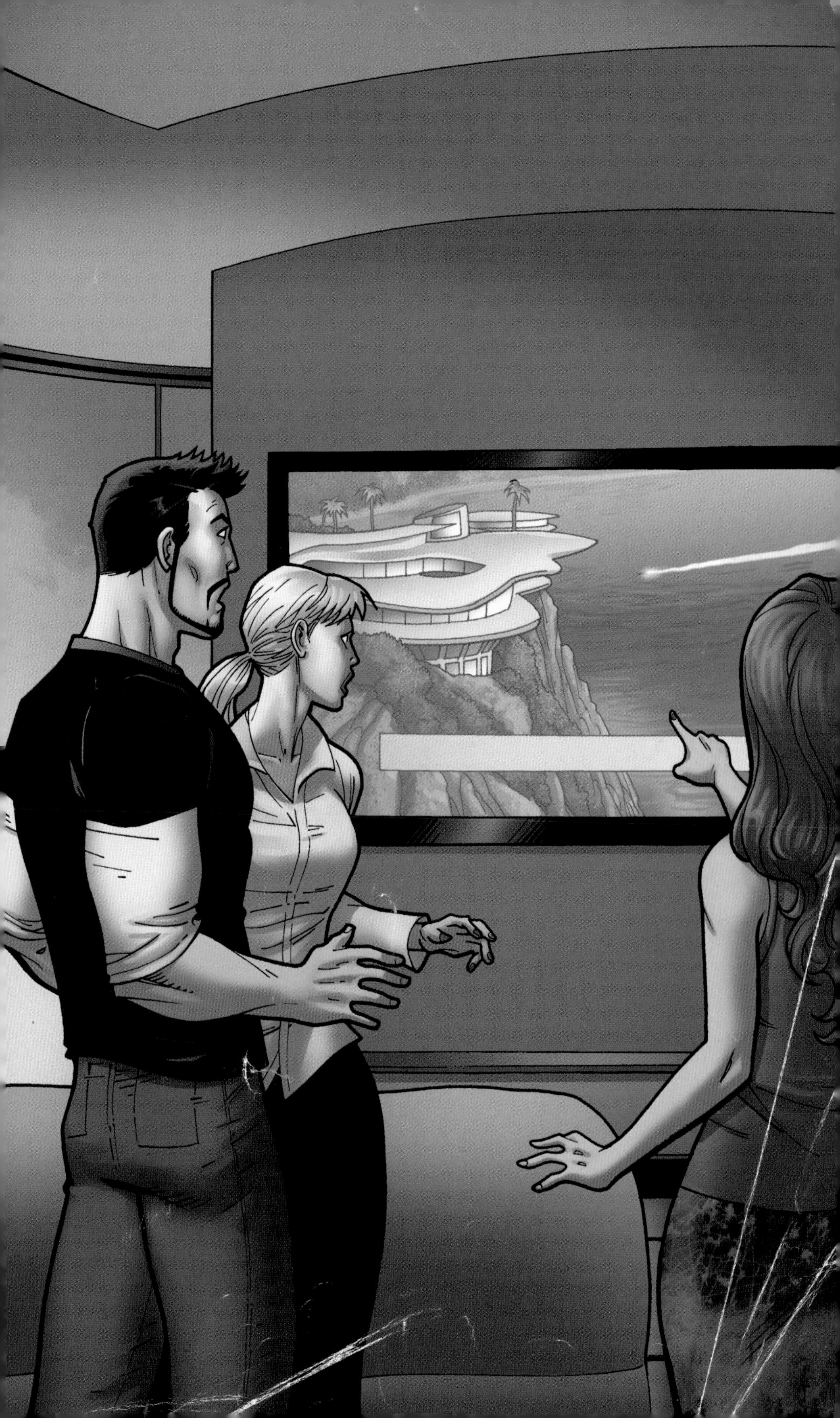

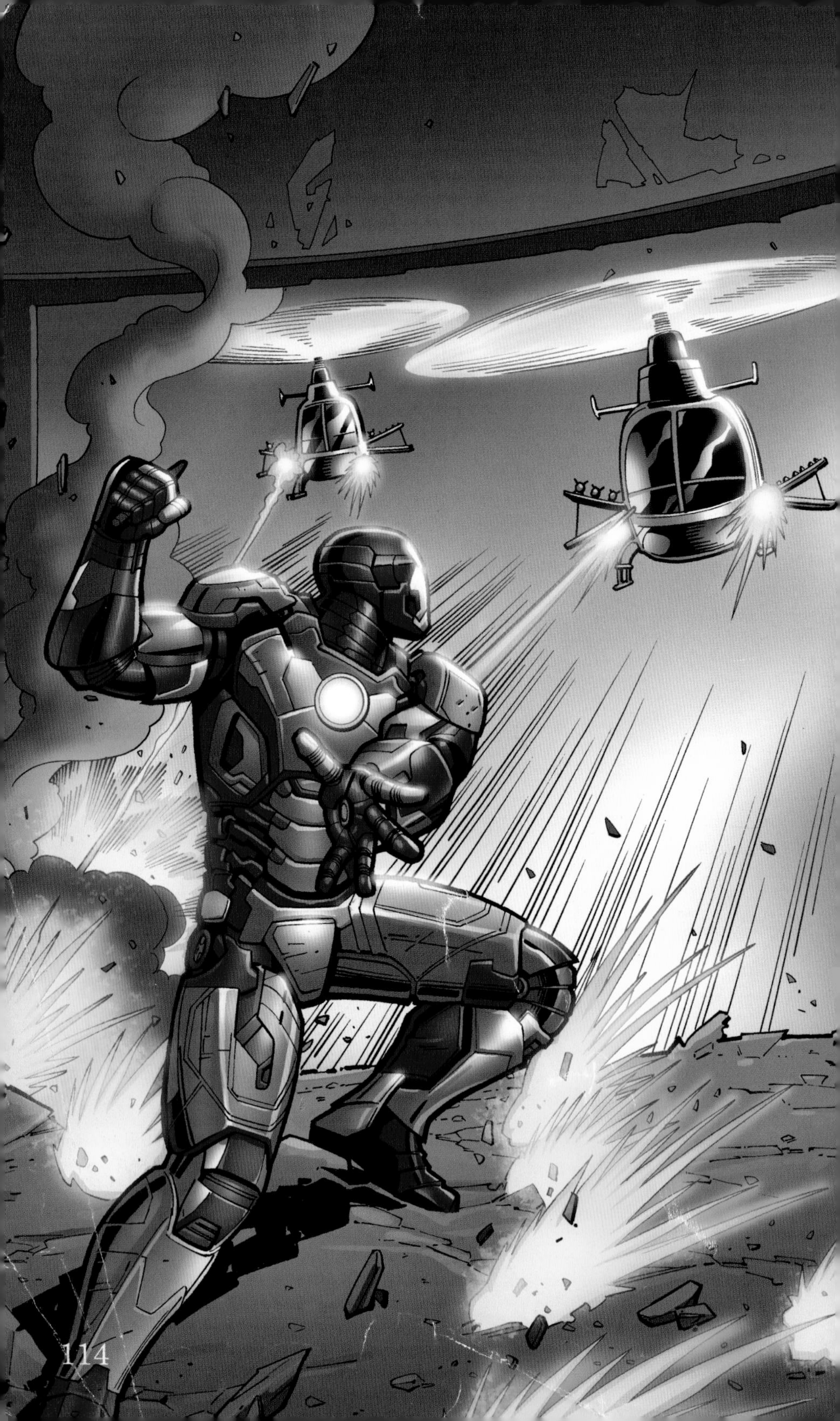

Tony's house was being destroyed.
His friends escaped,
but Tony stayed to fight back.
He put on his new Iron Man
armor and attacked!

But the Mandarin was smart.

His helicopters were really strong!

Iron Man's house fell into the ocean.

Iron Man was trapped inside!

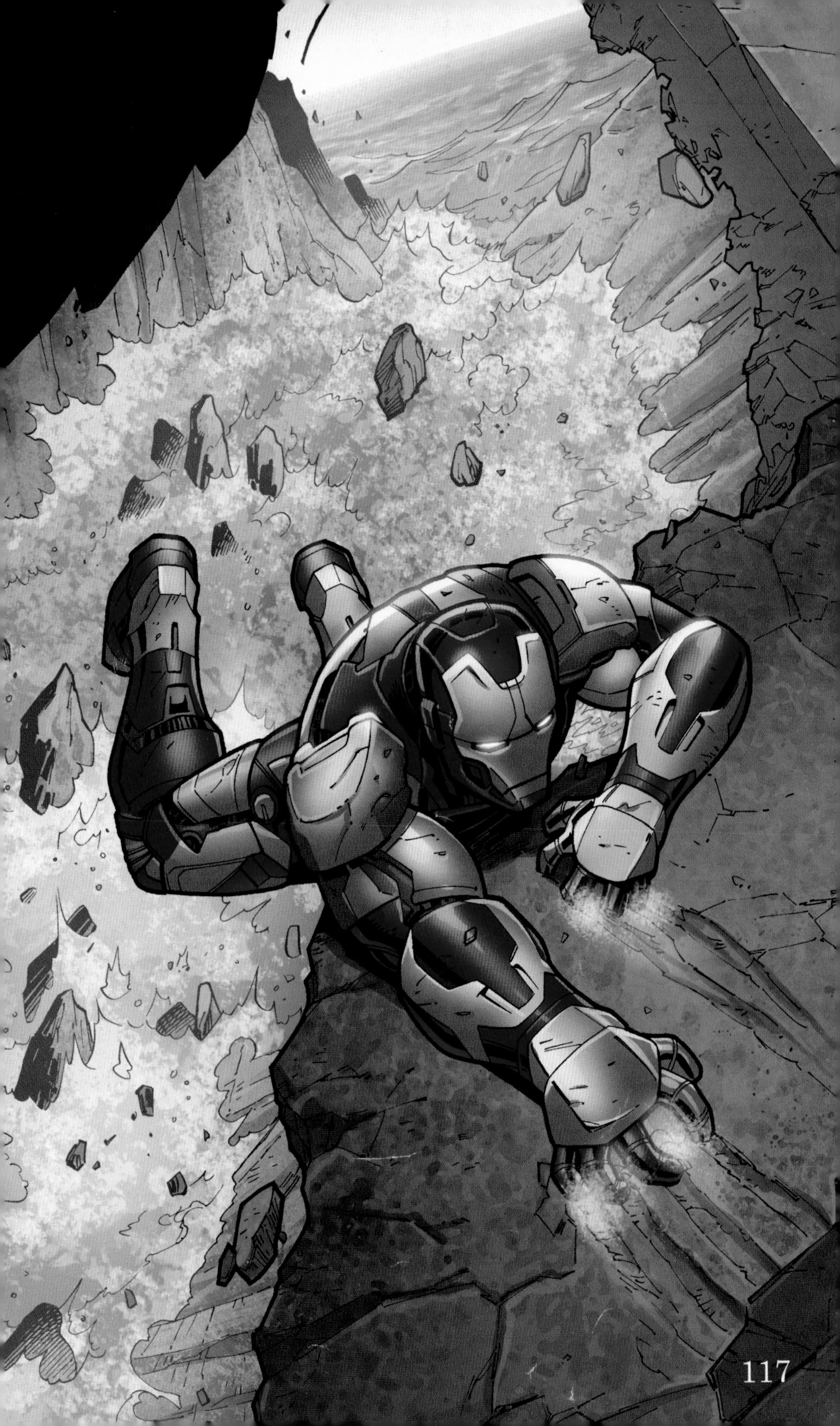

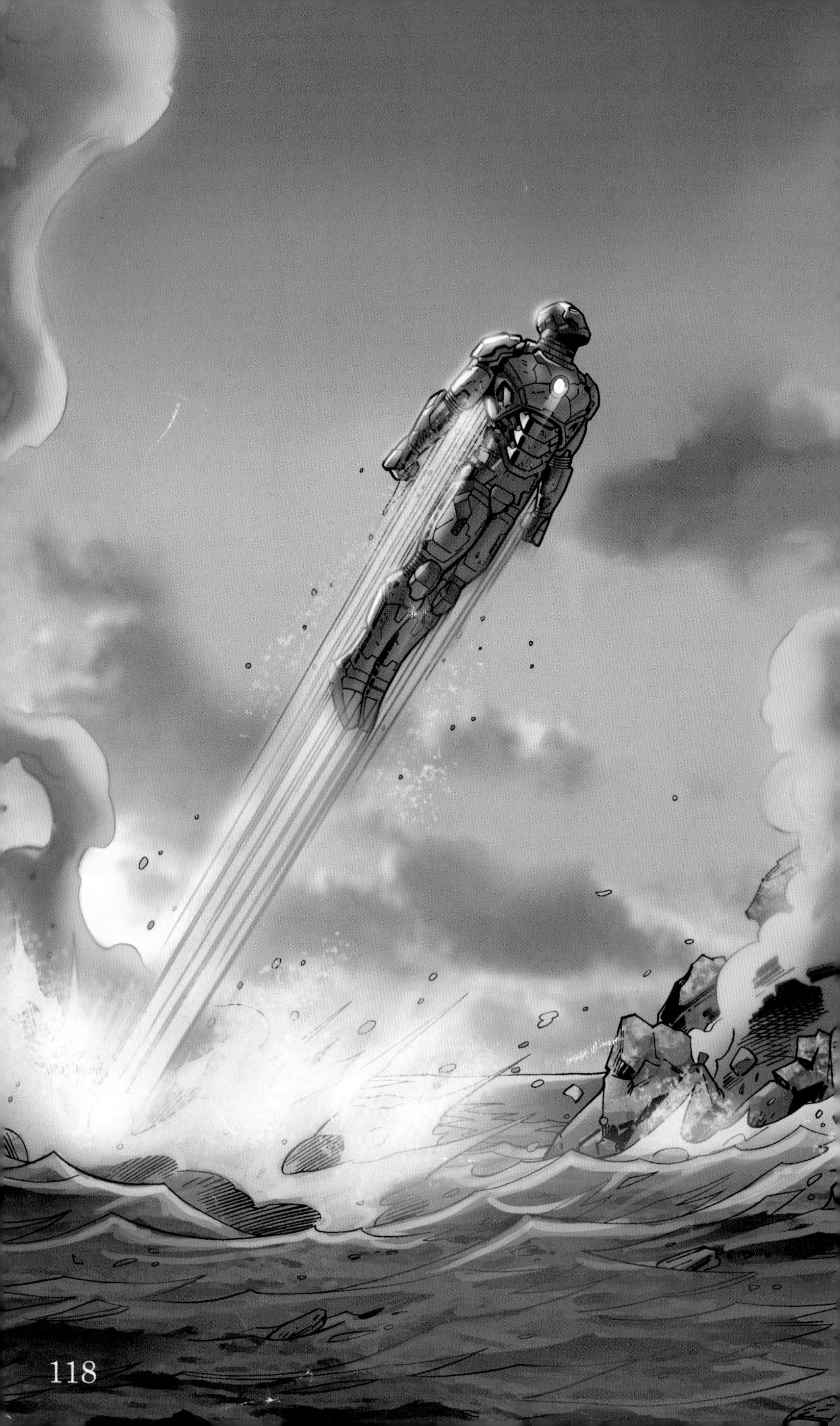

Tony escaped in his Iron Man suit.

His armor was damaged.

He flew as far away as he could.

The suit crashed into the snow.

It smoked and leaked oil.

It had stopped working.

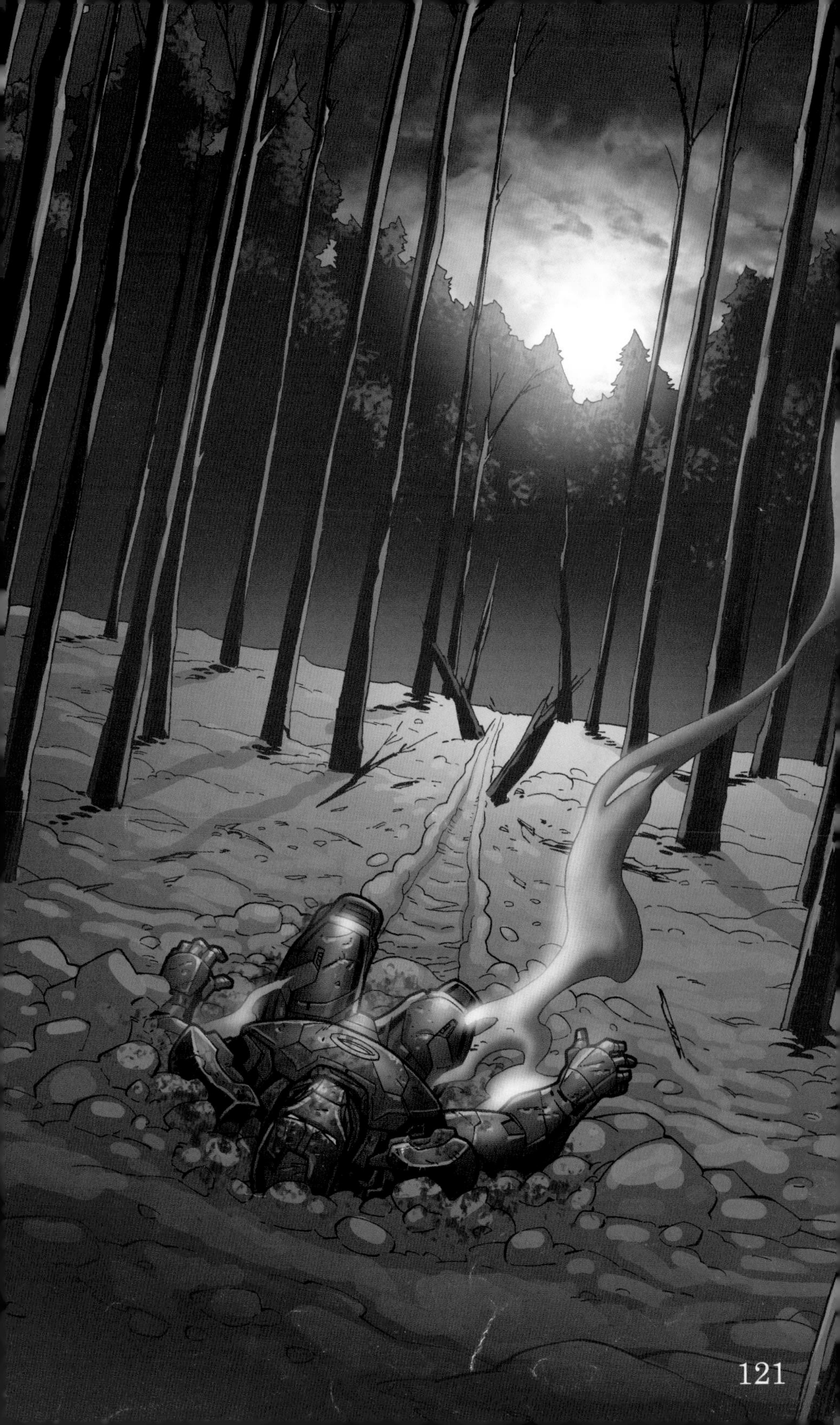

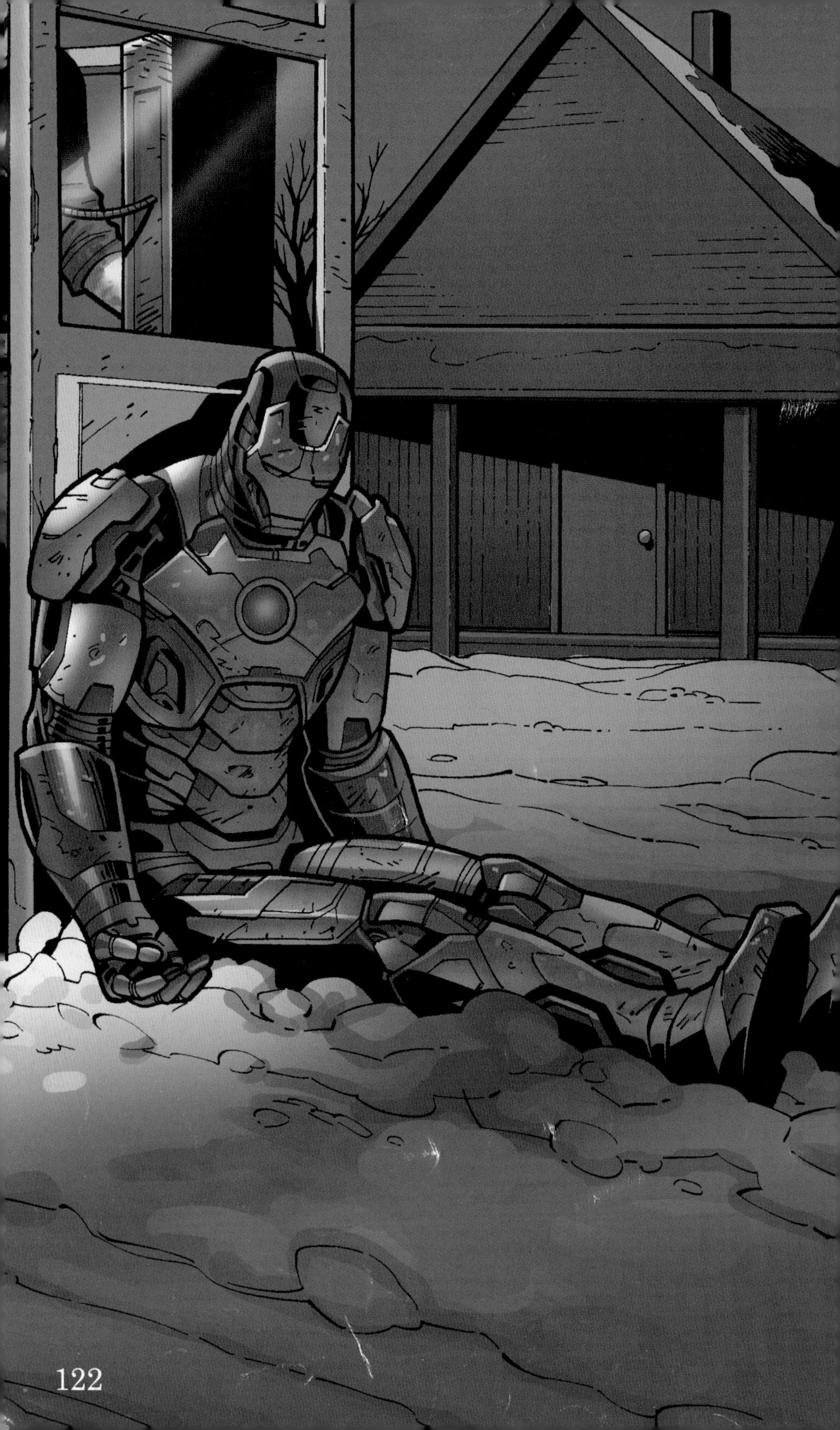

Tony dragged his suit to an old shed.

Tony knew he had to fix his armor.

It was the only way to beat the villain.

Tony worked very hard.

He tried to fix his armor.

He worked all day.

He even worked all night.

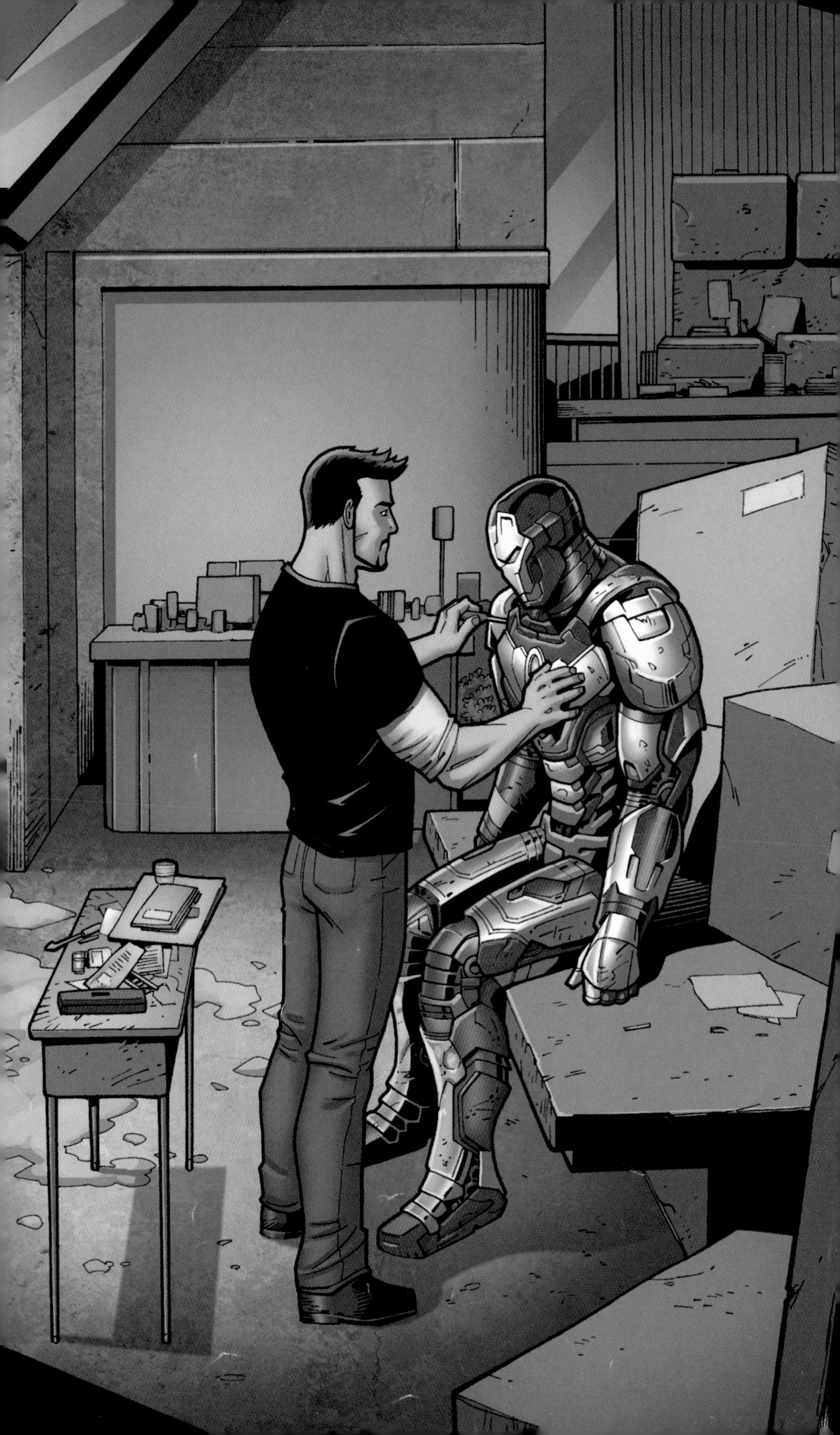

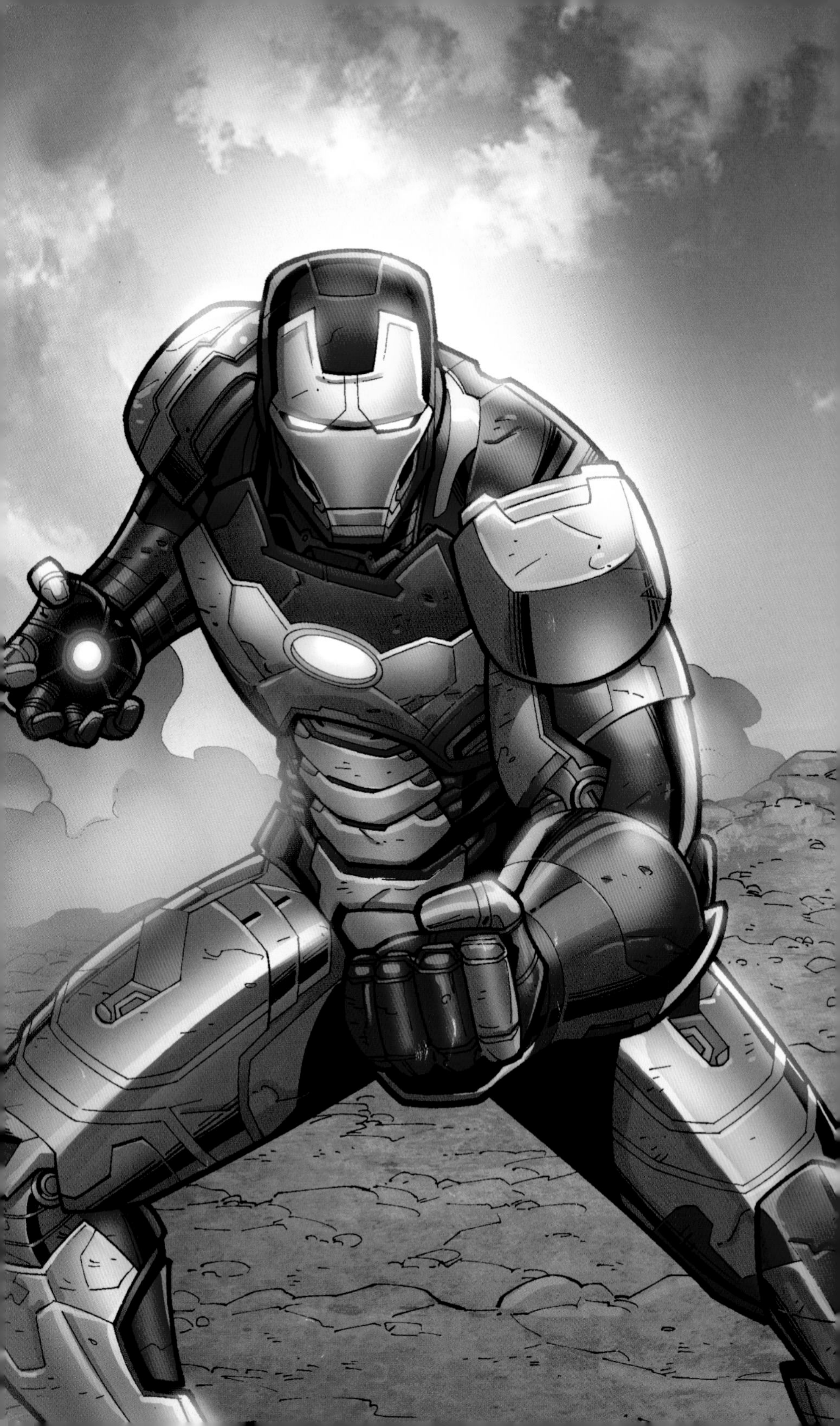

Tony's hard work paid off.

He fixed it!

Iron Man was back.

He was ready for a fight.

He flew up in the air.
He saved a lot of people.
He had made a bad day a little better.
Iron Man had fought back!

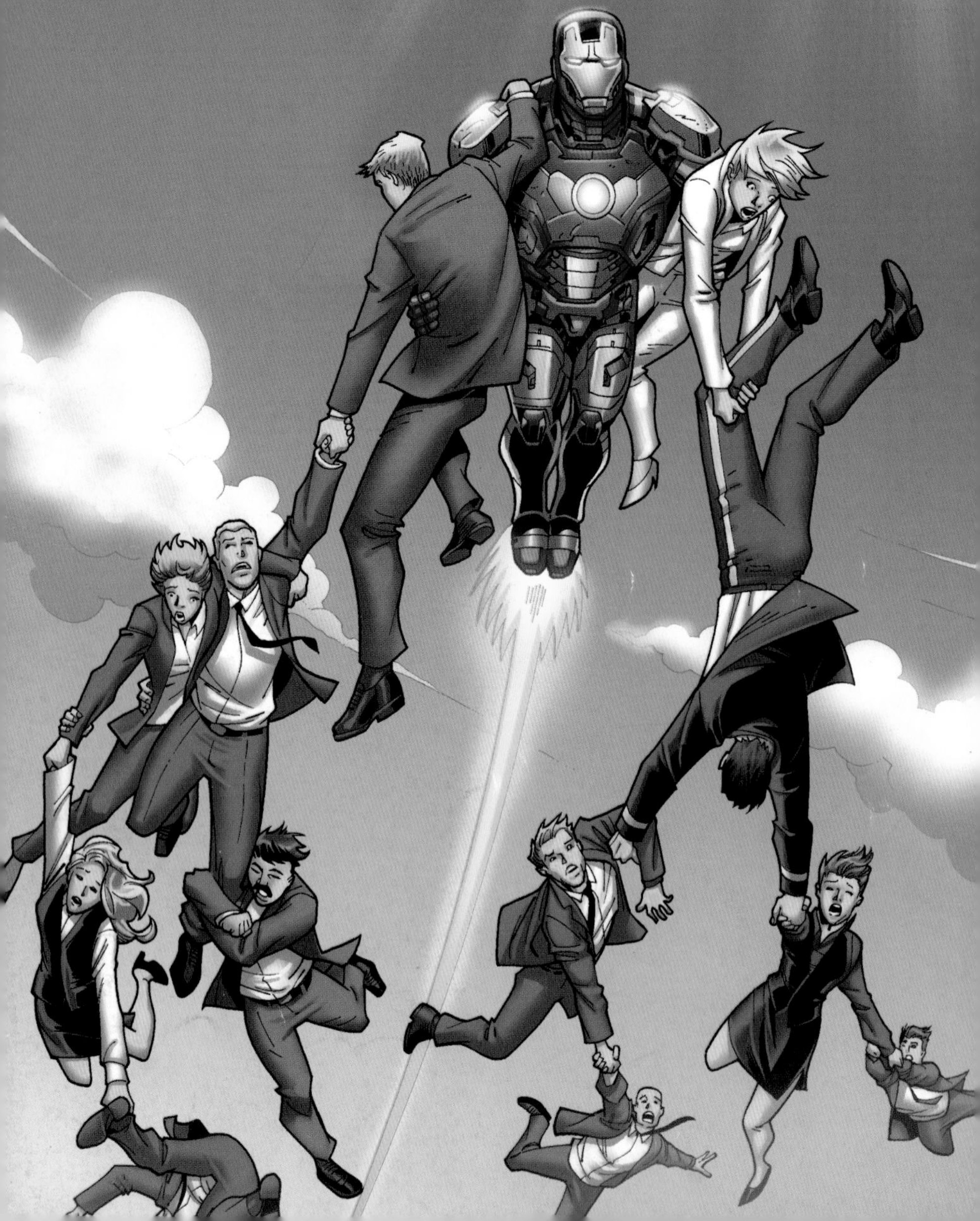

MARVEL
THOR
THE DARK WORLD
HEROES OF ASGARD

By TOMAS PALACIOS

Based on a Screenplay by CHRISTOPHER L. YOST
and CHRISTOPHER MARKUS & STEPHEN McFEELY

Story by DON PAYNE and ROBERT RODAT

Produced by KEVIN FEIGE, p.g.a.

Directed by ALAN TAYLOR

Illustrated by RON LIM, CAM SMITH and LEE DUHIG

There are all types of creatures
and monsters that live
in the Nine Realms.
Some are big and some are small.
Some are good and some are bad.

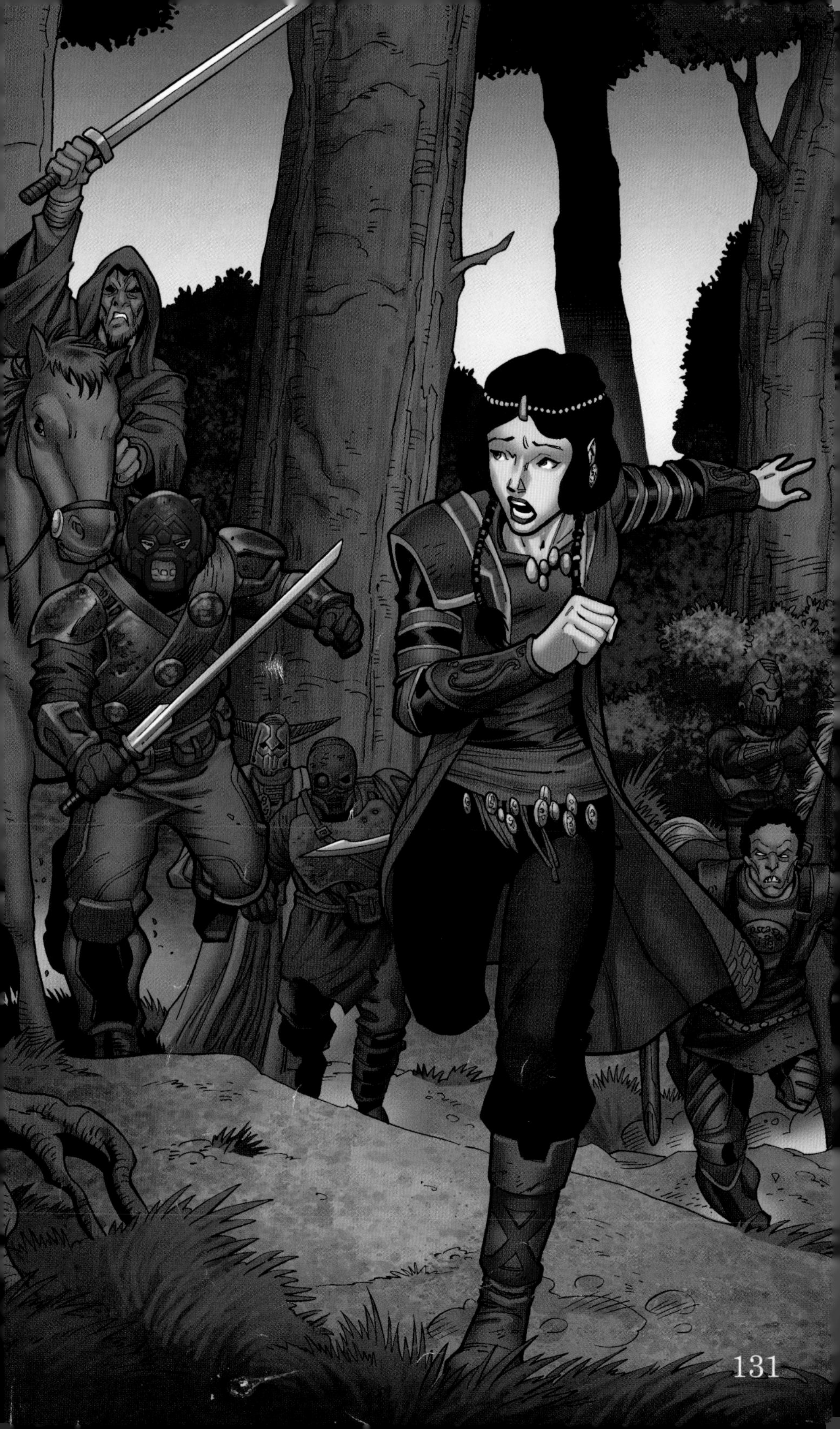

Sometimes, the bigger monsters
pick on the smaller creatures.
That is when the heroes are called!
Hogun the Grim is a part of the
Warriors Three.
He is strong and tough!
He uses his mace to battle
the monsters!

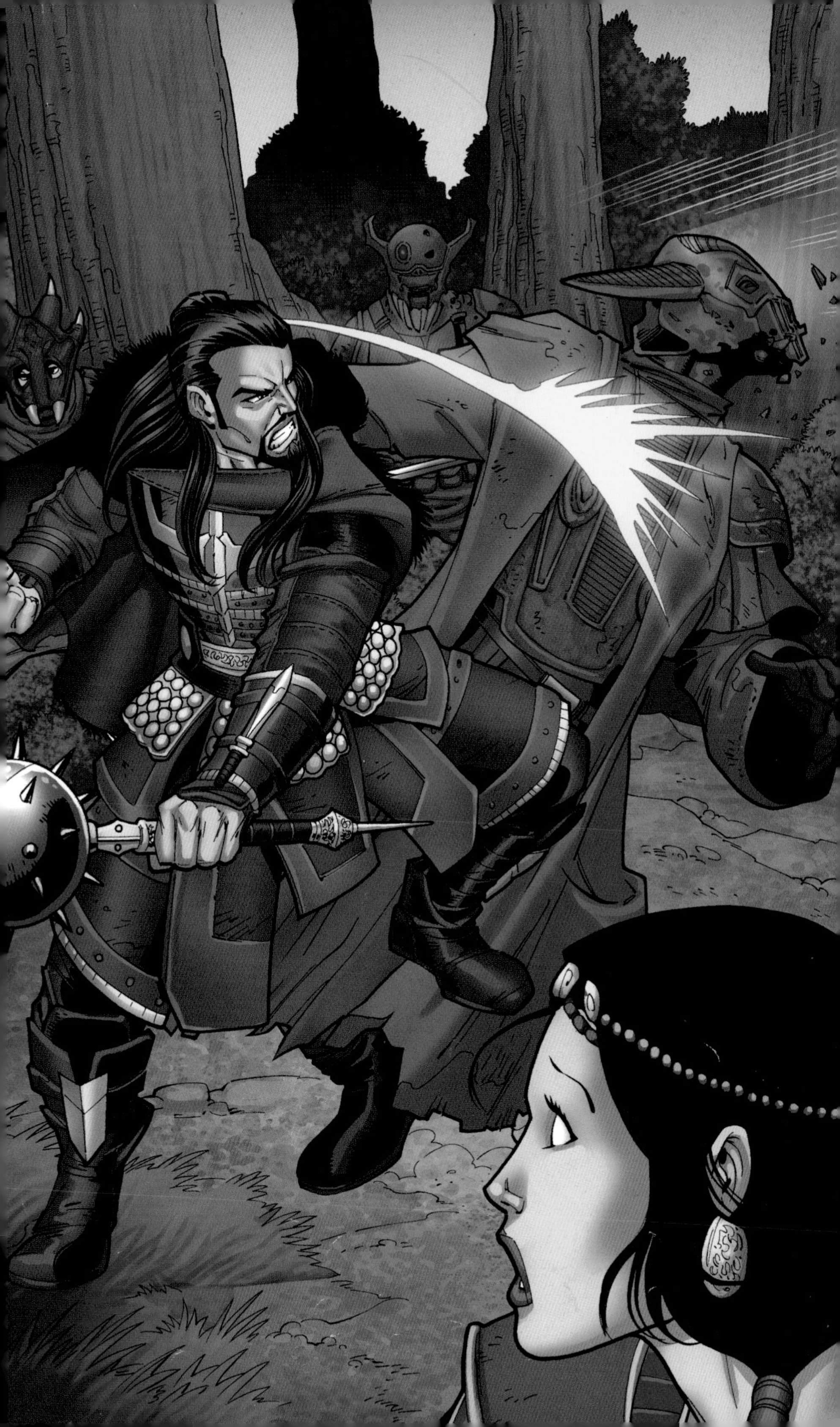

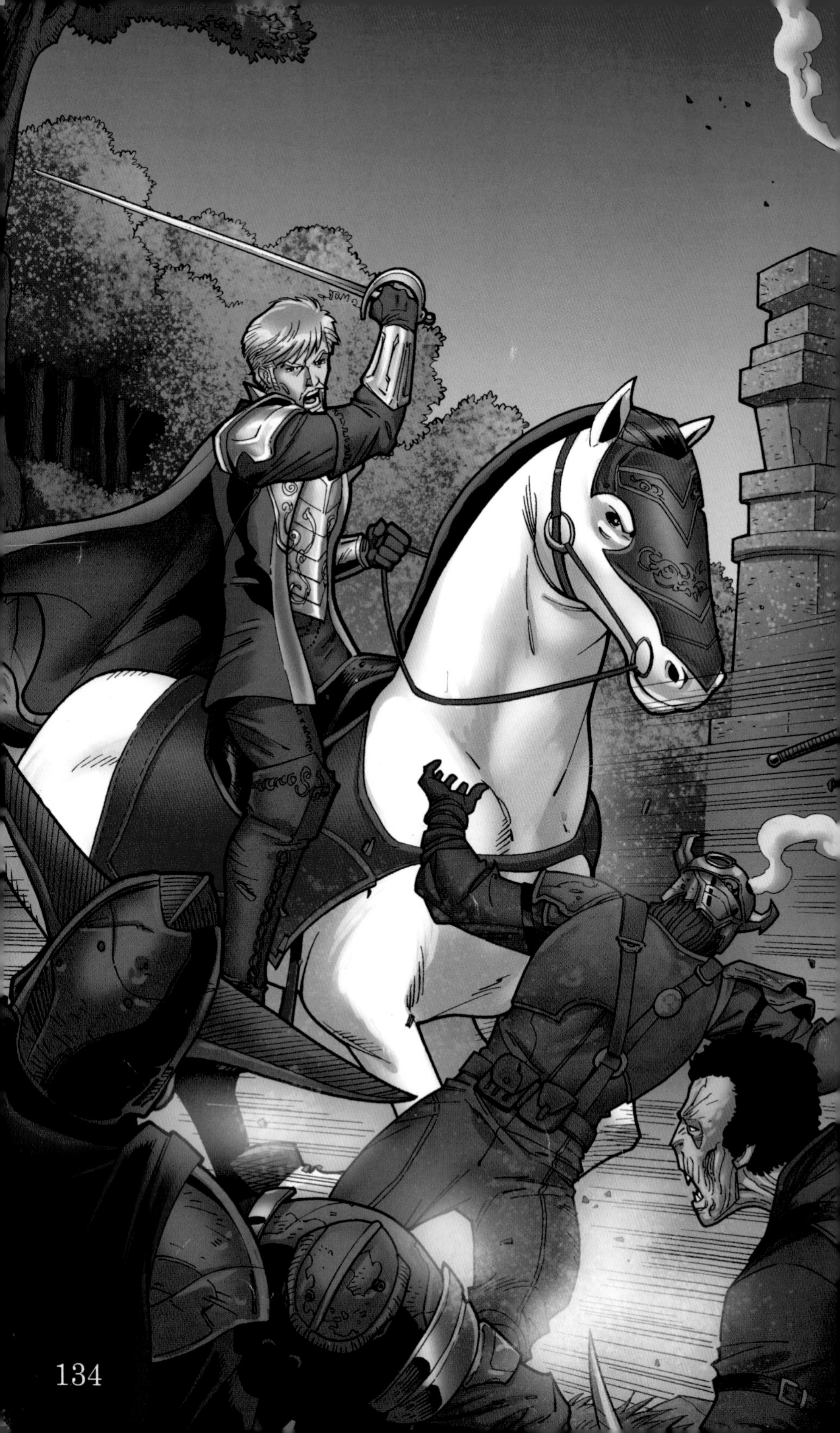

When Hogun needs help, he calls
on Fandral the Dashing!
Fandral is the second member
of the Warriors Three.
Fandral rides a white horse!
He flashes his sharp sword
to stop the villains!

Fandral and Hogun need help!

That is when Volstagg arrives!

Volstagg is the third member of the
Warriors Three.

He barrels down on the enemy!

He uses his big ax and swings away!

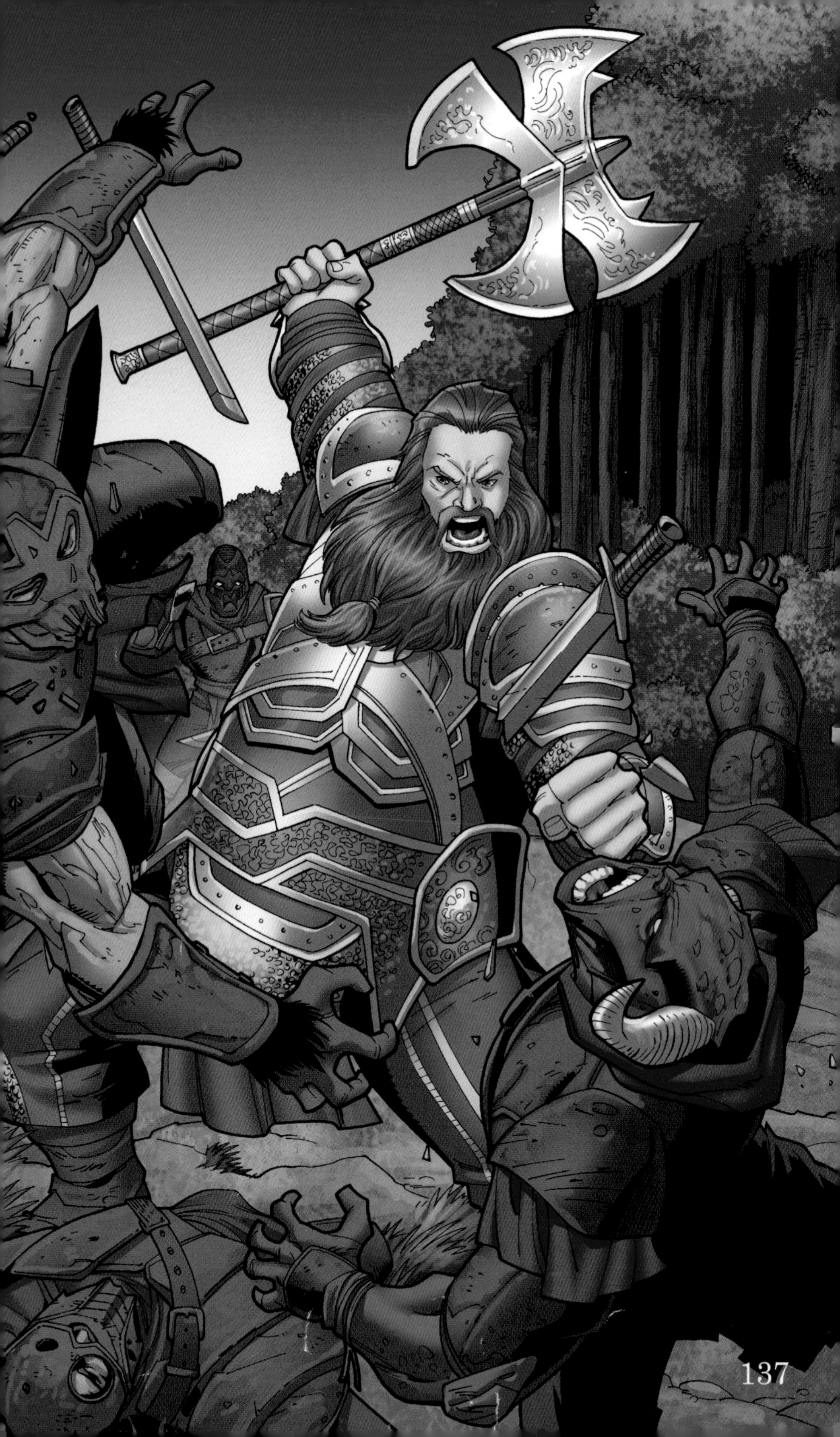

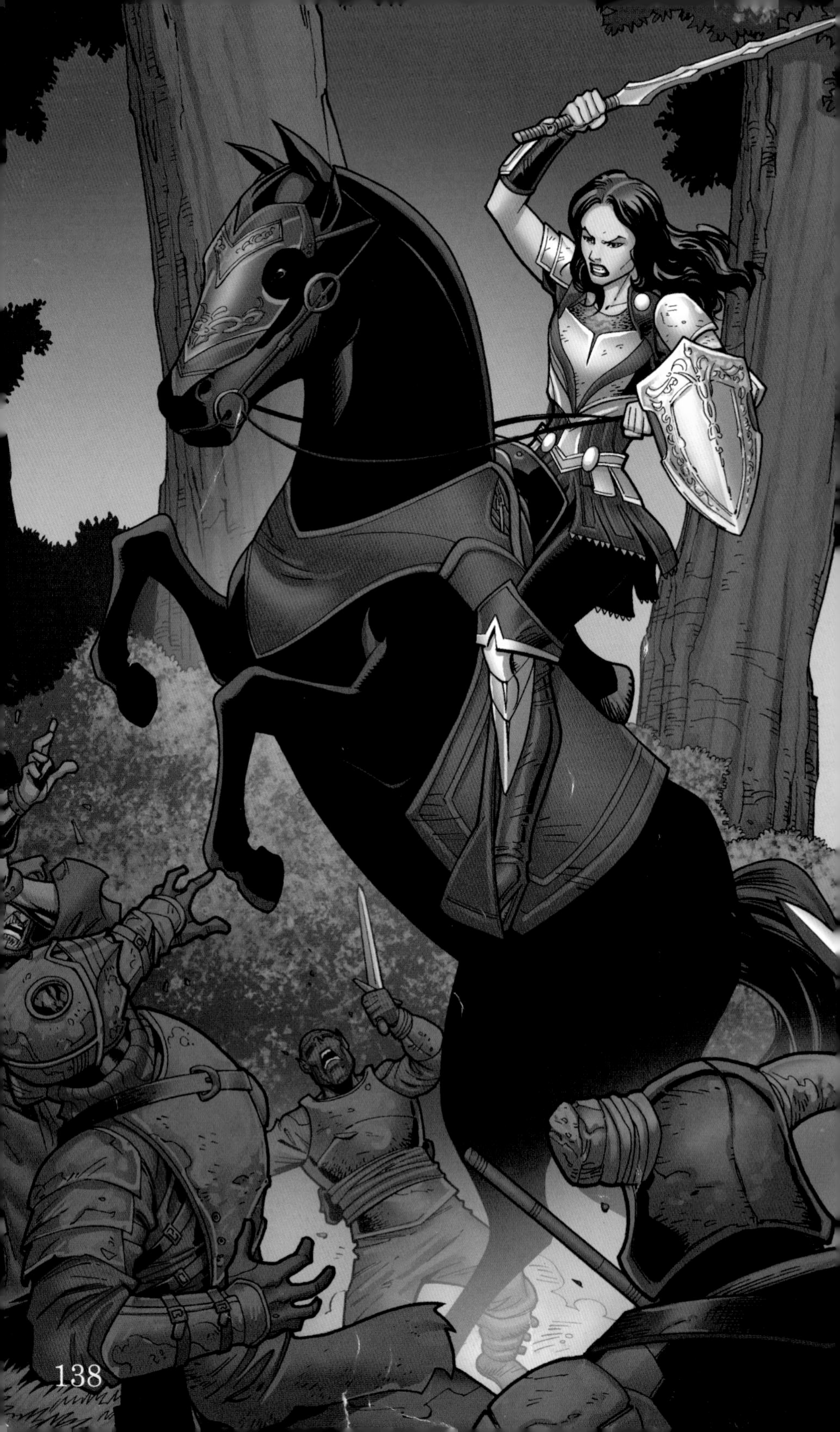

Now and then, even the Warriors Three
need a friend to lend a hand.
That is when Lady Sif arrives!
She is very quick and agile.
Lady Sif spins her bladed sword
to take out the bad guys!

Occasionally, the villains are even
stronger than the Warriors Three
and Lady Sif combined!
Sometimes, they need someone
to help all of them.
Who could that be?

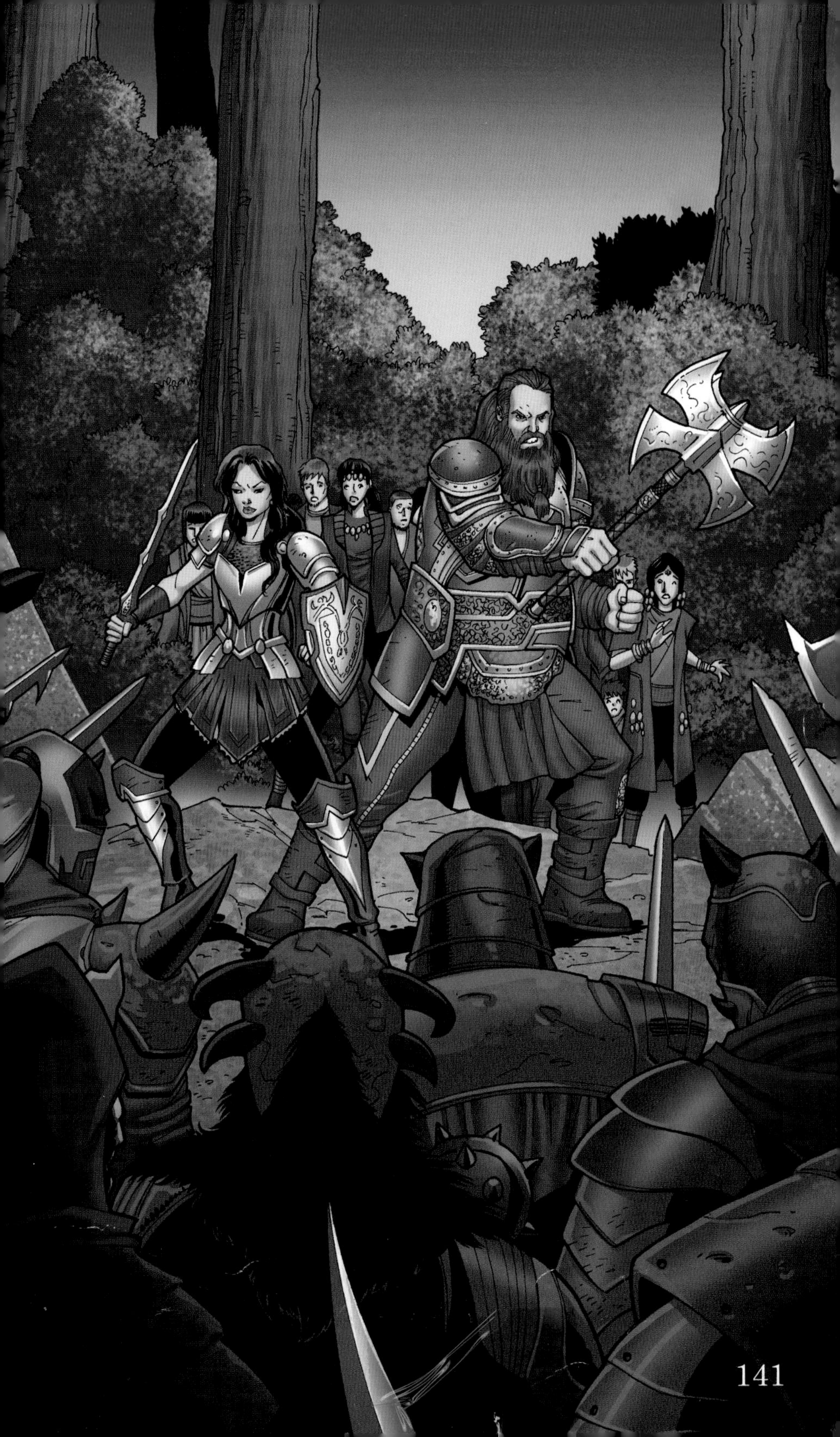

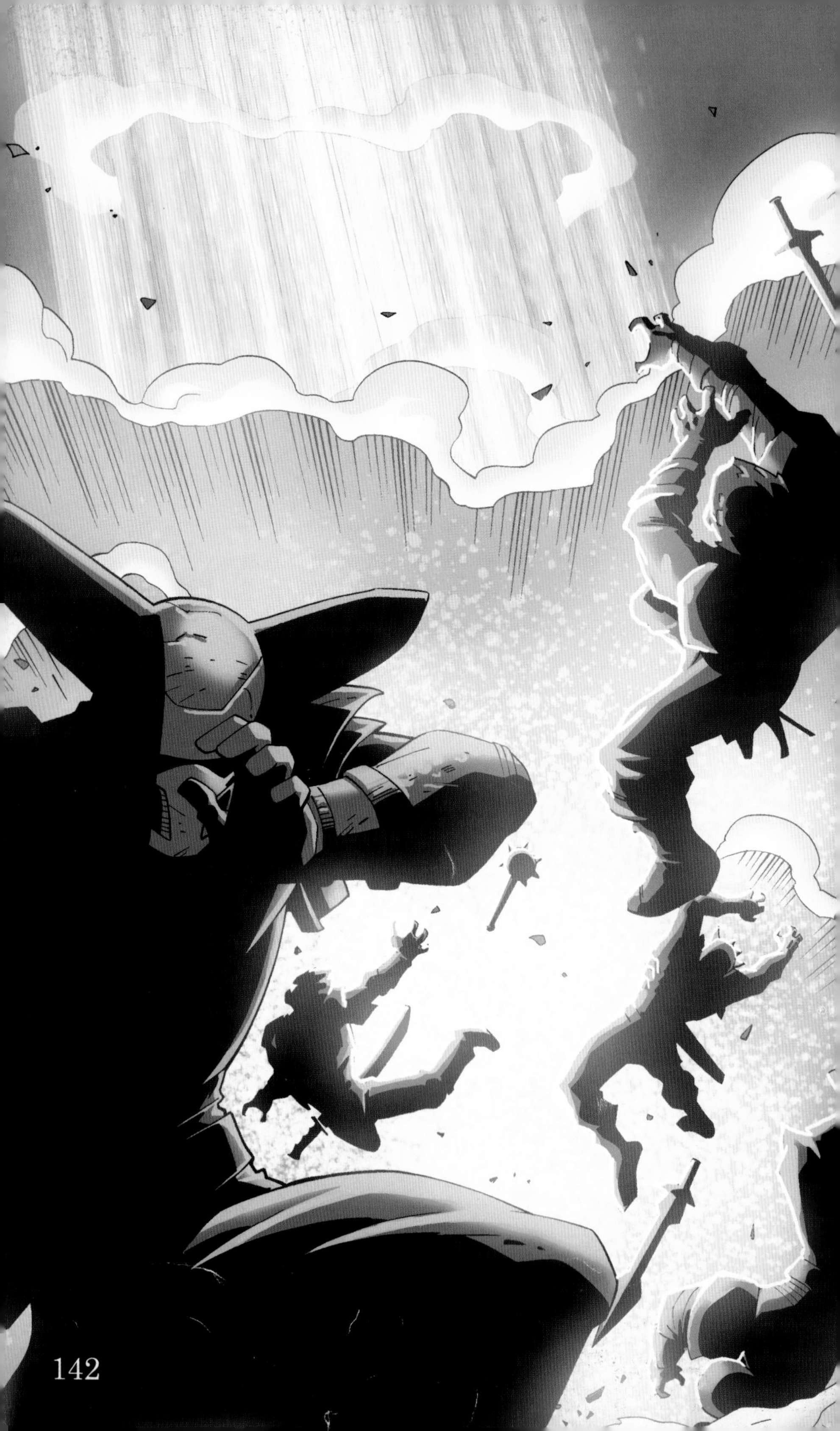

Suddenly, a portal opens up in the sky.

It is the Bifrost!

It is the bridge Asgard uses to travel from realm to realm.

The Bifrost is very bright!

The villains all run with fear!

They know the Bifrost means trouble!

Something flies out of the Bifrost!

It hits one monster.

Then it hits another!

Volstagg and Lady Sif see what it is.

It is Mjölnir!

Mjölnir is a mighty hammer.

It is so powerful that almost no one can use it or even hold it.

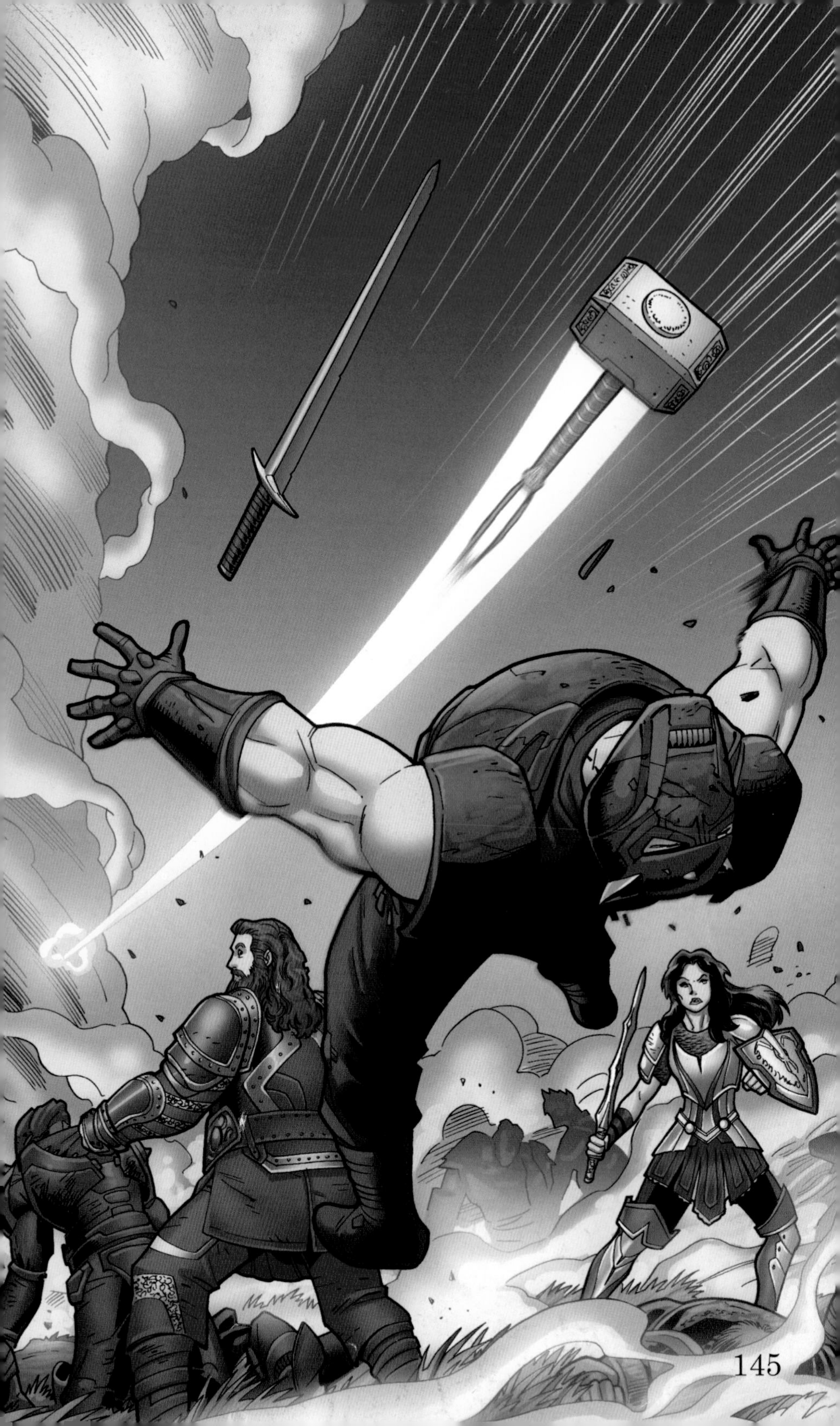

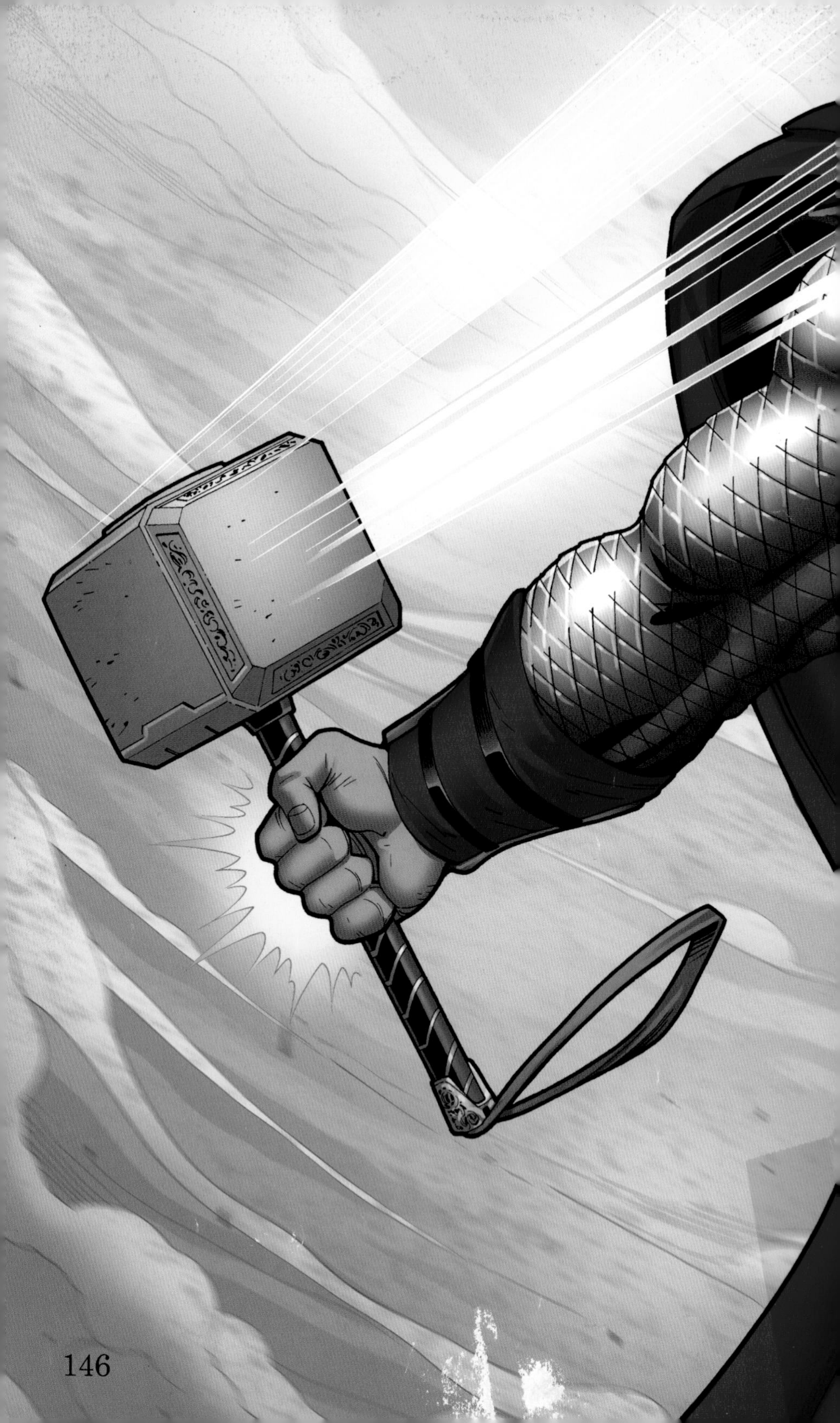

The hammer takes out most
of the Marauders.
The Warriors Three and
Lady Sif smile.
When they see Mjölnir, they know
they will also see a mighty friend!

A towering warrior steps out
of the Bifrost.
It is the Mighty Thor!
Thor is the strongest warrior
to ever live!
He grips his hammer and
faces the villains.
He will put a stop to them and
save the day!

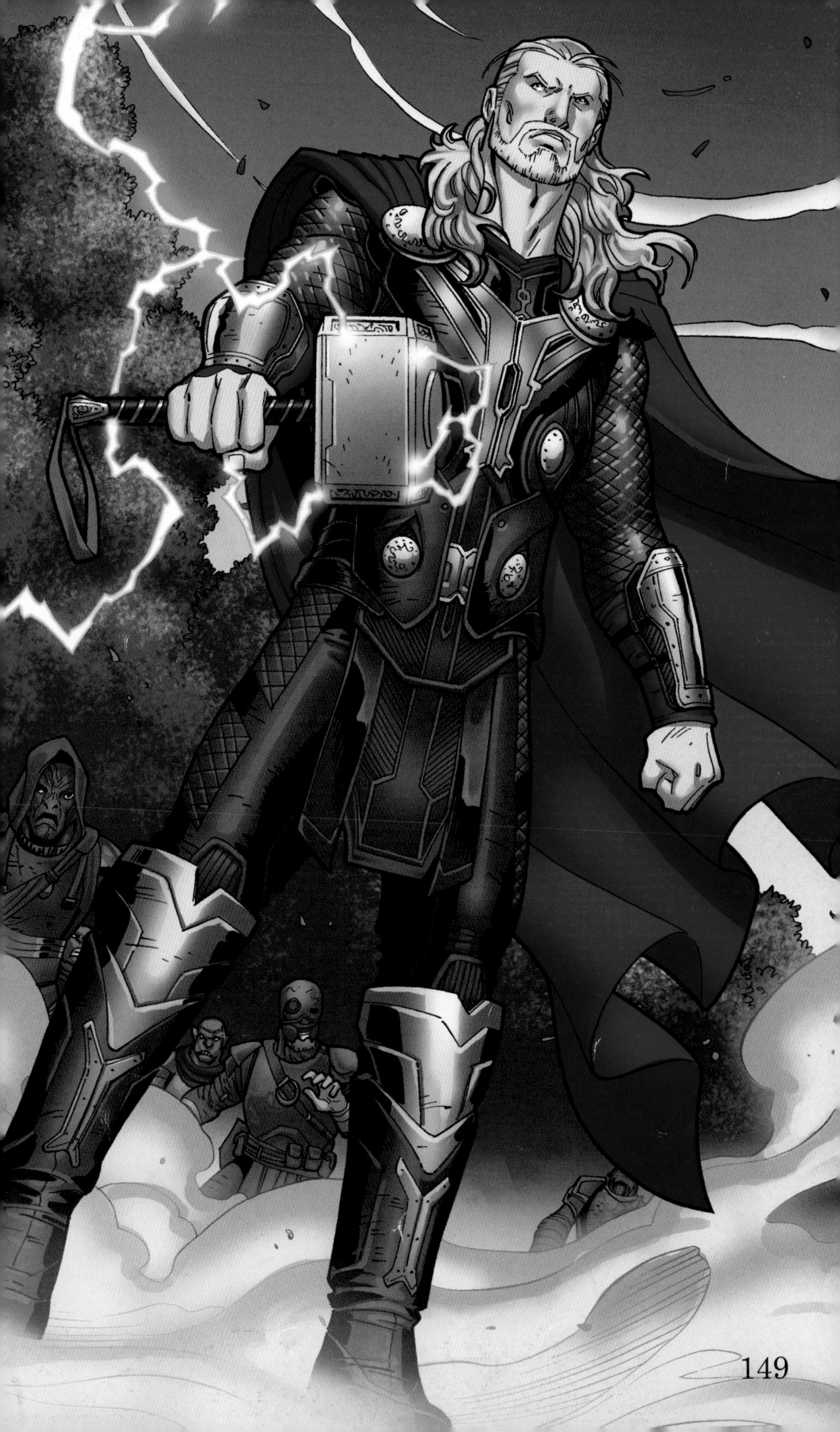

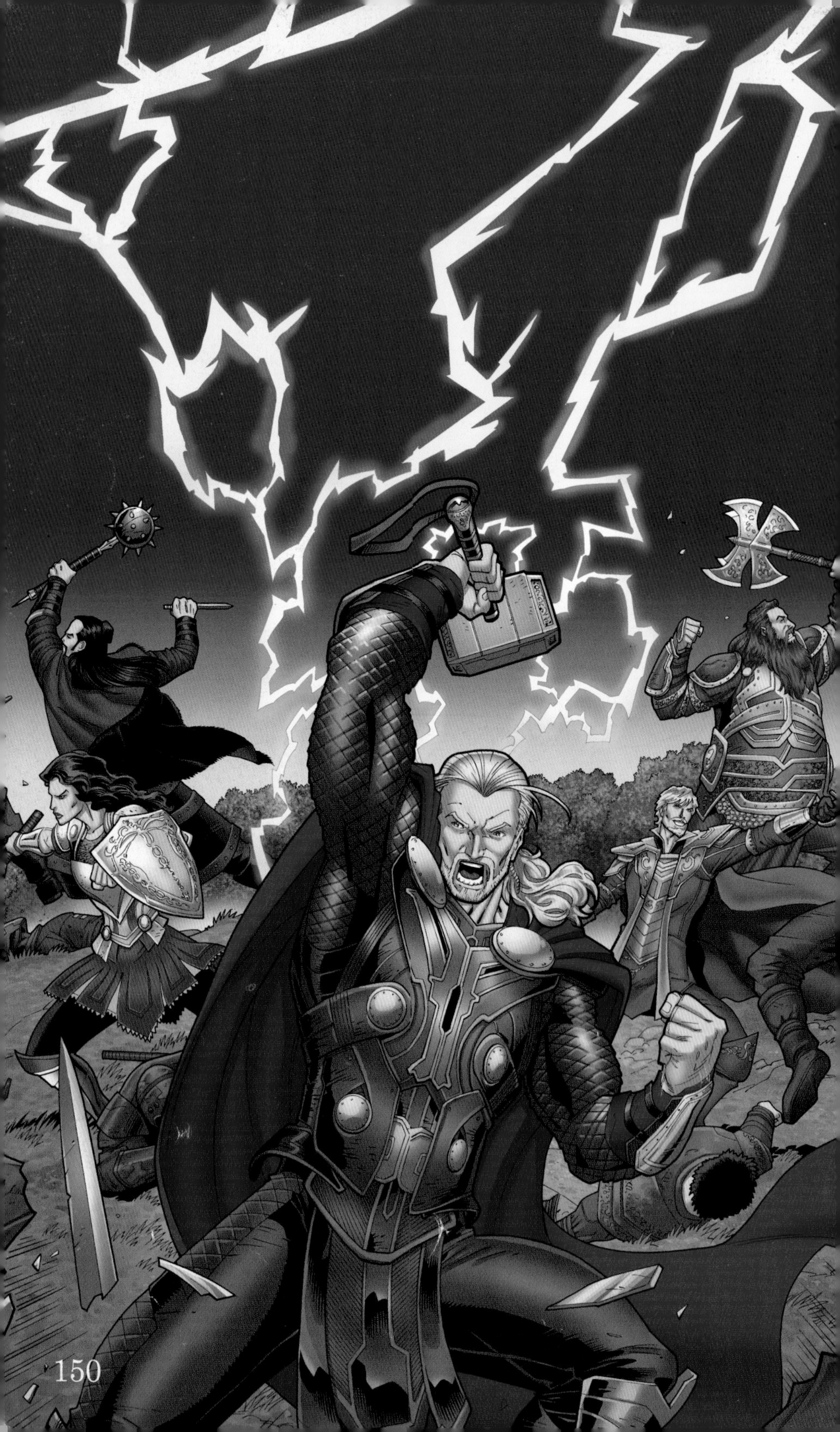

The Warriors Three and Lady Sif
join Thor in the fight!

They bash and smash the monsters!

Thor uses his hammer!

Lady Sif uses her blade!

Fandral uses his sword!

Hogun uses his mace!

Volstagg uses his ax!

They thought the fight was over.
That is when a huge rock monster
appears in front of them!
The creatures laugh and cheer.
The rock monster is their
secret weapon.
They are sure the huge beast
will defeat Thor!

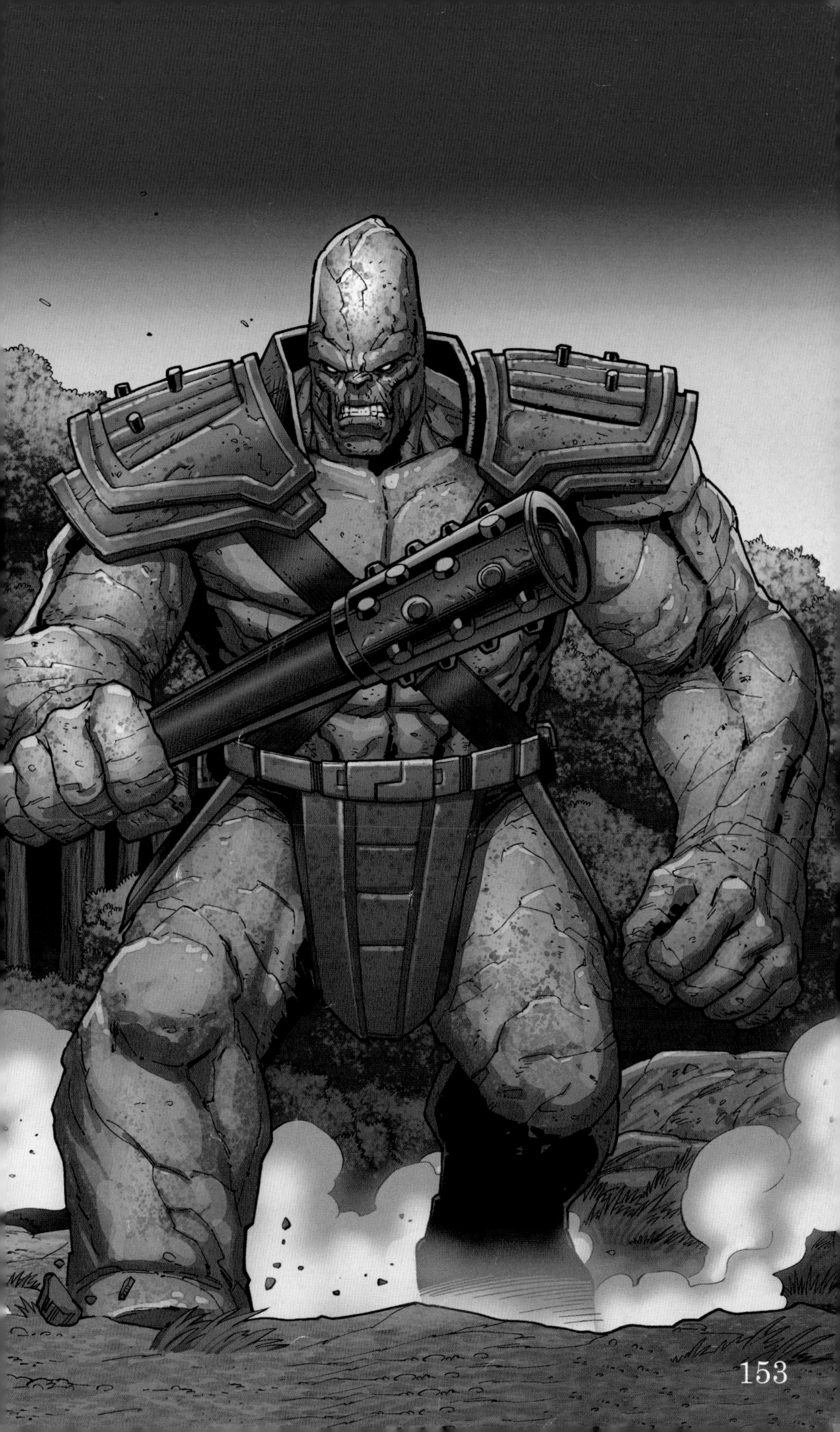

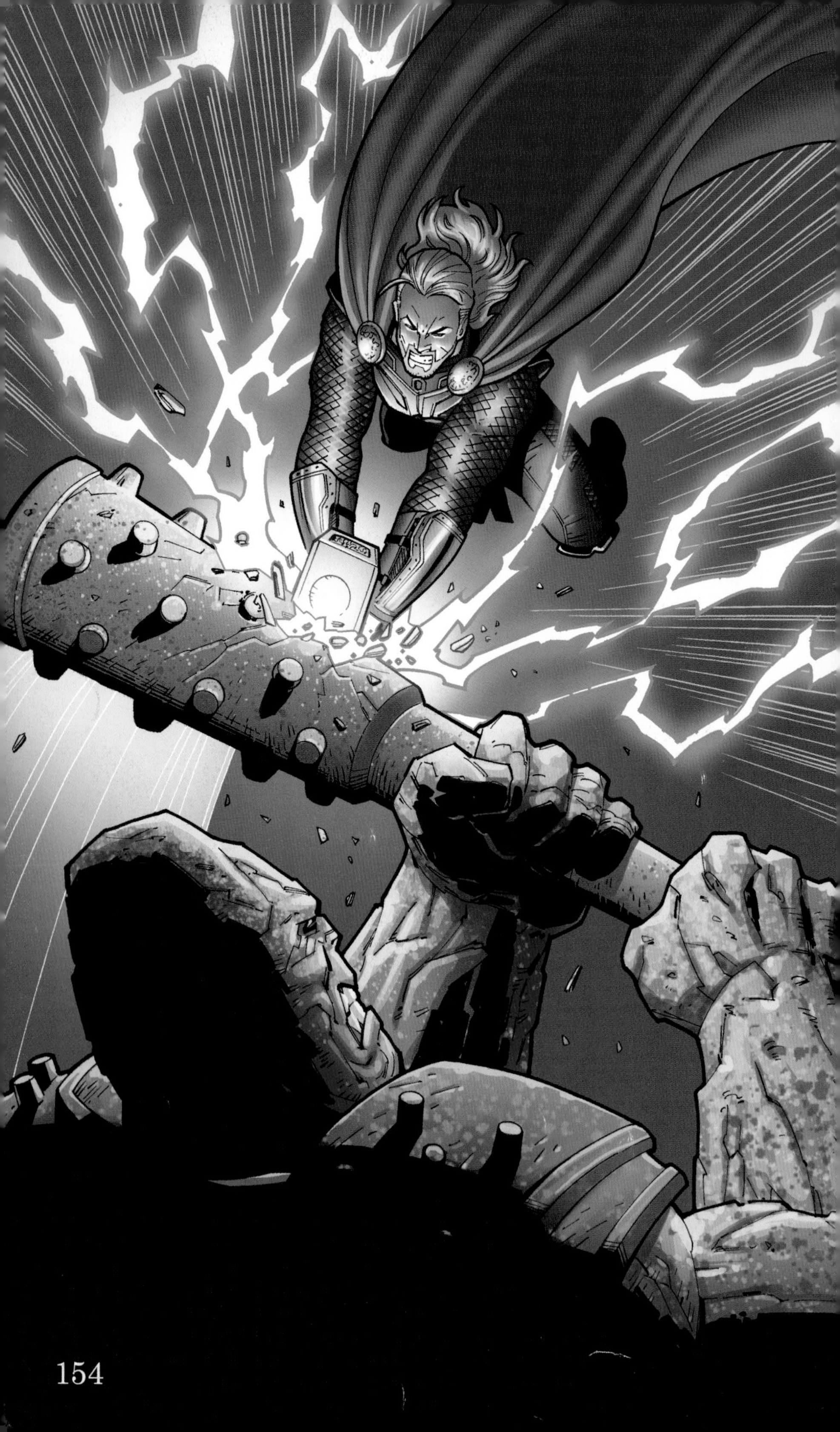

The rock monster is big and strong.

Thor will not back down!

The rock monster charges!

His club is ready to strike!

Thor also charges!

Mjölnir is ready to strike as well!

They clash,

and there is a huge explosion!

The smoke and dust clear.

The winner is the Mighty Thor!

Thor stands proud and strong.

He has defeated the rock monster

and helped save the day!

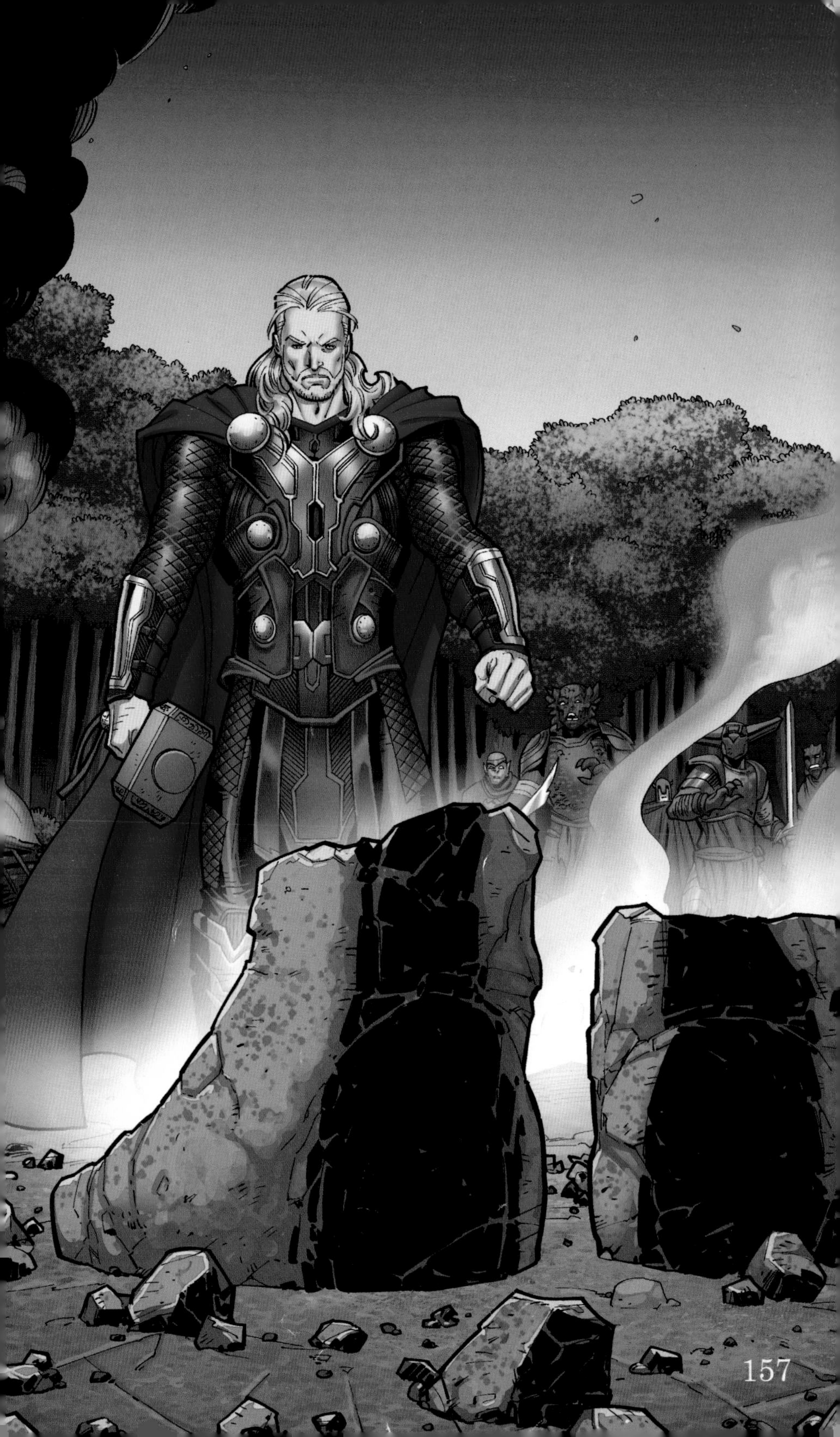

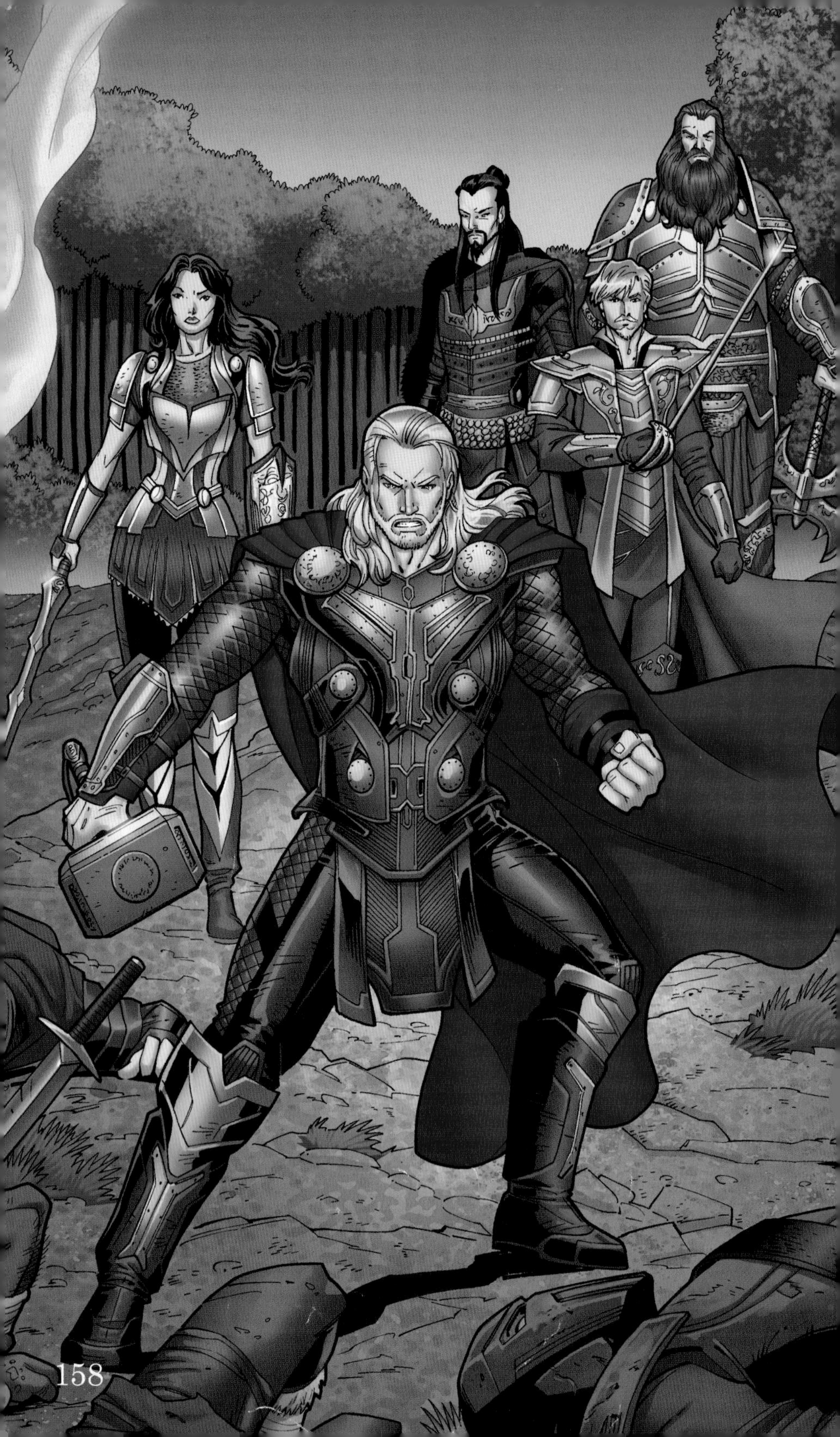

Thor, the Warriors Three, and Lady
Sif stand side by side.
They help the people and
save their land.
With the rock monster and
the creatures beaten,
they can rebuild and be happy again!

Thor knows more battles
will be coming his way.
Thor and his warriors will be ready.
They are the heroes of Asgard!

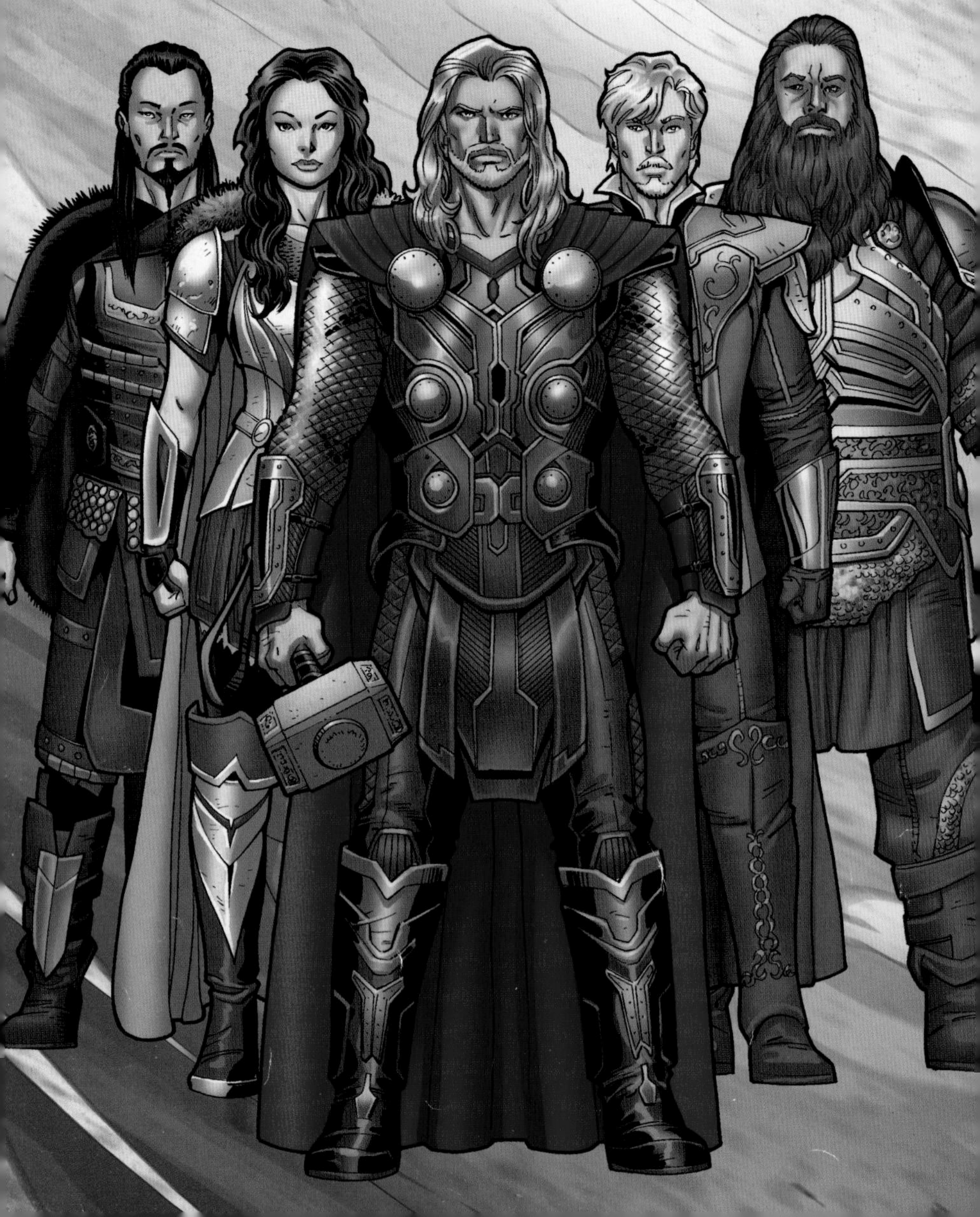

MARVEL
CAPTAIN AMERICA
THE WINTER SOLDIER
FALCON TAKES FLIGHT

BY
Adam Davis

BASED ON THE SCREENPLAY BY
Christopher Markus & Stephen McFeely

PRODUCED BY
Kevin Feige, p.g.a.

DIRECTED BY
Anthony and Joe Russo

ILLUSTRATED BY
Ron Lim, Cam Smith, & Lee Duhig

Captain America liked to run.

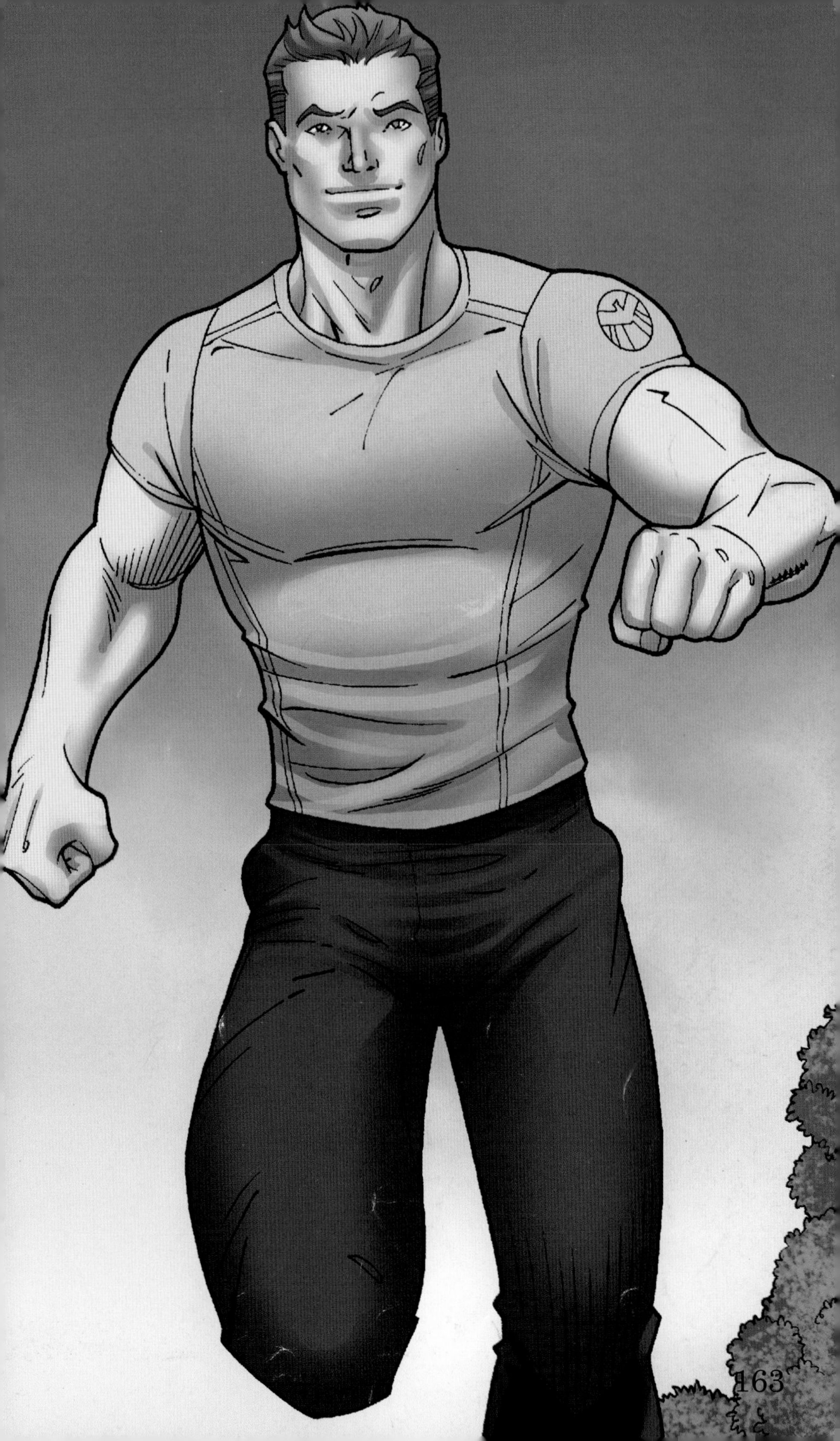

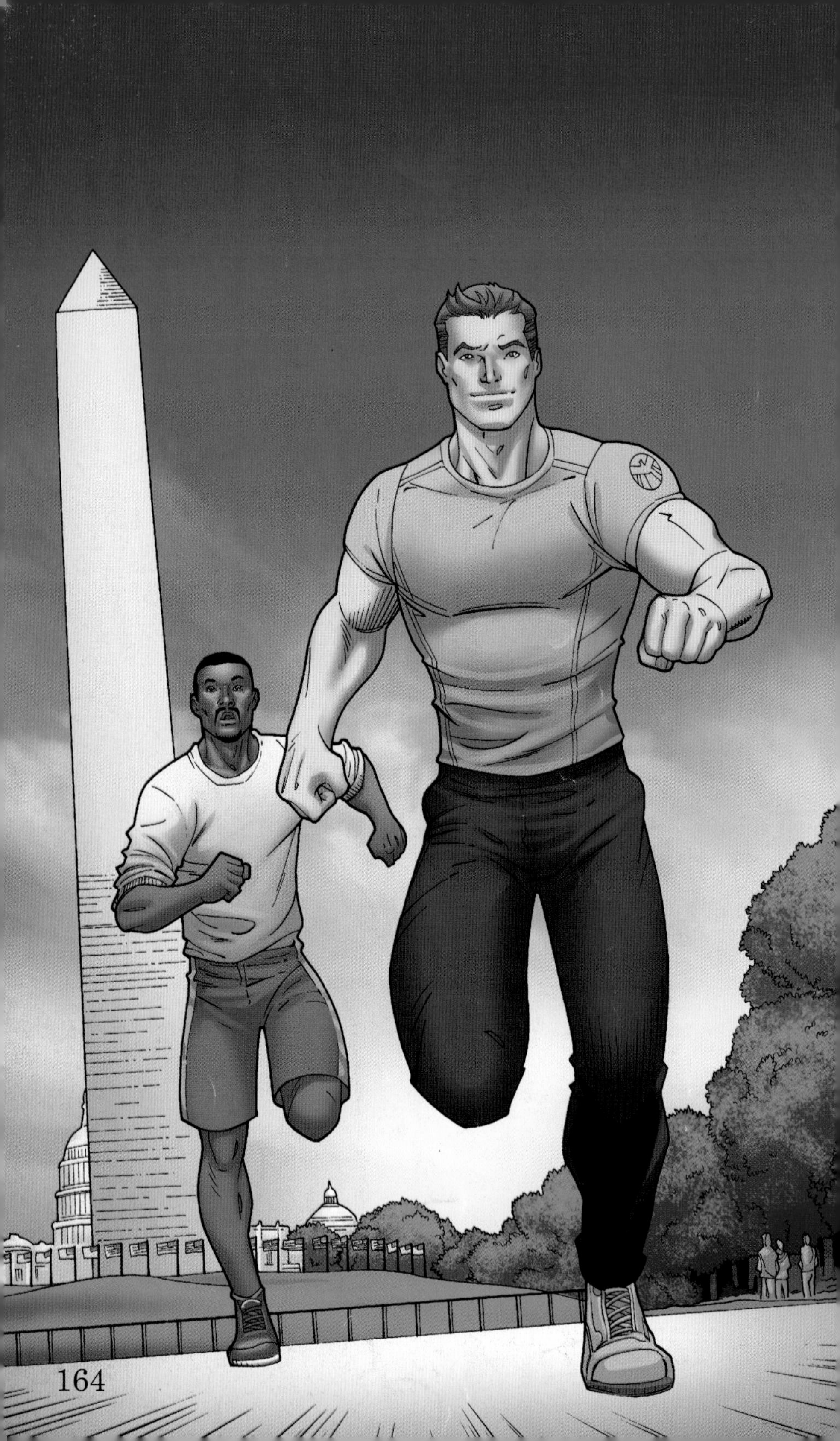

He ran every morning.

One morning, he met another person who also liked to run.

His name was Sam Wilson.

Sam and Captain America
had something in common.
Both were soldiers in the military.
Sam was now retired.
But Captain America
still had top secret missions.

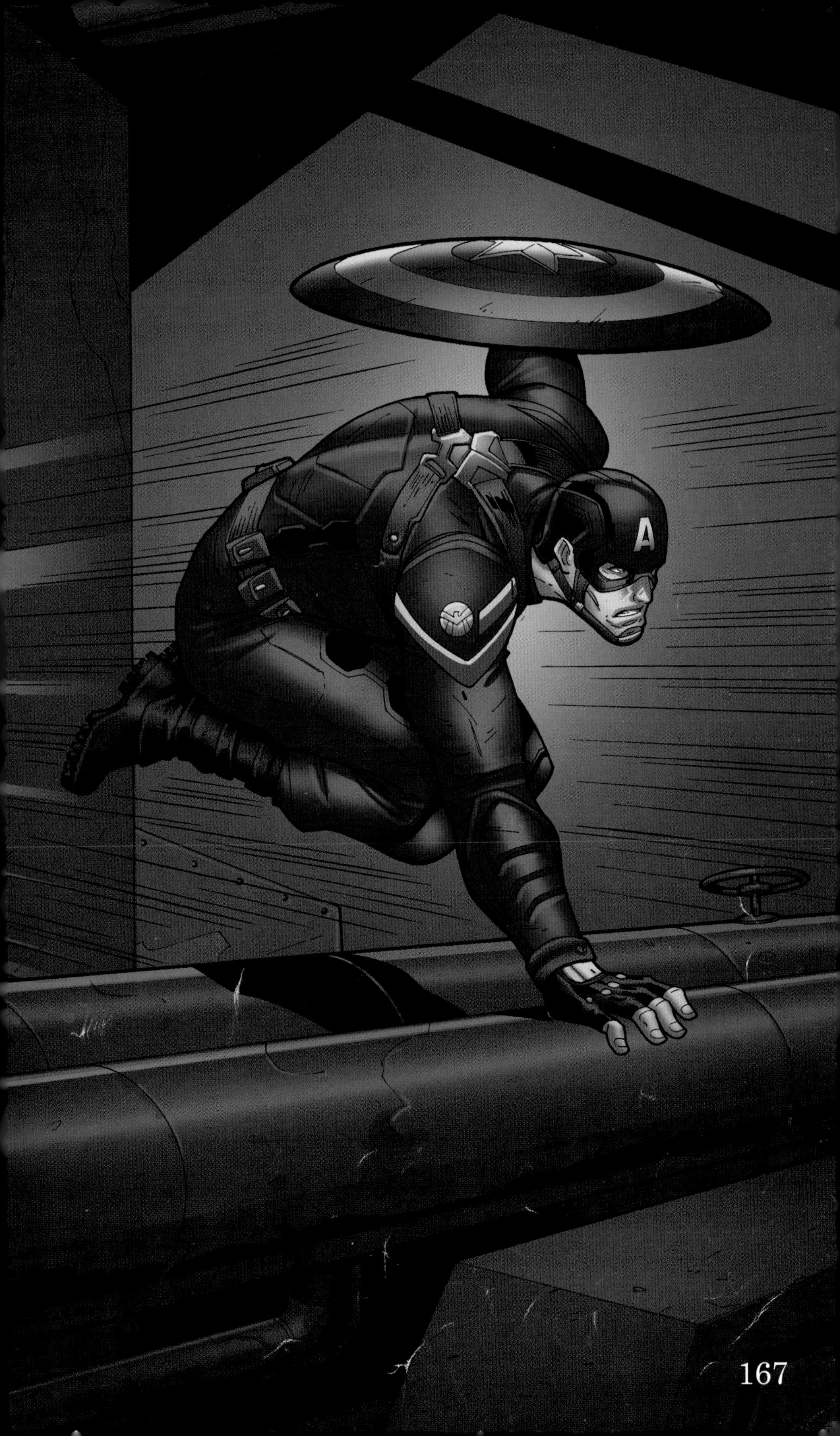

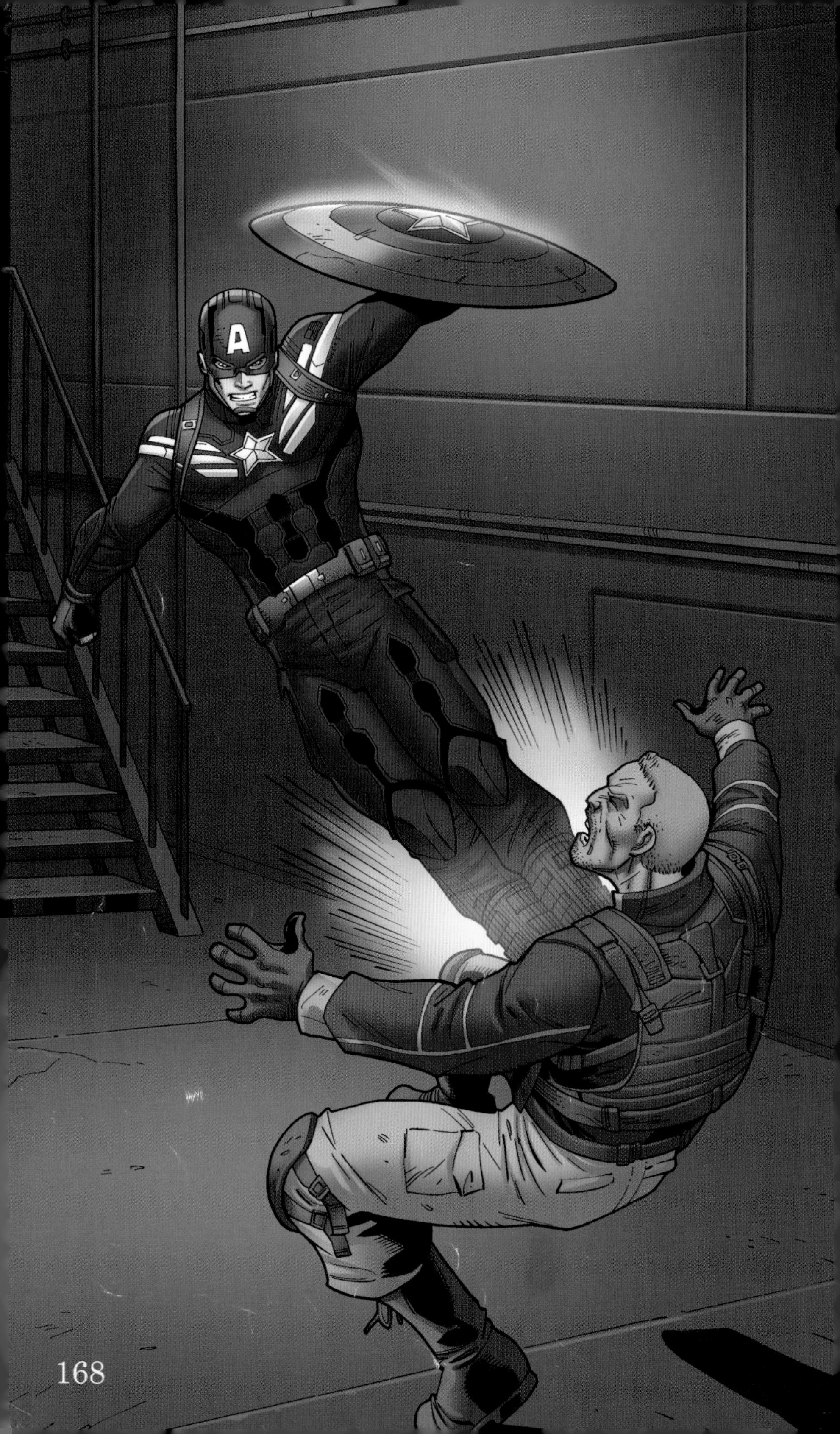

Captain America worked to
fight bad guys and rescue hostages.
Sam worked to help other
veterans like himself.
They had different jobs.
Yet both were important.

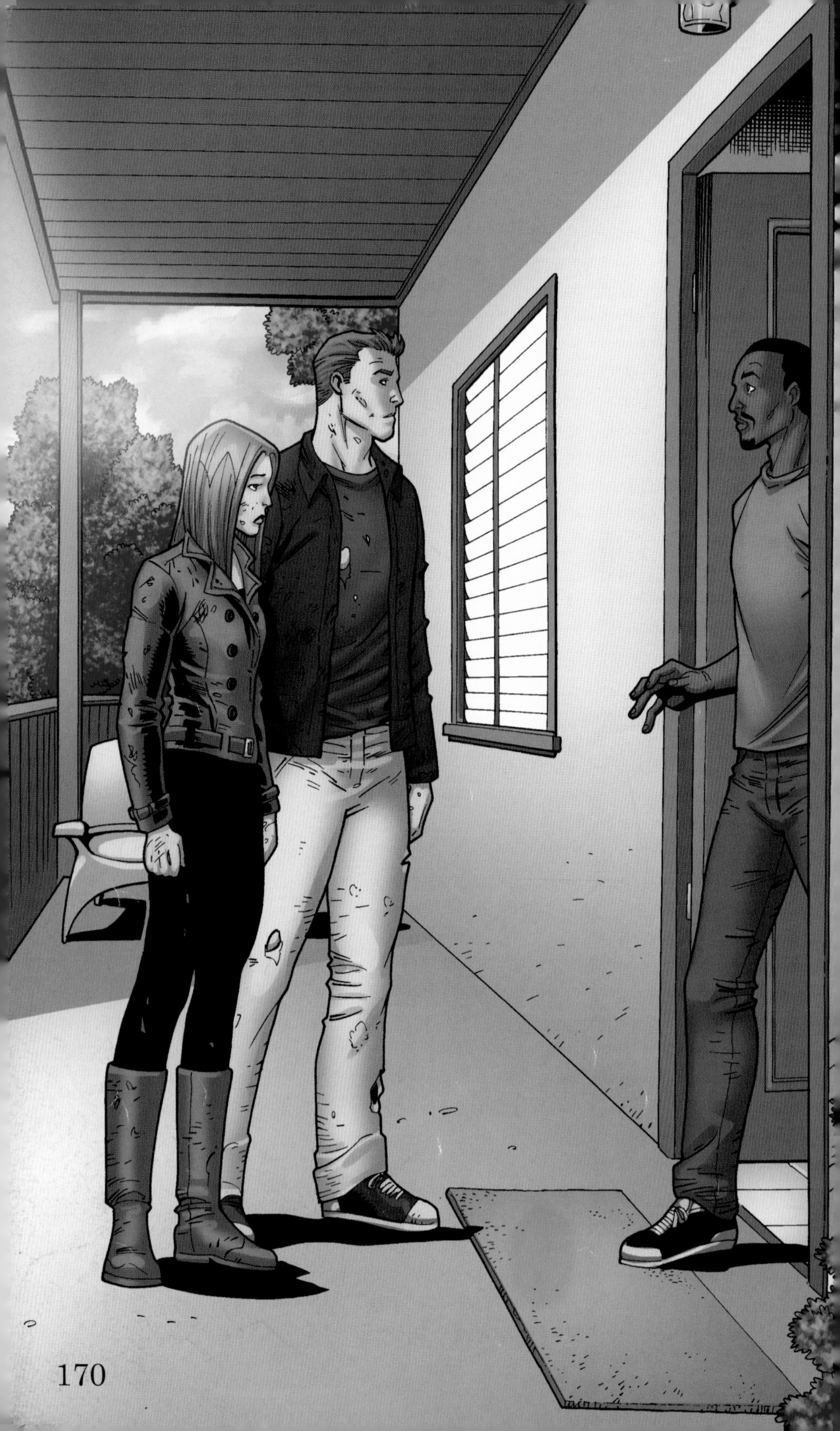

Captain America and
Black Widow went to Sam one day.
They had a problem.
They needed help.

Captain America was in a
fight with an old friend.
His name was Bucky.
He was also called Winter Soldier.
He had become mean.
He was out hurting other people.

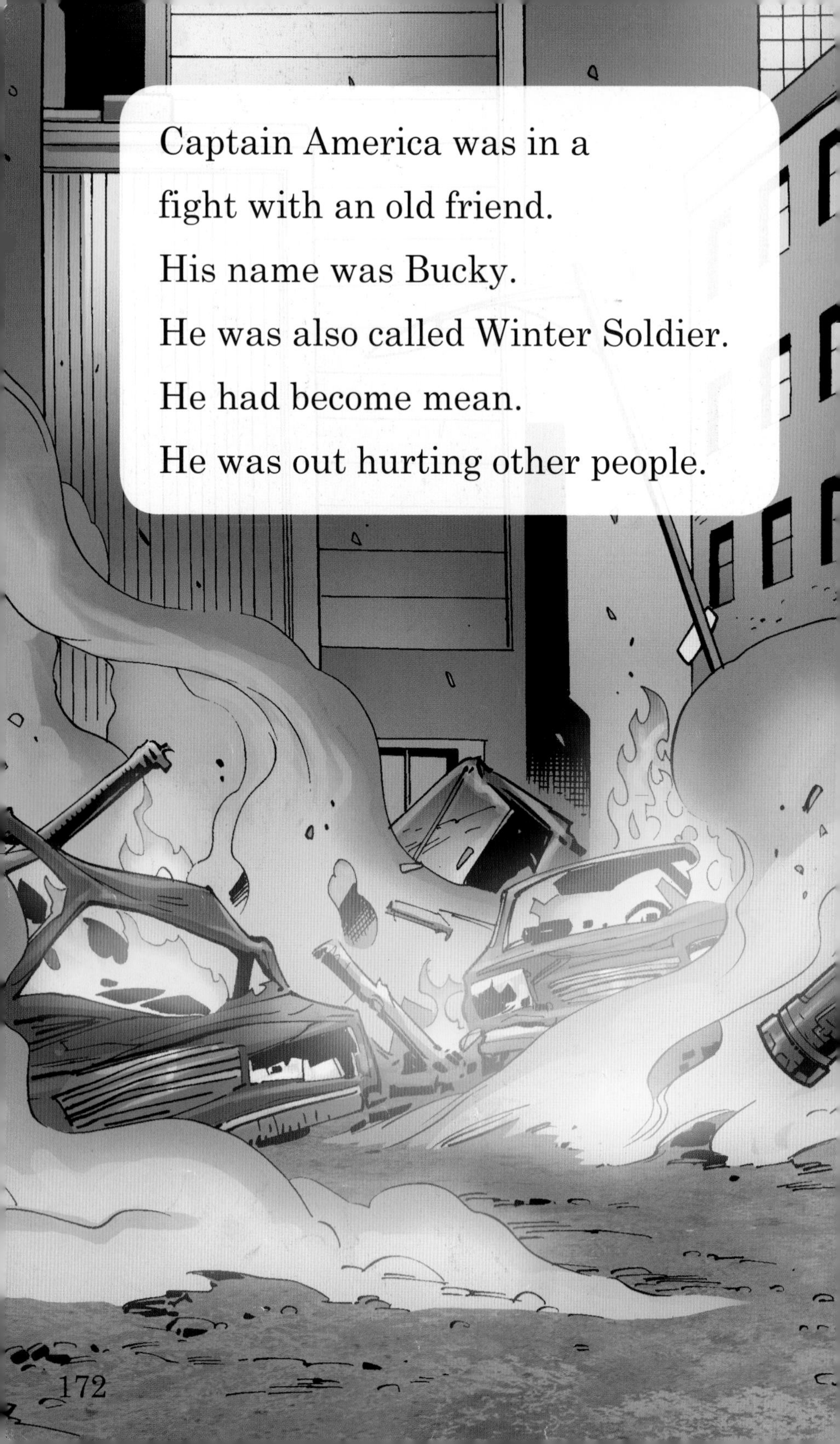

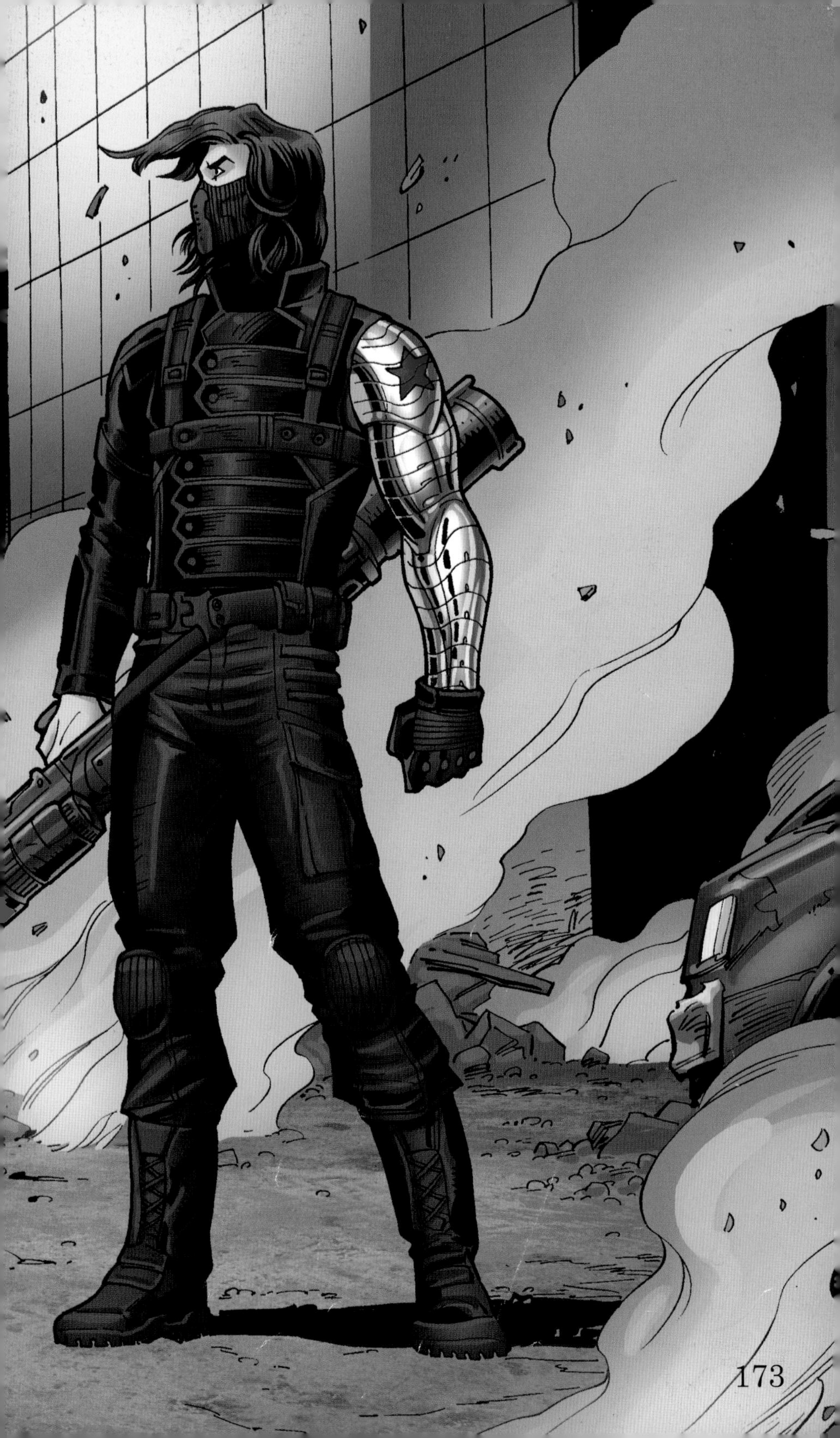

Sam did not have
to think about it.
Of course he would help!
Captain America was a fellow
soldier in need.
Sam Wilson would answer the call!

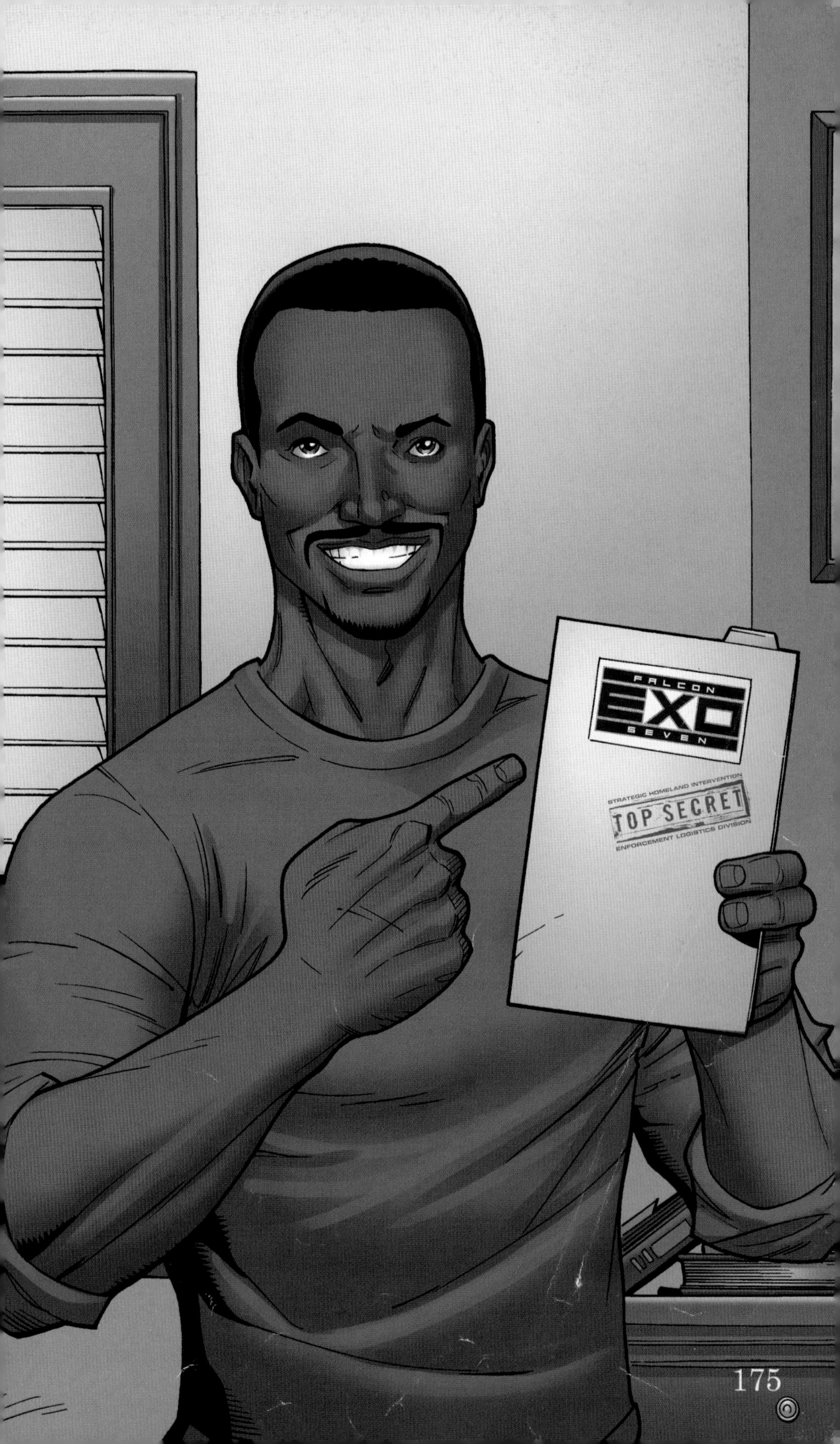
FALCON
EXO
SEVEN
STRATEGIC HOMELAND INTERVENTION
TOP SECRET
ENFORCEMENT LOGISTICS DIVISION

Captain America wore a heroic suit.

So Sam decided to wear one, too!

It was called the EXO-7 FALCON wing suit.

Sam used to wear one when he was a soldier.

It was time to wear it again!

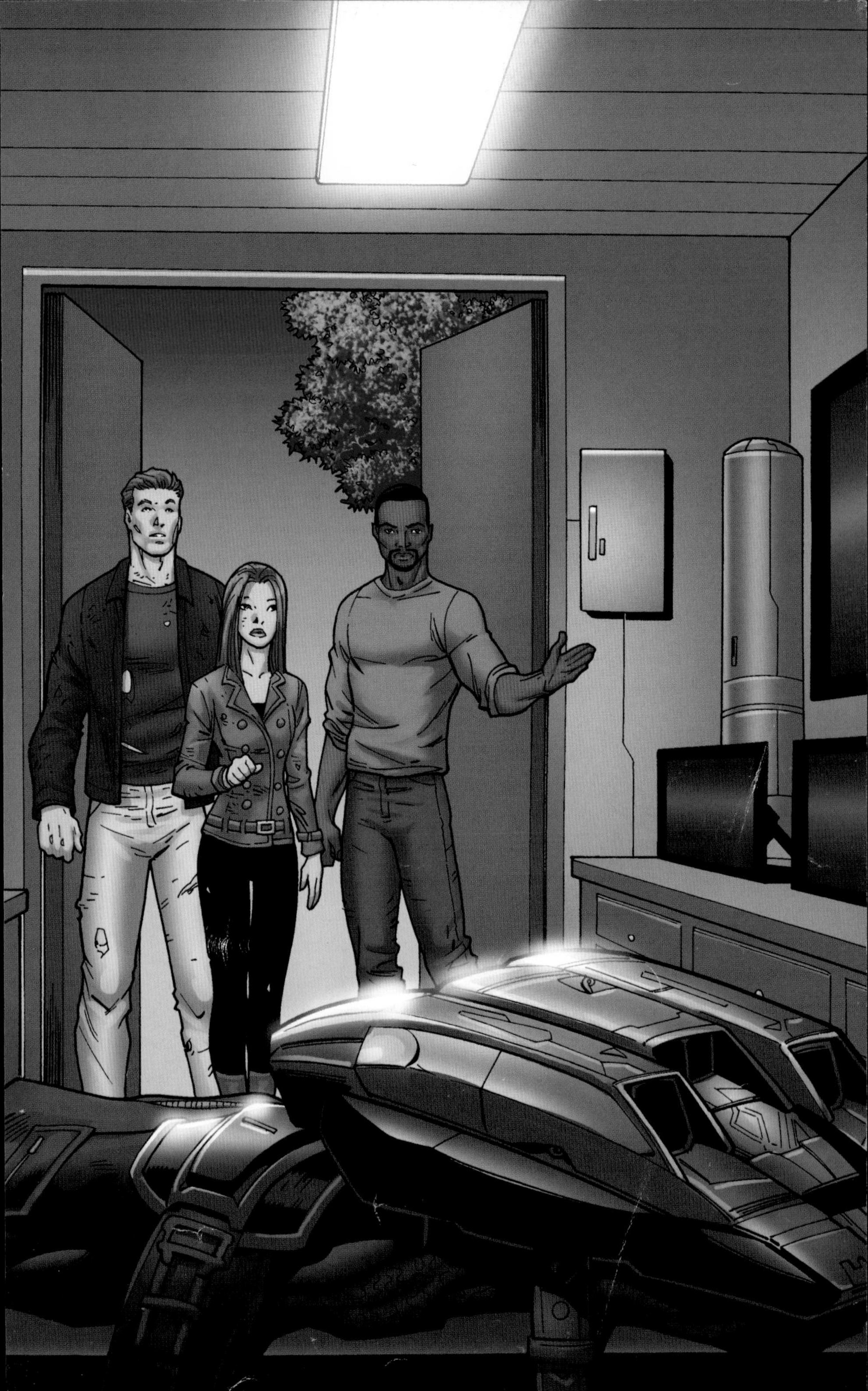

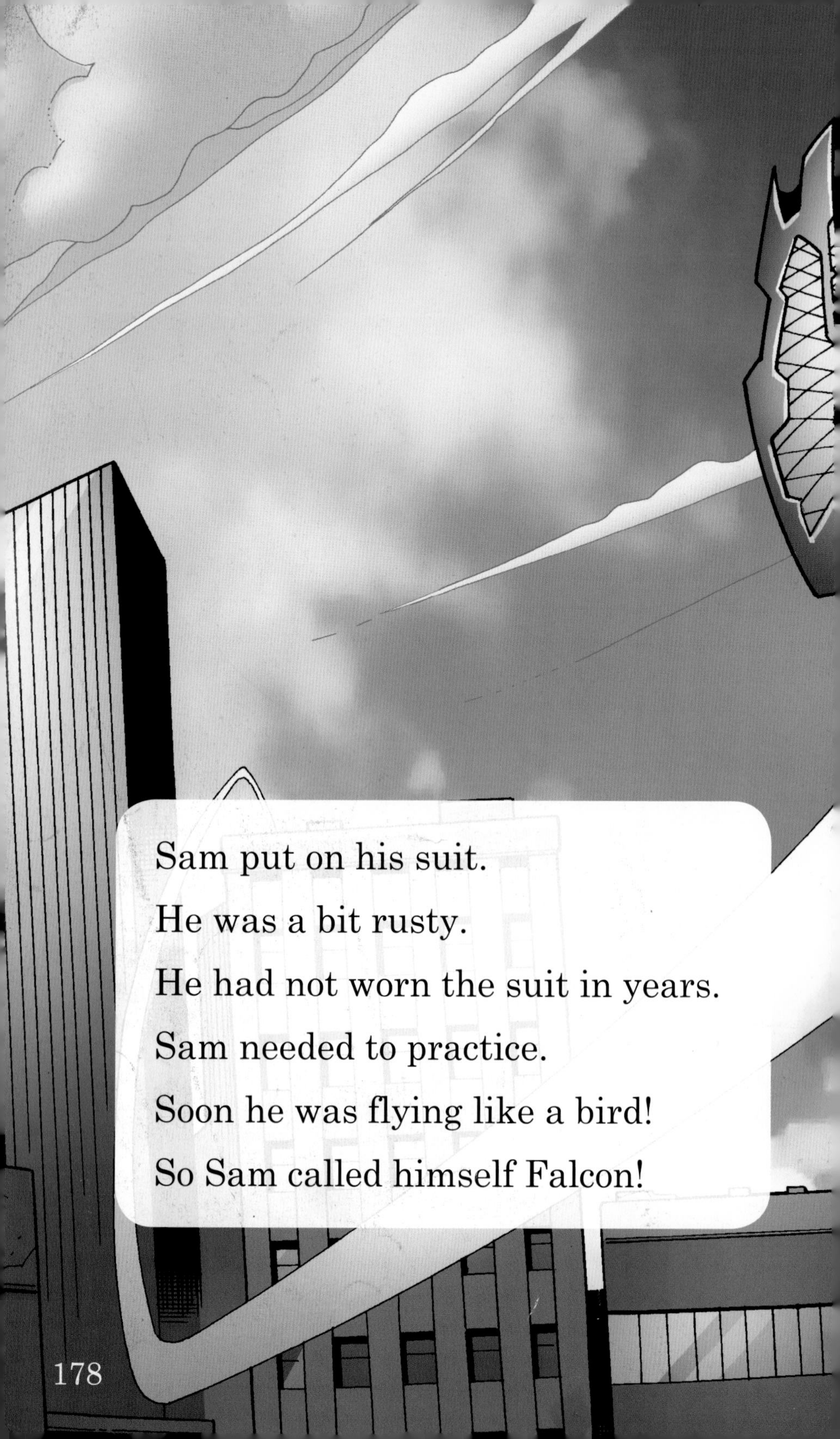

Sam put on his suit.

He was a bit rusty.

He had not worn the suit in years.

Sam needed to practice.

Soon he was flying like a bird!

So Sam called himself Falcon!

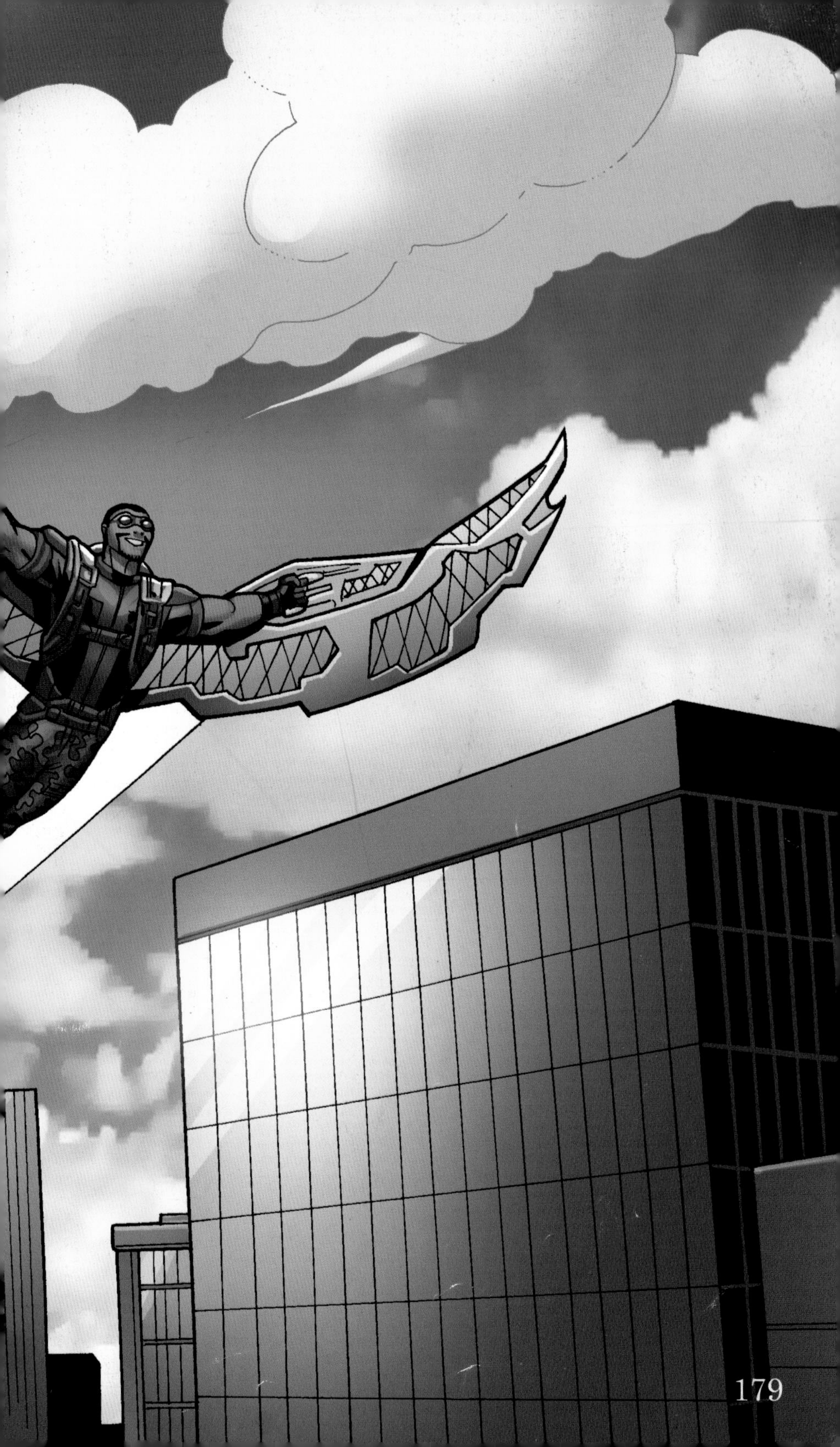

The Heroes searched for Bucky.

They did not have to search for long!

Bucky was in a helicopter!

He went after the Super Heroes.

Falcon picked up Captain America,
and they attacked the helicopter!

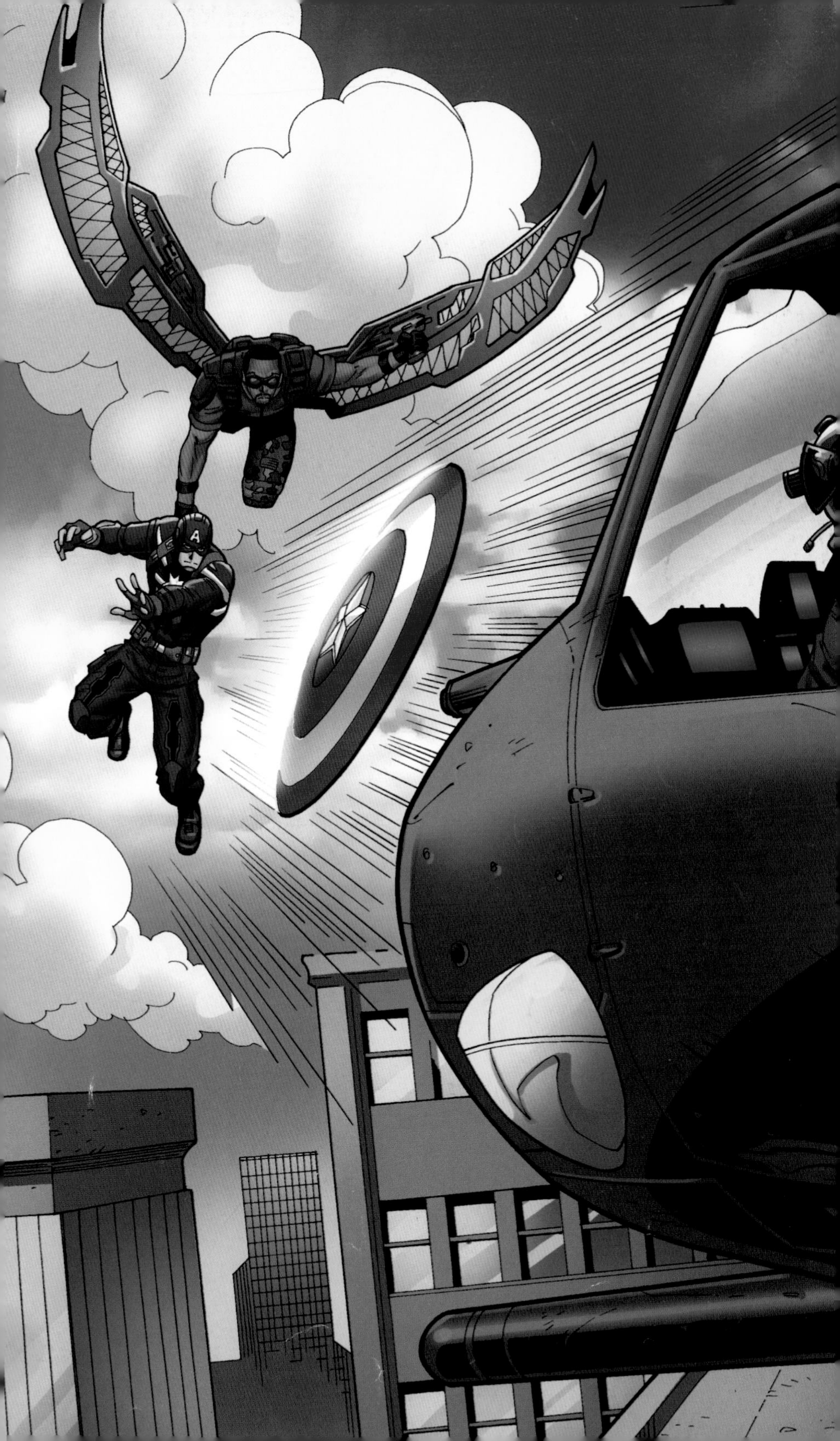

Bucky leaped from the helicopter.

He landed on the street below.

Black Widow attacked Bucky.

She fired her Widow's Bites.

He blocked them with his metal arm.

Bucky was strong!

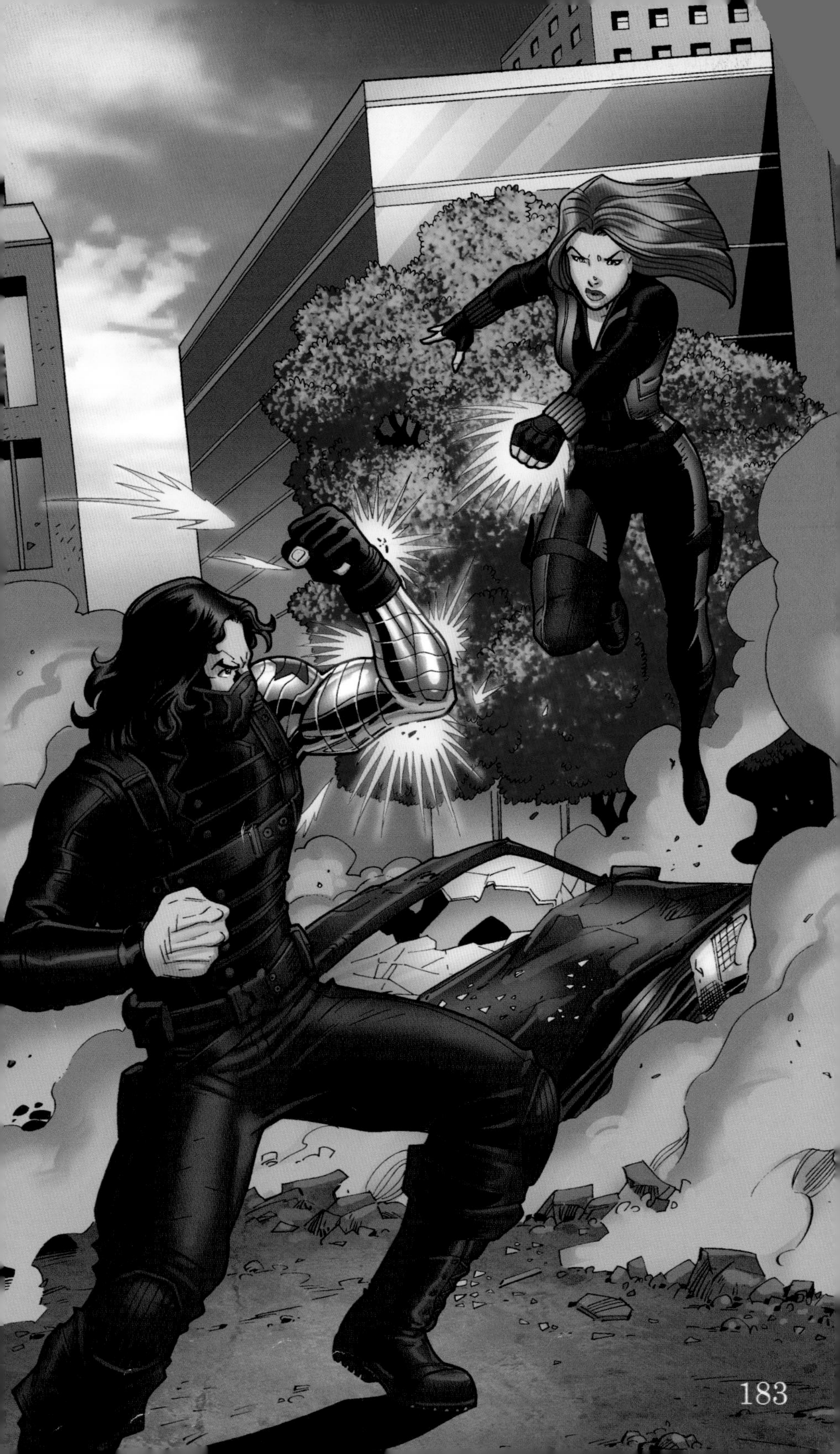

It was now Falcon's turn
to fight Bucky.

Falcon dived down from the sky.

He smashed into Bucky!

Bucky hit Falcon with his metal arm.

It was a great fight!

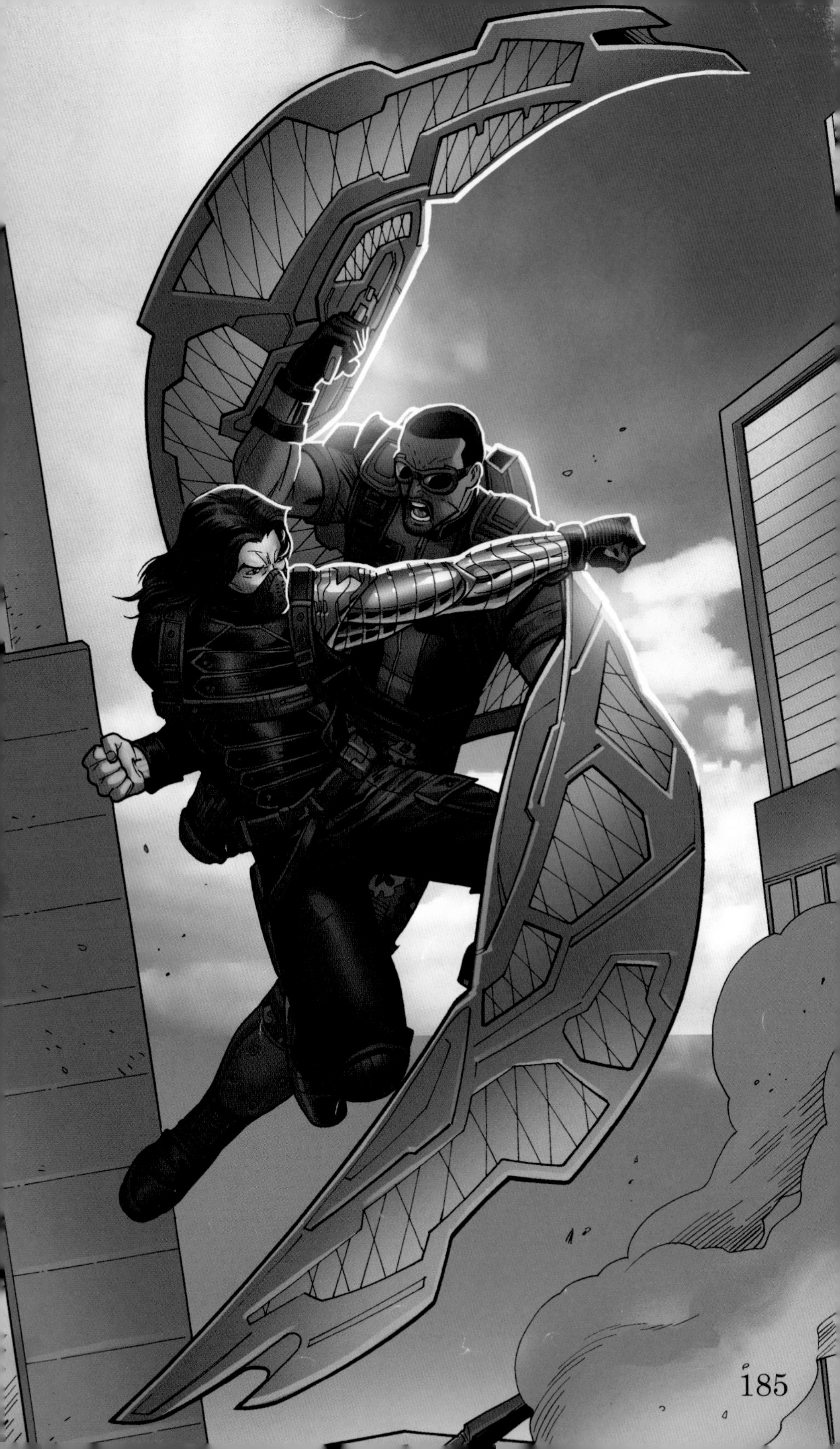

Next up was Captain America.
Cap attacked Bucky with his shield.

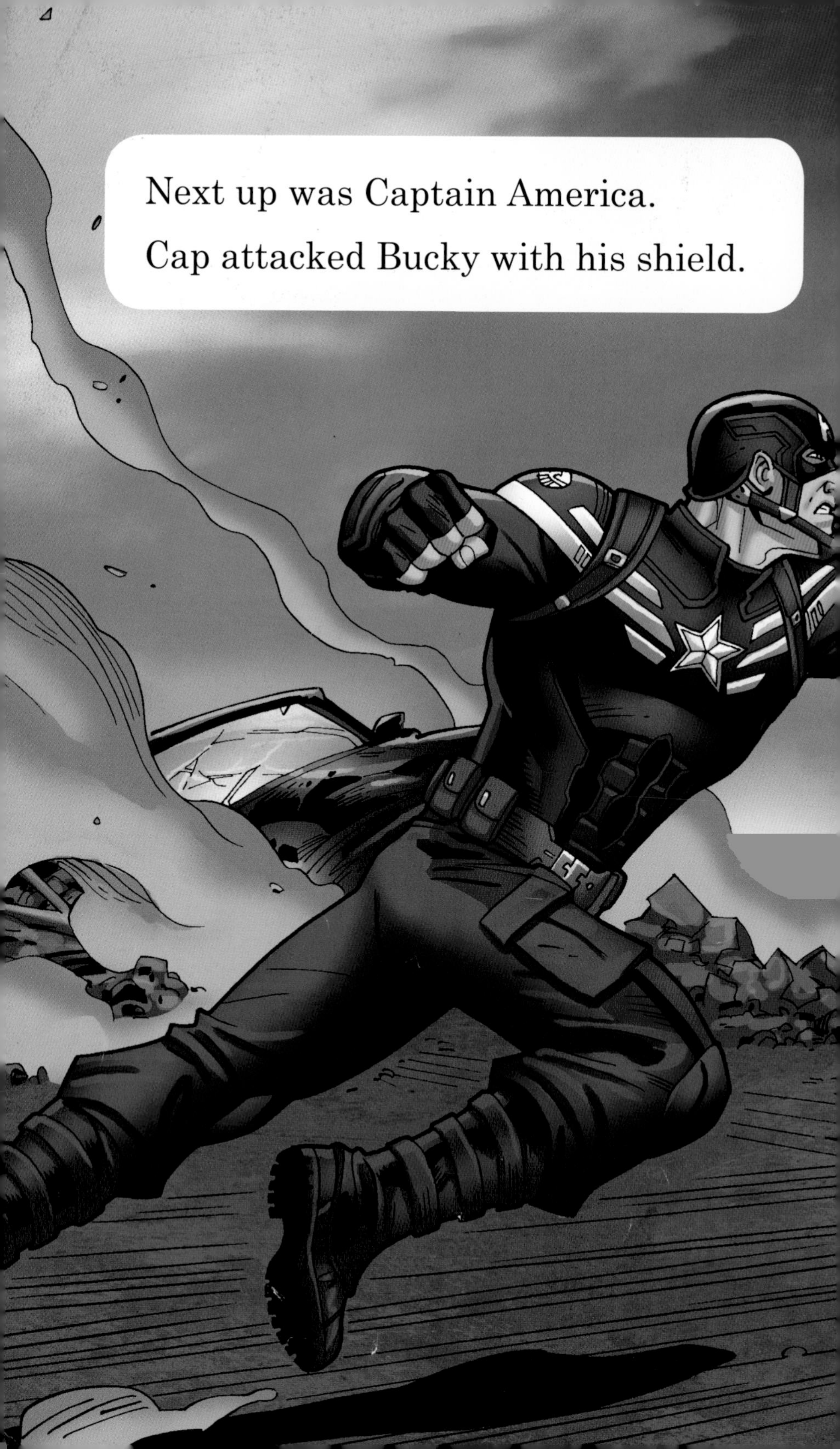

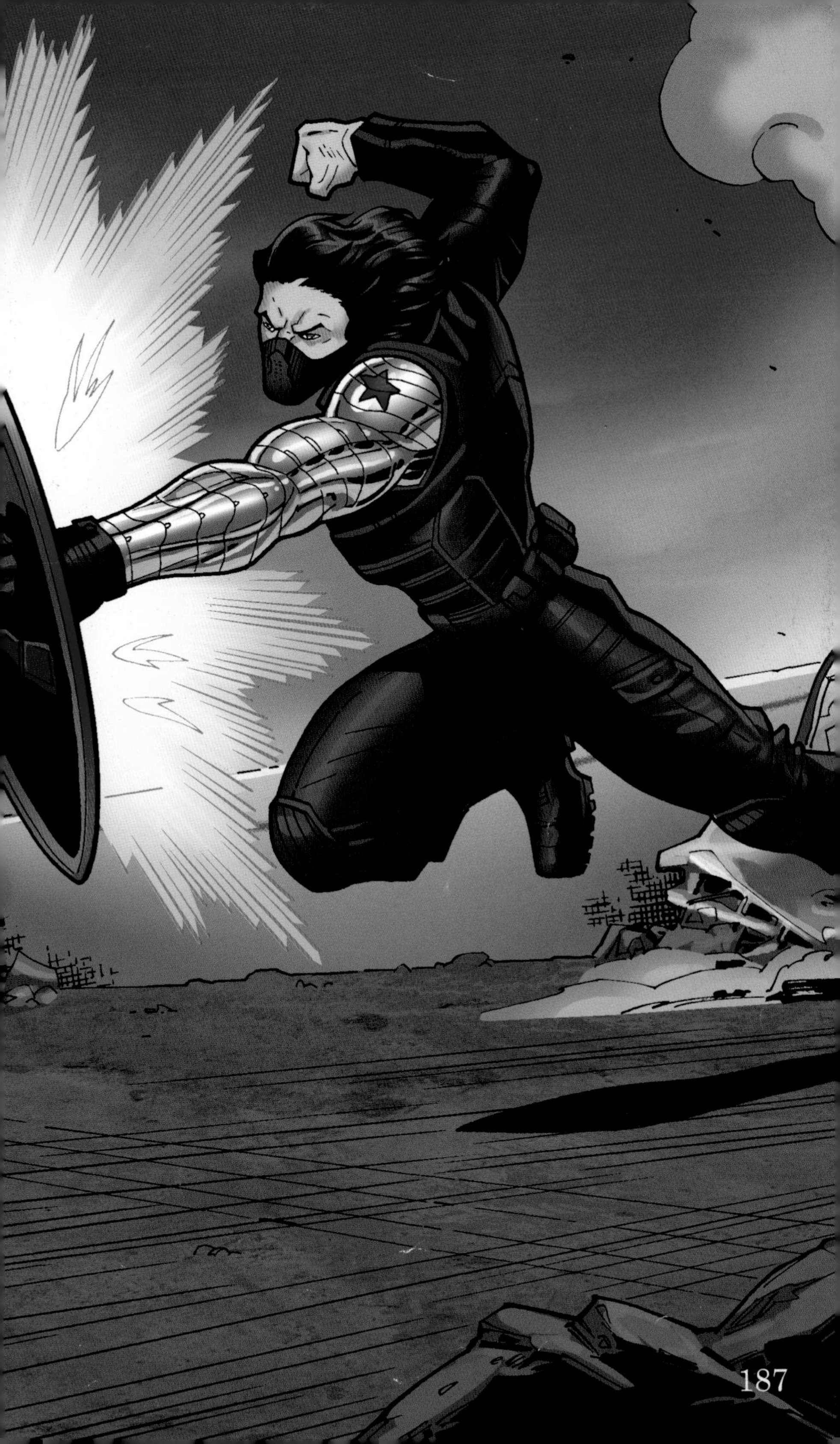

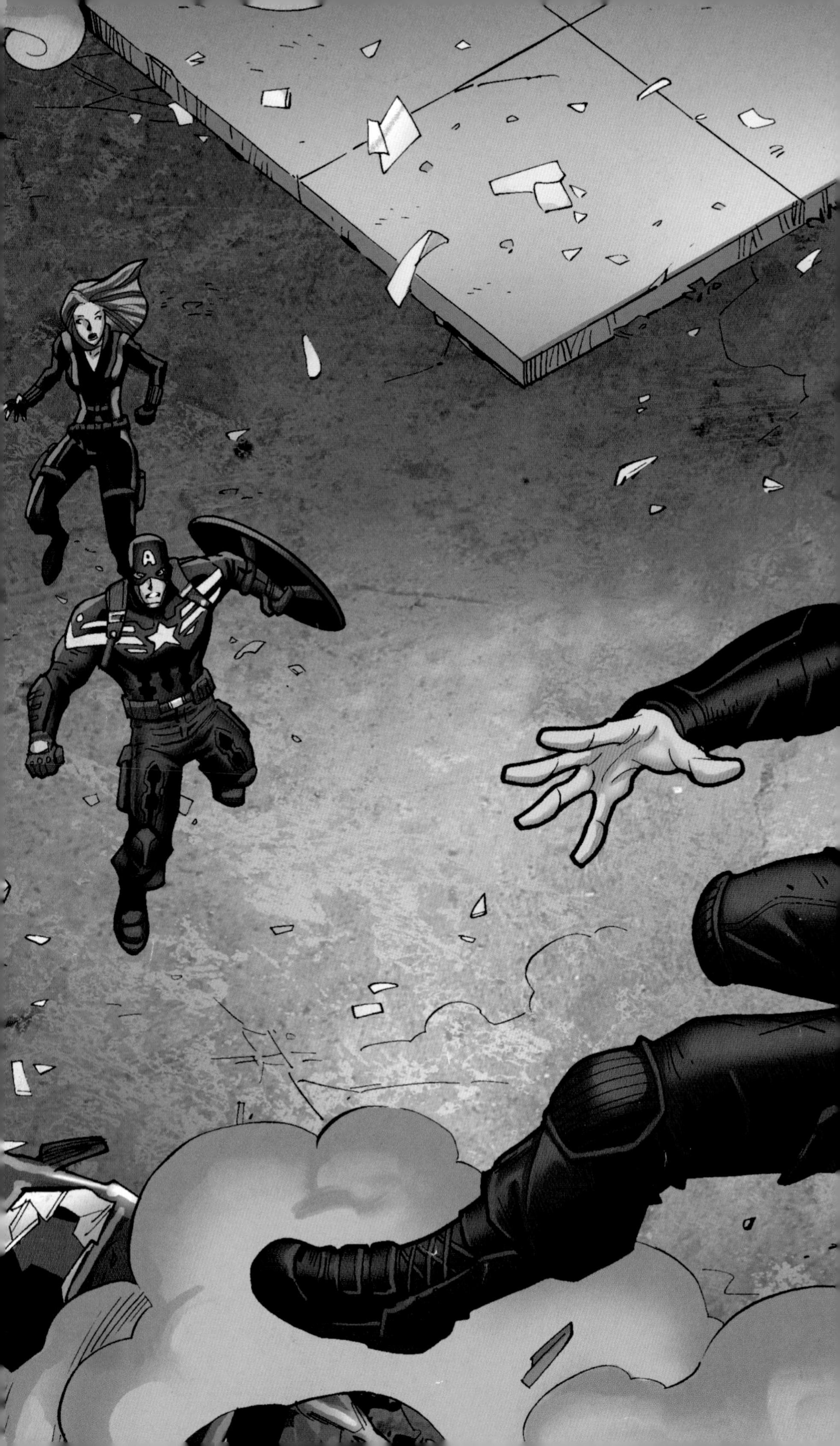

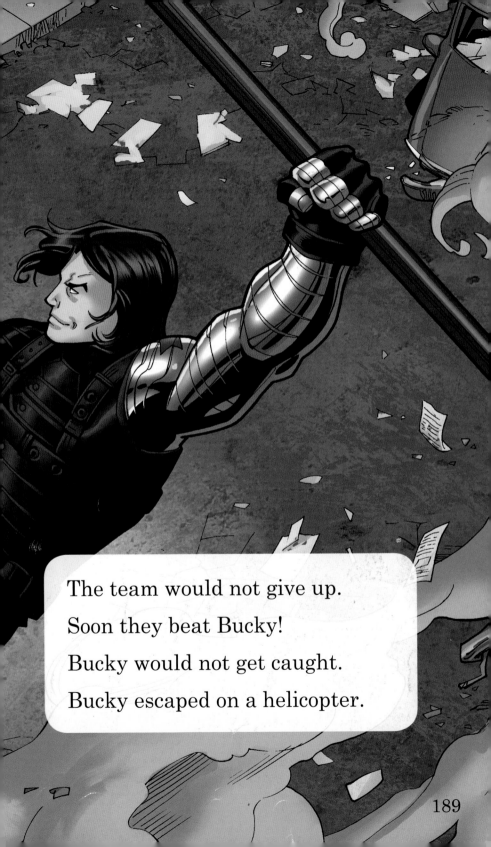

The team would not give up.

Soon they beat Bucky!

Bucky would not get caught.

Bucky escaped on a helicopter.

Captain America had lost a friend.

He also made a new friend.

His name was Falcon!

THE END

CHECKPOINTS IN THIS BOOK ✓

THE AVENGERS:
AVENGERS: ASSEMBLE!

WORD COUNT	GUIDED READING LEVEL	NUMBER OF DOLCH SIGHT WORDS
225	J	44

IRON MAN 2:
IRON MAN'S FRIENDS AND FOES

WORD COUNT	GUIDED READING LEVEL	NUMBER OF DOLCH SIGHT WORDS
628	M	89

IRON MAN 2:
MEET BLACK WIDOW

WORD COUNT	GUIDED READING LEVEL	NUMBER OF DOLCH SIGHT WORDS
680	M	99

IRON MAN 3:
IRON MAN FIGHTS BACK

WORD COUNT	GUIDED READING LEVEL	NUMBER OF DOLCH SIGHT WORDS
260	J	53

THOR: THE DARK WORLD:
HEROES OF ASGARD

WORD COUNT	GUIDED READING LEVEL	NUMBER OF DOLCH SIGHT WORDS
552	L	69

CAPTAIN AMERICA: THE WINTER SOLDIER:
FALCON TAKES FLIGHT

WORD COUNT	GUIDED READING LEVEL	NUMBER OF DOLCH SIGHT WORDS
364	L	62